D0197324

ALSO BY

JENNIFER A. NIELSEN

THE ASCENDANCE TRILOGY

The False Prince

The Runaway King

The Shadow Throne

THE MARK OF THE THIEF TRILOGY

Mark of the Thief

Rise of the Wolf

JENNIFER A. NIELSEN

MARK OF THE THIEF

BOOK ONE

SCHOLASTIC INC.

This book was originally published in hardcover by Scholastic Press in 2015.

ISBN 978-0-545-56155-6

10 9 8 7 6 5 17 18 19 20

Printed in the U.S.A. 40
First printing 2016
Book design by Christopher Stengel

A note to readers: Latin words will be italicized upon their first appearance in the text.

To Mrs. Flores, 1st Grade,
who gave me a love of words

ONE

In Rome, nothing mattered more than the gods, and nothing mattered less than its slaves. Only a fool of a slave would ever challenge the gods' power.

I was beginning to look like that fool.

I was a slave in the mines south of Rome and, generally speaking, did my job well. I worked hard and kept my head down and even took orders without complaint — unless it was a stupid order, one that risked my life. Then I was just as happy to ignore it.

"You will do as I say, Nic!" Sal's anger echoed inside this small underground chamber. "I've tolerated your disobedience far too long."

"Tolerated?" I snorted. If near starvation, beatings, and dangerous assignments were tolerance, then yes, Sal had been excessively generous to me.

As part of the grand joke that had become my life, the gods had given me a master with the wit of a withered carrot and compassion of a wasp. He also smelled like toe fungus, though that's less relevant. More significant is that of the hundreds of slaves who worked in the mines, Sal hated me the most. This was no great surprise, since Sal had always stood out to me as someone well worth hating back. With his whip and the ever-present chains on my wrists, he held absolute control over my life — or lack of it. So generally speaking, I did as I was told.

But I would not obey his ridiculous order to explore our latest discovery, a cave believed to contain Julius Caesar's lost treasure. The deep shaft that accessed the cave had killed the first miner to enter, and the second man, a friend of mine named Fidelius, was in the corner muttering incoherently and gnawing on his fist like a dog at his bone. Maybe the air was bad, maybe the cave was haunted, or maybe the gods just didn't want us mining there. I didn't know. I didn't care. I wasn't going inside.

Or maybe I was getting what I deserved. Earlier that morning, I had deliberately dropped sand into Sal's drink. He was still coughing up the grains he swallowed. I felt no guilt for what I'd done. Sal was getting what he deserved too.

My only regret was the worry I too often caused my sister, Livia, who also worked here at the mines. She was only a year younger than me, but when our mother was sold away from us, Livia became my responsibility. She wasn't allowed in the mine itself, but since our discovery yesterday, rumors had spread all over camp. She knew this was my work area, and would wonder now whether I was coming back. Actually, I had the same question.

"No, Sal. This is a waste of lives." It wasn't my best argument. Sal cared nothing for anyone's life but his own. Perhaps if I had told him this was a waste of money, I'd have gotten his attention.

"There's gold in that cave," Sal said. "The first man we sent down told us he could see it."

"Before he screamed for help and then died!" I said.

Sal pointed to Fidelius. "That one came back!"

Fidelius looked up, his eyes still as wide and bloodshot as when we'd first pulled him out. His hollow gaze turned to me. "Caesar's ghost walks that cave. It's forbidden earth."

Sal grabbed a fistful of my tunic and yanked me toward him. "Rome already knows about this discovery. General Radulf is on his way now to investigate that cave. If gold is down there, then I want my piece of it first."

"If you want it, you go down there!" He could beat me for refusing him, and he probably would, but that was better than obeying.

Across from me, Fidelius shuddered and mumbled the words, "Caesar. He'll curse you."

This was hardly a new thought. Every miner who worked the South Mountain already figured he was cursed. This mountain was close to Lake Nemi, home to a temple for the goddess Diana, where strange things were said to happen. Whenever a miner disappeared here, we all wondered if it was Diana, demanding another sacrifice.

"Enough disobedience!" Sal shoved me into the arms of his guard. "Toss his body down and get me another slave."

I heard the slice of a knife being drawn from its sheath, but I had no intention of dying at the hand of this swine. So I spread the chains around my wrists as wide as they'd go, then drove my elbows into the guard's gut and bolted for the tunnel exit. Sal and the guard collided to chase me, but I had worked this tunnel for five years and knew it better than anyone.

I brushed past a couple of miners as I ran, then, behind me, heard Sal yell for them to get out of the way. I slowed enough for the guard to see me take a sharp left down a dark corridor, then ducked into an even darker crevice, pressing tightly against the wall. The guard ran right past me, with Sal on his heels.

I wasn't free yet, not even close. I still had to make my way through the rest of the tunnel, and then find Livia in the camp. I always knew we'd eventually escape this place; today seemed as good a day for freedom as any other.

Just as I was ready to dart out from the crevice, the shadows of two men entered the main tunnel, their voices low. They ducked into the smaller tunnel, only inches from me. The men were Roman soldiers — that was obvious from their red cloaks and the leather boots — and likely the more decorated one was General Radulf. He had come earlier than expected.

Inside the crevice, I grinned. This was exactly what I needed. Radulf would distract Sal, giving me the chance to get away.

A man with a deep voice spoke first. "You'll wait here at the entrance. I don't want anyone in these tunnels until I'm finished."

"Yes, General Radulf. Are you sure about this? Emperor Tacitus will have your head if he finds out."

Radulf's laugh felt as dark as this tunnel. "The emperor fears me more than I do him. Besides, he won't know about any of this until I'm ready, and by then, it'll be too late for anyone to stop me. I will crush this empire in my fist."

"Assuming this cave has what you've been looking for," his companion added.

Radulf's boots stepped even closer to where I hid, and though he lowered his voice, I heard every traitorous word. "I can feel the magic here, just as Rome must feel its last gasps of breath. The discovery of Caesar's cave is going to change my life."

Magic? Nothing I'd felt in my years here could be described that way. Even still, though I closed my eyes and tried to disappear into the cracks of this crevice, somehow I knew my life was about to change too.

TWO

Someone must've notified Sal that Radulf had arrived, forcing him to give up the search for me. He met Radulf in the tunnel, breathless and full of apologies that he had not received the general properly.

When he bowed to the general, his sweaty head lowered directly in front of my face. Had he turned just an inch, he'd have spotted me. "General Radulf, you honor us with your presence."

"Clear this entire tunnel," Radulf said. "Then lead me to the cave."

"I have a man ready to explore the cave, as you asked." Sal motioned with his hand and a guard brought the man in. A quick peek out told me his chains were similar to mine, though his legs were also manacled. Sal must've expected him to resist.

But he didn't. The man fell to his knees and began howling like a lost child. "I beg you, *Dominus*. Don't send me into that cave. I don't want to die."

"I'll send a thousand slaves to their deaths if that's what it takes," Radulf snarled. "Get to your feet."

"I — I'm too big for the opening," the man said. "And too heavy on ropes. You want someone —"

Sal swatted his head. "How dare you refuse the general?"

The man fell to all fours, and when he turned to answer Sal, his eyes locked directly on mine. I shook my head, silently begging him not to reveal me, but his expression only darkened as a grin widened on his face. "Dominus, you want someone like him."

Sal followed his gaze and instantly grabbed my chains and yanked me from the crevice. "There you are, rodent. I'll deal with you later."

"Let me see this one," Radulf said.

My heart leapt into my throat. He must have known that I had overheard his conversation. So I kept my head down while he studied me, hoping if I made myself look weak enough, the general would lose interest. As one of the youngest workers here, I wasn't anywhere near the biggest or the strongest worker of the mines, and for that matter, I wasn't the stupidest either. At this point, the only chance I had was if he decided that I wasn't a threat to him.

None of it worked. The general pinched my face between his fingers and forced me to look up. He was tall, with dark hair that was graying over his ears, olive skin, and a square face that looked carved out of stone. His silver armor covered a broad, muscular chest, and I had no doubt he managed the sword at his side with perfect ease.

In contrast, my dark hair was ragged, as were the remaining shreds of my thin tunic. I was filthy and covered in the same bruises, scrapes, and cuts as any other slave miner. And I felt how low my status was compared to a man of Radulf's greatness. But at least I hadn't spent the last few minutes talking about treason against the Roman Empire.

Radulf turned my head from side to side. "You look familiar," he said. "Have we met?"

I nearly choked out a nervous laugh. Where would a mining slave possibly meet a Roman general? He and I had nothing in common. Nor was there anything I wanted to have in common with him, aside from one thing only: He was free, and I wore chains.

"Cooperate with me," he said, "and I might forget that you were eavesdropping."

I started to point out that for a treasonous man, he whispered rather loud, but before I could speak, Sal shook his head. "You wouldn't want him, Dominus. He displeases the gods."

No, I was their plaything, their entertainment in an eternity of boredom. This new twist was proof of that. Obviously, their idea of saving me from the punishment of escaping was to force me into that cursed cave. Because now it would be one or the other, and either way, Sal would win. That was intolerable.

Sal smiled. "On second thought, I can see why you would choose him." I immediately understood why he had changed his mind and glared back at him. There weren't many gears in Sal's brain, so it wasn't hard to watch them working. He had planned to dump me in the cave anyway.

"What's the boy's name?" Radulf asked.

"We call him Nic."

"Nicolas Calva," I answered. It was a freeborn name that I'd given myself five years ago. Calva had been my mother's family name. If I accepted my life with only a first name, like every other man here, that would be the same as accepting that I would never be anything but a slave in the mines. And I refused to die here, as if I were nothing.

Radulf said, "Well, Nicolas Calva, you will go into that cave for me. You will have to be brave, and obey my every order."

"You'll find no slave here braver than Nic, or more obedient." Sal nearly choked on the last part of his words. I wished he had.

"Then why was he trying to escape just now?"

Sal glanced at me, speechless. "You misunderstood," I said. "I went into that crevice looking for other runaway slaves. Luckily, I didn't find any."

"I can make him obey." Radulf smiled back at me. "You remind me of myself, when I was a boy in Gaul."

"I'm surprised you can remember back that long ago."

He crouched to my level. "I remember it well. There was always an uprising somewhere. Always an opportunity for Rome to crush us, again and again. You know what I'm talking about. I can see that in your eyes."

He was right. Rome had also destroyed my family in Gaul, before we'd fled deeper into the empire. None of my mother's attempts to hide us from the slavers had worked, though. We were sold into the mines five years ago.

Radulf's smile faded. "Who is your family, Nic?"

Sal answered for me. "He was born in Gaul of a Roman mother named Hortensia, and an unknown father."

Radulf's eyes flickered for a moment, but he continued to stare. "Unknown? Not even a name?"

Though it meant little to me, I did know my father's name, Halden. From my mother's description, he had died when struck by lightning. It was a senseless, useless death, one without honor. For that reason, I never said his name, not even to my sister. There was no chance of me telling this man now.

"Where is his mother?" Radulf asked.

"A few weeks after they all arrived here, I sold her to a family near Rome." Sal flicked his eyes at me and I glared back. It was on top of the long list of reasons why I hated him. "But the boy's sister is still here. Livia."

The way he said her name curled my hands into fists. Sal had never made it a secret that he was waiting for my sister to come of age so that he could make her an offer of marriage. The thought of it twisted my stomach.

Since it was too much to hope for favors from the gods, I decided that if I could not save myself, at least I would do something for Livia. Faking all possible innocence, I looked up at Radulf. "Sir, please allow Sal to come with us. If you want me to succeed in that cave, we must have his help."

Sal's face paled, then reddened as he tried to control his anger. He sputtered out an objection but it was already too late.

"Very well." Radulf nodded at Sal to lead us on. I wished I could've taken more joy in Sal's distress, but in truth, I felt anything but happiness then.

A roll of thunder sounded outside as we walked deeper into the tunnel, and I shuddered. It was a sign, reminding me that, like the rest of the world, the gods cared nothing for mining slaves. I felt the eyes of the other men staring as Sal dismissed everyone but me and Radulf from the mines. Their expressions were sympathetic, even concerned for my plight. But they were more relieved that it was me, and not any one of them, walking to his death.

THREE

The entrance to the secret cave was buried deep below the earth's surface. I knew because I was part of the small group that had discovered it. When we had broken the rock apart, it had revealed a long vertical shaft that had blown bitter cold wind out at us. That should've been our first warning. Now one miner lay dead somewhere at the bottom, and they'd had to carry Fidelius out of here, still chewing on his fist. Not that Radulf cared. In fact, considering that he knew what I'd overheard, he probably hoped I'd join their fates.

"Remove this boy's chains," Radulf ordered Sal. "He cannot do what is required of him while wearing chains."

But Sal shook his head. "You see how far he ran while wearing chains. Imagine if he didn't have them."

"It's never been chains that kept me here," I said. It was Livia's reluctance to leave. The idea of escaping frightened her just as much as it beckoned me. But she was younger, and didn't remember freedom like I did.

"Unchain him," Radulf said.

Sal reached for his keys and did as he was told. He was then ordered to tie a long rope around my waist. It would be his job to lower me to the bottom of the cave. *If* there was a bottom.

Looking down into the cave's black entrance, I was sure Fidelius had been right. This was forbidden earth. My chances of returning weren't good, and where would that leave Livia? Without me, there was no one to take care of her. Except for Sal, which was worse than having nobody at all.

After Sal tied the rope, Radulf dismissed him so that we could talk in private. He checked the knot, but offered no sympathy for the likelihood that I would die, nor did I expect any. He only said, "If it truly is Caesar's lost treasure down there, then you will look for only one thing, a *bulla* made entirely of gold. Do you know what a bulla is?"

I rolled my eyes. Every freeborn boy in Rome wore the pendant around his neck. Not having one identified me as worthless to the empire. So yes, of course I knew what it was.

"Good. The one I want will have a griffin carved on one side and Caesar's initials on the other. Do you know your letters?"

"All the important ones." He smiled at my comment, though I hoped he wouldn't make too much of it. My mother had taught me to recognize Latin letters, but got no further before she was sold away. I had no idea what to do with them beyond that.

"That bulla is all I want," Radulf said. "The rest belongs to the empire."

I squinted back at him, recalling the conversation I had just overheard. If Radulf wanted a way to crush the Roman Empire, a bulla would do him no good. Bullas were given to wealthy young boys as charms against bad luck. Personally, I doubted they worked. Since they had been born wealthy, I figured those boys already had all the luck they needed in life. Regardless, once a boy became a man, he put away the bulla along with his other childish things. Caesar would have done the same.

Radulf grabbed my arm and leaned in closer. "I know what you overheard from me, and you would be wise to forget it. If you defy me, it will not go well for you."

I believed him. He'd been in my life for less than an hour and my hopes had already taken a significant turn for the worse. "All I care about is getting back to the surface," I said. "The rest is your concern, not mine."

His expression warmed to that. With his grip on me tighter than ever, he said, "Once you find the bulla, do not put it on; do not hold it too close. Just carry it back to me. If you do as I ask, then I will take you away from this place, even bring you back to Rome with me. Your sister too."

My mouth dropped open in surprise. I didn't like Radulf, but I'd rather not like him in Rome than stay here in the mines for another minute. That made it harder to ask the question still hanging in the air. "What if I don't find the bulla?"

"Then Sal won't bring you back up."

My hands began shaking, and I pressed them against my leg to calm the nerves. "I might not come back anyway. Others have tried."

Radulf looked me over again, and the barest hint of a smile escaped his stern expression. I wasn't sure if that was a sign of hope, or one of cruelty.

With that, Radulf called Sal back in to join us. Then he hoisted me up to the cavity in the rock, handed me a torch, and ordered Sal to lower me inside.

The darkness was blacker than anything I'd ever seen. Blacker than night, or even the deepest mine tunnels. Light was an enemy to this place. The torch I carried helped a little, but it was so bright, I could see nothing else. An icy breeze assaulted me next. As miners, we had all become used to cold, but this air seemed to flow right through me, and I half expected the torch to freeze in place.

I held my breath at first. Mostly from fear, but also because of the possibility that the air was poisonous. We'd seen it before in the mines. Air that is trapped underground for centuries sometimes kills the first few miners to breathe it in. It had never been a question in my mind that I would die young. Killed during an escape attempt or during an uprising, maybe — those were honorable deaths, at least. But I refused to have stories told about me dying from bad air.

As Sal lowered me down, I tried to think of what I knew about Julius Caesar. My mother had once told me a story about when Caesar was kidnapped by pirates on the Aegean Sea. Offended that they asked only twenty talents of silver for his ransom, Caesar demanded they increase it to fifty. Once it was paid and he went free, he returned to the island where he'd been held and executed the pirates himself. Then he recovered his fifty talents, and all their possessions too. It was no surprise that he went on to become a military general who won every war he ever fought.

If Caesar was that powerful, then who was I to dare enter his sealed cave?

The rope above me was sliding against a very sharp rock. Using the torch to look up, I saw strands of it beginning to fray. And when I swung the torch down, I was still too high to see the cave floor. I wondered if I had any chance of landing before Sal ran out of rope. If he did, would he pull me back up, or cut it? Without Radulf standing right beside him up there, he probably would've cut it already.

Finally, I had no choice but to take a breath, and was relieved to discover that the air was stale, but not poisonous. My relief was short-lived, however. The same breeze I drew into my body also snuffed out my torch, leaving me in complete darkness.

I called up to Sal that the light was gone, but he either didn't hear me or didn't care. Since he was using this cave to get rid of me, it was safe to assume the latter. And I continued to drop lower and lower. Into nothingness. Into the underworld.

After several long minutes, my feet collided with something hard. The ground, I hoped, but I didn't trust it yet. So with my hands, I groped around blindly. I found rock beneath me, but different from the type of rock we mined higher up. It was less porous, and sharper. It also seemed fairly flat, but before I had the chance to test a step, Sal lowered me down onto it. Whatever this was, I was committed now.

I was on my knees, and put my hands down again to determine how much room I had, but I touched upon something different than before. It wasn't dirt, but it wasn't as hard as rock either. It felt more like wood, a rounded, carved piece as smooth as — my breath caught in my throat. It was as smooth as bone. And round . . . like a skull. I ran my hands along the ground and felt more skulls and other bones.

I choked on my own breath, suddenly ill. Who were these people? Were they sacrifices made at Diana's temple? Or invaders whose discovery had become their tomb? A worse thought still: Was I meant to join them?

Horrified, I leapt to my feet and ran. I didn't know exactly what I was running on, but my feet rolled more than once, so I had a pretty good idea of what lay below. I would've apologized to the dead as I ran, but I didn't like the idea that someone here might answer back, so I kept my mouth closed and continued running.

After some distance, I came to solid ground and began to breathe easier. I'd hoped that my eyes would gradually adjust, as they always did when I was mining. But not down here. There simply wasn't any light for my eyes to adjust to.

So I took careful, halting steps, always keeping one hand

on the rope as my last connection to the surface high above me. But that was little comfort. I had never been so alone in my life.

Except, I was beginning to think I wasn't actually alone. Somewhere in the blackness, something was awake. Its breath came in even and deliberate strokes. Whatever it was, it knew that I was here too.

The bones I had stumbled over weren't from people who had died in here. They had all been killed.

FOUR

I felt my way through the cave like a blind man. And like most blind beggars, I knew my fate if I didn't find some sort of mercy. Darkness was part of any life in the mines. But I'd never been so deep on my own, and rarely without the hope for a lit torch somewhere shortly ahead.

The breathing continued, so quietly that I might not have heard it if everything else wasn't so still. And though I tried to move away from it, the echoes in this cave made it sound as if the creature was always ahead of me, just out of my reach. Or if there were no echoes, then the creature was moving, like a cat waiting to pounce.

I wanted to call to Radulf to pull me up, but I didn't. Not only was I certain he would ignore my request, but I also doubted the wisdom of giving away my exact location to the thing inside this cave. That was ridiculous, of course. No matter how blind I was, it clearly knew exactly where to find me.

Somewhere ahead there appeared to be some sort of light. It cast a faint gleam toward me, enough to see the fallen body of the first miner who had entered. He was on his back with his hands like claws frozen in place. His skin was white like the moon, as if all blood had drained from him, but I couldn't see any sign of injury. It was the look of a man who had died of fear.

I stepped carefully around him, then continued moving. It wasn't much, and I ignored the bigger question of how there could possibly be any light at all this far below ground. But I felt the pull of the light, calling me toward it. I was a moth to the flame.

When I had first started working in the mines, the dark had frightened me. But my mother had shown me how there was nothing in the darkness that didn't also exist in the light. Since then, I had never been afraid of moving in the deepest shadows . . . until now. Because this time, I was certain that she was wrong. Not only was some mysterious creature down here with me, but the closer I came to the light, the more I believed it was coming from Caesar's spirit. I felt him, still here, drawing me forward.

As real as that seemed, when I got closer, I saw the true source of the light. I was standing in the doorway of an enormous cavern, more vast than any place I'd ever seen underground. The room was filled with piles of gold. There were toppled stacks of coins, thousands of them, and heavy gold bars, each one larger than all the gold we might carve out of the mine in a year. Tossed carelessly amidst the rest were goblets, rings, and trays, all made of gold. But they weren't the source of the light. The glow came from something on the very top of the highest pile, something I only saw when I stood on the tips of my toes and arched my neck. It was a golden bulla, the size and shape of my fist, with a brown leather strap to hang from the neck. It seemed no different from any other, except for the glow. Admittedly, that was odd. I'd mined gold before, and it never, *never* glowed. Without a doubt in my mind, I knew this was the object Radulf wanted. It was Caesar's bulla.

I tried to step into the vast chamber, but by then I had reached the limits of the rope. If I was going to retrieve the bulla, there was no choice but to untie it. My plan was simple and undoubtedly stupid: move fast, grab the bulla, then race back to the cave's entrance. With any luck, the creature down here wouldn't fit through that doorway, and if it did, then I hoped Sal was faster with the rope than the creature was on his feet. I *hoped* for that. But I didn't truly believe it.

The instant I was untied, I set off on a full run toward the gold. My mind couldn't even begin to process the value of everything down here. One handful of gold could buy freedom for my sister and me. With another handful, we'd have a life of luxury. The sweetest foods, the softest fabrics. Even sandals for our feet. Radulf had told me to ignore everything but the bulla. But . . . what if I didn't?

The bulla was square in my vision as I continued running. If it had jewels inside, as most bullas did, then they could be as valuable as two handfuls of gold. Maybe more.

But the moment my foot touched the first gold piece, I was attacked from the side by something that knocked me to the cave floor. My head banged the ground hard enough that my vision blurred while the creature flew away. I tried to focus my eyes. Whatever the thing was, it had powerful wings, and a long, muscular tail.

I rolled to my stomach, then pushed myself up onto all fours while I got a breath. When I did, the creature swooped down from above, flapping its great wings hard enough to create a wind that rattled the gold pieces. It snatched me up with a giant talon that squeezed my lungs. I didn't care what this thing was — I'd have it for dinner before I gave up fighting. So I kicked back, landing a foot into its soft underbelly.

The animal dropped me almost on top of the pile of gold and screeched in anger. Only then did I turn to my back where I could see it better. It swept upward and fixed a furious eye on me. The animal had the head of an eagle, only it was as large as a horse's. When outstretched, its eagle wings commanded the cave, and the creature circled around, always with an eye on me. Once it crossed behind me, I saw the rest of its body, that of a lion.

I knew what this was. The king of all birds and the king of all beasts, joined in one animal.

It was a griffin.

My mother had told me about them, but had insisted they belonged only to the gods. If that was true, then this must be a very special griffin, for she guarded Caesar's treasure.

That was fine by me. For all I cared, she could guard the entire pile of gold, minus just one thing. That bulla was my only chance of getting back to the surface. Without it, I might as well give up now. My bones would join the rest down here.

The griffin flew to a ledge high above the cave floor and stared down at me. Then she squawked and the rear claws pawed the rock beneath it, ready to attack. I didn't have much time.

I eyed the bulla, almost within reach. The initials were clearly visible from here. G.J.C. Gaius Julius Caesar. This was the one Radulf wanted. I made another run up the stack of gold, placing my feet on the gold bars, which would hold my weight better than the coins. Once I was high enough, I dove for the bulla while straightening my body. With the bulla's strap clutched in my hands, I rolled down the pile.

Shrieking louder than before, the griffin shot off the ledge and aimed herself directly at me. No arrow could've been faster, or more direct in its target. A talon swiped for me, but I tossed up a golden pitcher, blocking the attack. The heavy pitcher fell, landing on my chest hard enough that I nearly blacked out for want of air.

Now at the bottom of the pile, I only had a short run to get out of this room. Then I'd find the rope and make my escape.

So I got to my feet and ran again, but the griffin found me with her tail, and swiped it so powerfully that it threw me against the cave wall. Never in my life had I taken a hit that hard. With many more hits like that, I might not have much life left. I had to escape this room, get away from that beast. The rope was out there in the darkness. I could still find it, and have Sal pull me up.

The griffin made several circles in the air before landing, then faced me with a low growl that could have come only from something born of the gods. I was trapped.

If I was going to fight this beast — regardless of how poor my chances were — I needed the use of both hands, so I put the bulla around my neck.

A wind swirled up around me when I did. "It isn't yours," the wind seemed to say. "It will curse you."

The threat didn't bother me — my present situation was worse than any curse from a dusty amulet. My bigger concern was that the wind spoke to me at all.

The wind came again, and bored through me. I felt it inside my bones, and it chilled my very heart. This was what had killed the other miner, what had driven Fidelius mad, I knew it. And though I felt it start to take me too, I clutched the bulla with both hands, instinctively using it to hold on to my life, until suddenly, the wind stopped, almost as if someone had closed a door to lock it out.

Which would have been a fine end to my worries, except for the griffin directly ahead, watching me. That wasn't natural. At least when she was attacking, I knew what to do, but what was the proper response to a dangerous animal that only stared? I tried speaking to her, hoping to fake enough calmness in my voice to make her relax.

"They call me Nic. It's only a hiccup of a name, I know, but it means 'victory of the people.' One day, all people will be free, and then they'll call me by my full name, Nicolas Calva."

The griffin didn't look all that impressed. Or at least, she took several steps toward me until I could almost reach out and touch her if I wanted to. Which I didn't, by the way.

I kept talking. "You need a name too." It wouldn't matter to the griffin, but it did to me. No matter what she might do next, I couldn't deny she was the most beautiful creature I'd ever seen. She deserved a name, and nothing ordinary. "I'll call you Caela, because you are from the heavens. You have flown with the gods."

Maybe it wasn't smart to remind her where she had come from. She might not like the idea of living amongst humans now.

The griffin screeched again, revealing the sharpness of her beak. Sure enough, I had reminded her.

"I won't take any more of your gold," I said. So much for my plans for a life of luxury. All I wanted now was any life at all. "But you must let me have this one piece. Please!"

Caela flapped her wings angrily, then quickly drew them in again when another wind swirled through the cave. It distracted her, and I took my chance. I darted beneath one wing on a full sprint for the exit. I might've had a small hope of escaping, except now that it was around my neck, the gold bulla seemed heavier than before and the weight of it pulled me to the ground.

It shouldn't have. More than once, I had carried heavy sacks of raw metal to the surface on the strength of my back. One bulla shouldn't be this hard.

Seeing me start to fall, Caela swiped a claw at me, which cut across my shoulder like a knife. I heard the rip of my tunic and immediately felt as if my shoulder had exploded. With a cry of pain, I fell to my hands and knees while black splotches marked my vision. I raised my arm and was half surprised it didn't fall off. How could it hurt so much and still be attached?

With my other hand, I fumbled about for the bulla to be sure it was still there, but this time, it had become warm. The heat from it poured into my hand and traveled up my arm, straight to my injured shoulder, still throbbing with pain. What I felt there was so fierce that I would've sworn fire had licked it. I tried to grab my shoulder and massage the pain away, but I couldn't reach it, so I had to content myself with letting it burn. The only good news was that I didn't feel any blood, which seemed impossible considering that it felt like the griffin's talon had touched bone.

I rolled to my back and saw Caela staring down at me. Why didn't she take one final swipe? I knew now how deep those claws could go. It wouldn't take much.

Caela screeched again, but this time her tone had changed. This wasn't anger. It was a warning. The ground beneath us shook, some sort of earthquake. I scrambled to my feet and stumbled toward the opening from where I'd entered. With the bulla's glow on my chest, it was easier now to see. I found the rope, but a rock instantly dislodged from above and landed directly on it, not far from my feet.

I needed that rope. It was my only chance to escape this cursed place. So while trying to dodge other falling rocks, I clutched at the rope and pulled with all my strength.

It was a mistake. I didn't see the rock coming straight for me until it was too late. Even as it crashed onto my head, I thought about how meaningless my life had been, and how quickly I would be forgotten. This was never the way I had wanted to die.

FIVE

There was no possible way to explain my waking up.

I lifted my aching head long enough to guess at which of the nearby rocks had struck me, but it didn't much matter. Any of them were large enough to have finished me off.

The scratch on my shoulder still burned, but less than before. Maybe in the chaos of fighting a griffin, it had seemed worse than it really was.

And I felt for the bulla around my neck, breathing easier once it was in my hand again. It was already hard to imagine myself without the bulla, which was absurd, of course. But it should be mine. I had claimed it from the bitter wind. From Caesar's ghost.

I wished I knew how much time had passed since the earthquake. Was it minutes, or hours . . . or days? Was it worse on the surface, or had they even noticed it?

I heard breathing again and realized the griffin's warm body was right behind me. She must've dragged me away from the entrance after I fell, or else I'd have been buried there. Either she had nestled into me now, or somehow in this cold cave I had moved closer to her. She seemed to be asleep.

Being so close to a griffin should've horrified me, and my instincts should've begged for me to run. But they didn't. In fact, all I felt was the desire to stay close, as if this creature who had so recently threatened my life was now the only one who could save it.

Or more likely, thoughts like these had been the beginnings of Fidelius's madness. If I moved carefully, maybe I could find a way out of here without disturbing her. But then what? Another cautious peek made it clear that the opening from where I'd come had collapsed. This room was sealed. And somewhere above us, more cracking sounds could be heard. I knew those creaks from other mine shafts that had failed and taken many good men with them. Whatever held the rest of this cave together was slowly crumbling to dust.

As slowly as I dared, I sat up, but I was only halfway to my feet when the griffin lifted her head. I backed up and raised my arms, a pathetic way to fend off another attack, but it was the best I could do in that moment.

She sniffed me, and I tried to convince myself it was only out of curiosity — not hunger. If she had wanted to eat me, she'd had plenty of time for that while I slept.

"Listen," I said, continuing my ridiculous strategy of speaking in Latin to an animal that communicated in screeches. "There must be another way out. This cave isn't safe anymore. If you don't fly us out, we'll both be crushed when the rest of it collapses."

Caela cocked her head as if she understood me. If she could, then she probably also knew that I had told her a half-truth. Yes, the cave might collapse, and yes, she'd be crushed if it did. But flying me out of here wouldn't make any difference to her. I was absolutely irrelevant to her survival. If I was lucky, she wouldn't figure that out.

Before I dared get her help, I needed her to trust me. Or more important, I needed to trust her. So I started walking around Caela, brushing my hand along the black feathers of her neck, and then running my fingers through the short brown fur along the lioness half of her. Caela arched her back at my touch and I felt a rumble inside her. The lion was purring, and I dug my fingers deeper. She crouched lower, but did not lie down. Was she moving so I could better reach her, or inviting me to climb on her back? I took a deep breath and tried to shake any doubts from my mind. Maybe I was wrong, and the consequences for misjudging a griffin couldn't be good. But the cracking sounds were growing louder. I knew how my story would end if I did nothing.

I continued scratching her fur until I came to her other side. Then with a whisper to the gods for help, I grabbed the hook of her wing and swung onto her back. Would the gods help me now? For surely if anyone had ridden this griffin before, it was them. The wound she had given me protested my movement, but I ignored it. Being crushed by falling rock would hurt a lot worse.

I held on extra tight, expecting she would try to throw me off, but she didn't. Instead, she widened her wings and flew upward on a steep climb. Some mornings, as I prepared to delve deeper into the earth, I watched the birds soaring upward in the air. I often wondered what their journey must be like, so weightless, so powerful. But feeling it now for myself was so much greater than anything I had ever imagined. When we were as high as we could possibly climb, Caela arced around and then dove at a sharp angle toward the floor. Near the bottom, she straightened out and I was certain we were about to collide with the black cave wall. Only when we were upon it did I see the change in shadow. It was a tunnel, plummeting even deeper into the earth. Deeper wasn't what I had in mind.

Caela couldn't use her wings in here, but she had built up enough speed in the dive to carry us through the length of the tunnel. I noticed water building on the ground below us. It seemed shallow at first, but the longer we flew, the more there was. Eventually, she had no choice other than to fly directly into the water, which she seemed perfectly comfortable with. I was less enthusiastic about where we were headed. I had the swimming skills of a lead pipe, and wherever we were, I needed Caela's help now more than ever before.

From the first moment we went completely under, the water pressed in on my lungs like a vise. Caela was moving so fast that I could see nothing other than bubbles and blurry images, and could think of nothing but how fond I'd always been of air. After only seconds underwater, I was already in trouble, but finally I saw a light above us. We were heading to the surface, and just in time.

When we finally broke through, I was so breathless I nearly let go, but with a wide lake below us, that would hardly be helpful. Now that we were in open air, Caela slowed in her flight. She skimmed the lake's surface, letting one talon cut a line across the water.

I leaned my head against the back of her neck. "Thank you," I breathed. "Thank you."

Her gentle caw back at me wasn't angry anymore. Either Caela had become mine, or I had become hers. I didn't know why or how this had changed, or whether it would last. But for now, I didn't need an answer. This single moment was enough.

We were crossing Lake Nemi, called Diana's Mirror by most of the other miners. They had warned me never to look at it, and never to ask questions about Diana's temple, which I easily spotted on the hills of the opposite shore. I couldn't see why any of their warnings mattered. It was beautiful here, and the bulla glowed through the grip of my fingers. I took it as a sign from Diana that she approved.

As we flew back toward dry ground, I began to wonder again how much time had passed since I had first entered the cave, and what surely had happened since then. Radulf would've blamed Sal for the collapse of the cave entrance and probably punished him. In turn, Sal would punish the other miners for not making the entrance stronger. They'd report my death to Livia and then tell her not to mourn since she should've been expecting it.

Livia.

If it weren't for her, I would have begged Caela to keep flying forever. To a place without mines or chains or whips. Somewhere I had any chance for a future. If such a place still existed in this world, I knew Caela could find it.

But I wouldn't leave without Livia — I had promised that to my mother, and it was a promise I intended to defend with my life. Left alone at the mines, Livia would be swallowed whole.

I wrapped one hand around the bulla again and pressed it to my chest. My heart seemed to beat just to get closer to it. Or maybe it was still beating *because* I was close to it. This was no ordinary bulla. I understood that now, though I couldn't figure out exactly what made it so different. Was it the reason I had survived when hit by that rock underground?

I had to return to the mines for Livia; there was no question of that. But if Radulf was still there, I would have to give him the bulla, and that infuriated me. I hated that Radulf would be able to take this from me. I hated that it would become his simply because he was a general and I was nothing.

Once I got back, I would give the bulla to Radulf, then beg him to fulfill his promise to take Livia and me to Rome. I would ignore what I had overheard of his threats to the empire, and pretend he hadn't smiled when I told him I might not return from the cave. Even if we were his slaves in Rome, it was better than working in the mines.

By now, Caela was flying us over a grassy knoll on the west side of the lake. The gray mines already seemed far away, only a memory of another life, another me. It was a good thing I had already decided to return for my sister, because if I hadn't, nothing else would've convinced me to go back.

Suddenly aware of how hungry I was, I began scanning the valley for any sign of food. As if the gods had granted my wish, almost instantly I spotted a large patch of wild strawberries, ones so fat and red I could see them from up here. How could they feed us nothing but tasteless crusts of bread each day when so much fresh fruit was this close?

"Put me down, Caela." I pointed out the strawberries. "Over there."

Rather than take my orders, Caela merely tilted her body and literally dropped me off. Luckily, we weren't too high off the ground, or it might've hurt worse, and the second I landed, she speared forward, probably hunting for food of her own. I was glad for that. It meant Caela wouldn't be eating me. More good news.

I ran down the hill where she had dropped me and dove into the patch. I ate greedily, stuffing whole handfuls of berries into my mouth and swallowing almost without tasting. Although it wasn't often, Sal sometimes got strawberries. He ate them right in front of us, and we privately grumbled that he wanted us to see him eating so that we would understand how far beneath him we were. Since I would probably never have this chance again, I ate until my stomach ached with pleasure. Was this how the wealthy felt after every meal, ill with happiness? I couldn't imagine what it must be like to live a day without hunger gnawing at each step.

If I could have, I would've stayed forever in that strawberry patch without a worry in the world. I stretched out on the ground to soak in the sun and to rest from the ordeal in the cave. I tried to feel for Caela's scratch again, but couldn't quite reach it. Finally, I gave up trying.

As my eyes grew heavier, I realized there might be another option than giving Radulf the bulla. I had fought the griffin, not him, and nearly died in the cave because of it. The bulla was literally the only thing in the world that was mine. Maybe I could claim that I'd never found the bulla, that if it ever was in the cave, it was lost to the ages now. With that thought, I tucked the bulla beneath my tunic and twisted it around so it hung under one arm and fell to my side, where it was less noticeable. The bulla lay against my skin with a comfort and familiarity as if it had always been with me. And if I was successful in keeping it hidden, it always would be.

The foolishness of attempting to hide the bulla was only outmatched by the likelihood of failure. So in the end, if I had to give it back, then I hoped it was cursed, just as Caesar's whisper had suggested inside the cave. Only then could I tolerate losing it.

Caela eventually returned to my side, and nestled in the brush beside me where she immediately fell asleep. I curled into her soft feathers, surprised by how calm I felt when she was nearby. Miners are never allowed enough of anything, especially sleep, and with the fragrance of ripe berries, warm sun, and my full stomach, my eyes were quickly lulled closed.

That was where they found me.

SIX

There were a few moments of disorientation while the guards from the mines yanked me back to reality. I immediately yelled for Caela, but other guards already had her in ropes and were trying to control her thrashing about.

Privately, I was angry with myself for falling asleep. Hadn't I learned by now that sleep was dangerous? Those who let down their watch for an instant were the ones we never heard from again. And yet, I had done exactly that.

I should've noticed the creak of the wagon as it approached the berry patch. I should've heard voices, or footsteps jumping to the ground. Had I really been that deeply asleep? Or was this group of guards so cunning that I could never have hoped to escape?

They weren't all that smart, I decided, as the first guard swatted me back to the ground with the side of his arm. I recognized him from the mines. His brutality made Sal look like a nursemaid. These men were rats. Getting caught was my fault, which probably meant I was a rat too. But they were ugly rats, and that was worse.

"Trying to escape?" one guard asked. "You must think you're pretty clever."

If I had been trying to escape, I wouldn't have lain out in the middle of a strawberry patch. And no, at the moment, clever was the last word I'd have used to describe myself.

"I was helping General Radulf." I rubbed the back of my hand against my mouth where he had hit me, but when I pulled it away, I couldn't tell if it was strawberry juice or blood. My mouth stung, though, so I didn't get up. I didn't want to risk him hitting me again.

"The griffin is getting away," one of the men shouted just as Caela angled her body sideways, slapping the man to the ground with her long tail.

"Then kill it," the guard standing over me ordered.

"No!" I cried, earning a kick to my side.

But the man who had been hit was preparing to obey the order. He reached into the nearby wagon for a bow and a handful of arrows.

I stood and yelled at Caela, who was squawking with fury. "Stop fighting them! Caela, stop this or they'll kill you!"

Either she couldn't hear me or she didn't care. The man nocked his arrow.

Ignoring the threats of the guards, I ran between the man's bow and Caela, and put a hand on her side.

"You have to stop fighting," I told her. "Caela, please, you won't win here."

She came down to all fours and was staring at me again. I was sure she could understand me, which was no surprise since she had once belonged to the gods. But understanding my words wasn't the same as obeying them. She cast an angry glance toward the guards, then screeched so loud it made my ears ring. But she stopped fighting. The bow was lowered and the other men surrounded her with more ropes. I could only hope she would allow them to safely take her. They grabbed me next, rougher than was necessary considering I wasn't fighting either.

"Be careful, you brutes!" a voice said from behind me. "Don't hurt him!"

At first I had to twist to see who was speaking, but it was a boy not much older than me. He marched to my side, forcing the guards' hands off me. He was tall, with curly golden-blond hair trimmed neatly around his face. I had no sandals at all to compare with his fine leather pair, and my tunic was plain, oversized until I grew a little more, and torn in the back where the griffin had scratched me. The boy's fine clothing was perfectly white with purple trim, and for good luck, around his neck he wore a golden bulla. It wasn't too different from the one hidden beneath my tunic, though I doubted his bulla glowed.

"Crispus, you shouldn't have run up here! Stay back from that animal!" Another man came forward in a similar white-and-purple toga. Only senators, or their sons, were allowed to wear those robes, but what was a senator doing out this far from

Rome? I noticed his shoes next: high buckskin boots colored black, rather than the red ones or sandals other, lower-ranking citizens wore. He had kind eyes, and thinning blond hair that seemed to be graying sooner than it should. His face was a series of worry lines, though he also seemed to have an easy smile.

But Crispus nudged his head toward me. "I told you I saw a griffin, and this boy controlled her. You should've seen it, Father!"

The guard next to me stepped forward and bowed. "This boy is an escaped slave, and must be punished, Senator . . . er . . ."

"Valerius." He walked closer to me. "Did you run from your master, boy?"

"No." Not this time.

A guard grabbed my arm again, but Valerius brushed it off and ordered the guards to stand back. "Why are you here, then?" My eyes darted away and he asked, "Did they hurt you?"

I glanced at Crispus, who looked genuinely concerned, and I wondered about his life, so different from my reality. I'd never met someone of his status who cared about anyone of mine. Maybe all patricians weren't the same.

I wasn't injured, but Valerius lifted my head with both hands anyway, which I hated. When he turned me for further inspection, he noticed the tear in my tunic. "What happened there?" he asked.

"It's only a scratch," I mumbled. Why couldn't they go away already?

He pushed a finger through the rip to examine the scratch, and then drew in a breath. Once he did, he whispered, "Crispus, come see this."

His son obeyed, gasped, and then asked, "What is that?"

A scratch, I wanted to say. The senator and his son were thin-skinned people who probably considered dressing themselves as a form of physical labor. I'd received plenty of scratches before, and this wouldn't be my last. Perhaps such strange concepts as bruises, cuts, and scratches were entirely unknown to soft patricians like them.

Valerius started to question me, but I cast my eyes away, instinctively not wanting to talk about it. It wouldn't take much to guess that Caela had given me the scratch, and then they might start asking why. The bulla against my hip felt warmer than it had before, almost like a warning against me letting those secrets be discovered.

Before he completed his sentence, however, another senator walked up behind them, dressed in the same white-and-purple toga. He was a round sort of man. Round eyes, round nose, and a round belly that probably consumed more cakes in a day than I had seen in a lifetime. Valerius greeted him as Senator Horatio, then quickly faced me forward again. He placed a hand over my torn tunic, covering the scratch. It sparked when he pressed down on the wound, and I winced, but with his other hand, he squeezed my arm, warning me to stop moving.

"How much is it to buy this boy?" Valerius asked the guards. "Who is his owner?"

"You wouldn't want him," Senator Horatio said, speaking of me. "This boy is filthy. Show us your teeth."

I'd heard how slaves were treated at auction, and this small taste of it was bitter in my mouth. They didn't even bother talking to me, and spoke about me as if I wasn't right in front of them, hearing every word they said. I clamped my mouth closed and tried to turn away, but Valerius's hand was still covering the scratch on my shoulder and he pulled me back. I wished he wasn't holding me so tight — the sting in the scratch was getting worse — but he wasn't giving me any room to squirm free.

One of the guards stepped forward. "He belongs in the mines south of this lake. We must bring him there for punishment."

Senator Horatio's only interest was in punishing me now. "Show me your teeth!" he demanded.

"Show me yours," I muttered. Once we returned to the mines, Sal could give me whatever punishment he wanted. It would be a pleasure compared to any service of this gasbag *ructuose* pig.

Despite both Valerius and Crispus persuading him to move on, Senator Horatio was becoming angrier. "I am the presiding magistrate of the Roman Senate," he said. "You will obey me!"

"He isn't worth your trouble," Crispus said dismissively. "If this boy was obedient, he wouldn't be here right now."

That caused Horatio to pause, and privately, I rejoiced. If my lack of obedience caused him to leave me alone, then it had just become my finest trait.

Without another glance at me, Horatio arched his neck. "Senator Valerius, this entire day has been a waste of our time. Those rumors of a discovery of Caesar's treasure were clearly false. I will return to Rome at once."

"Of course." Valerius gave him a curt bow but still did not release me. After Horatio was gone, Valerius then stepped toward the guards. "Perhaps we can arrange a deal. For enough money, you might forget you ever found this boy, or saw me here."

The guards blinked at one another as if they were considering his offer. Not that I had much choice in the matter, but I was considering my options too. Sal was at the mines. But then, so was Livia.

One of the guards finally brushed the senator's hand aside. "We'll return this boy for his punishment, or else we're the ones to receive it. You can negotiate for him back at the mines."

"Very well." Senator Valerius leaned down to me and whispered, "I am your friend, but do not trust that anyone else in Rome will feel the same way. I will try to get to the mines before dark. Until then, understand that the mark on your back is no scratch. It doesn't matter how you got it, only that there are people who will kill you if they see it."

Despite the rudeness of looking directly at him, my eyes met his. "Why?" I asked. "What's there?"

But there was no time for him to answer, for the guards grabbed my arms and pulled me into the wagon. The last thing I saw before we rounded a corner was his son, Crispus, who merely shrugged apologetically at me. Maybe because of Horatio's rude behavior. Or more likely, because he knew his father had just attempted to buy me in order to save my life. And failed.

SEVEN

As we rode back to the mines, the guards joked at the various punishments Sal might give me for running, but I hoped they were only jokes. Sal knew the truth about how I had come to be so far away. Less certain was whether the truth mattered to Sal.

Once we arrived, the guards shouted out for Sal to come, that they had found me. I heard my name being called like an echo around camp, and within minutes, I heard Livia's voice behind me. I squirmed around until I saw her.

Livia looked like a younger version of our mother, which made it hard to look at her on the days I missed our mother the most. Livia was tall for her age with gentle features and kind eyes. She had a round face with curly golden hair that she usually bunched up in a knot at the base of her neck so it didn't get in the way of her duties. Just as my mother had done. Despite the hard work and worries of a life in the mines, Livia was uncommonly pretty. I supposed that was its own sort of curse, because it drew Sal's attention to her, something she hated almost as much as I did.

Tears were running down Livia's face and they only increased when she saw me. I hated seeing her so upset and wished she could've hidden her feelings better. Because unless we escaped, I would die in the mines anyway, and when I did, my last thought would now be the picture of what that would do to my sister.

Sal came from the other direction and the guards pushed me out of the wagon and then set me on my knees. I immediately noticed that Sal was limping and his cheek was badly bruised. I wondered if those injuries had come from Radulf after Sal lost me in Caesar's cavern.

Sal greeted me with a kick directly to my gut. I had expected something like that and, frankly, was glad he didn't do worse. I took the kick with my eyes down and tried to recover my breath without falling over. The bulla was as heavy as it had been when I tried to run with it inside the cave, far heavier than gold should be. If I was going to take a beating for the bulla, then I figured that confirmed my right to keep it. So when I sat up, I angled my body to hide it better from him.

Livia was closer to me now. I only saw the edge of her skirt, but her cries rang in my ears. I tried telling her to leave but still didn't have enough breath for words. All I had to do was explain myself. Things would return to normal.

"So you're alive?" Sal didn't sound entirely happy about that fact.

"He was trying to escape," a guard said. "We found him near the lake." They didn't mention our encounter with the senators. Neither would I.

"I was only eating berries!" I looked up now. Sal's face was bruised worse than I had first thought. No matter my feelings for him, I still wouldn't have wanted him injured for something I'd done wrong. "When the entrance collapsed, I had to find another way out, and I did. I would've come back here."

"Why would anyone return to this place?" Sal said. "You're not only an escapee, but a liar too."

My eyes darted over to Livia, whose face had drained of color. She often told me that if I ever had the chance to escape, I should do it, even without her. I always replied that I wouldn't leave her behind.

"I belong in these mines," I said. "This is my life."

"There's no life here, Nic! When will you understand that?" He was screaming at me now, but I had to let him do it. Once he calmed down, he'd allow me back in.

I nodded toward the guards. "Have them untie me and I'll go back to work right now."

"Are you asking me to forget about your disobedience before? Or your attempted escape?"

Well, no, not asking in words. Though it would've been nice.

He continued, "And what happens if I return you with the other slaves, with your story about an exit deep inside the mines, and your belly full of berries? What will they think of that? What will they believe about their own chances to escape?"

I could have promised not to say anything, but he wouldn't have believed me and besides, the story would get around anyway. Whispers that I had survived the cave's collapse were probably already floating through the mines.

"Brand his forehead," the guard behind me said. "Let him be a lesson to any others who think about escaping."

"No!" I cried. "Please, Sal, don't do that!" If there was even the smallest chance of my becoming free one day, I could never build any sort of life with my face marked as an escaped slave. Branding my forehead would steal away my last hope. But maybe that was the exact reason why Sal would do it.

Sal brushed a hand over his bruised cheek as he thought it over. Then he crouched near me and parted my hair to reveal my forehead. He tapped the skin and smiled. "We'll put it right here, in big, black, burned letters."

"Don't do it, Sal." My heart pounded wildly, causing my hands to tremble. "You know I wasn't trying to escape. If I had intended to go, I would've succeeded."

"I know that." He removed his hand from my head. "General Radulf was furious when you disappeared. I told him that after everything settled in a few weeks, we could dig out the cave entrance again and get another man to go in. But that wasn't the reason for his anger. He was upset because *you'd* be dead by the time we got back inside. Tell me, Nic, why does a general of the Roman army care if you're alive?"

I shook my head, genuinely confused. "I don't know. I think you misunderstood him."

"And did you get whatever he wanted you to find in there?"

Letting Sal even touch the bulla was intolerable. He'd stain it with the grease of his hands, and tarnish it with his own corruption. "No, sir," I said, looking him straight in the face. No matter how wrong it was to lie to a master, I couldn't give the bulla up to him. Not to anyone.

Sal searched my face for any sign I was lying, and I was certain he would figure me out. I didn't care. Where I should've felt guilt for my lies, I only felt anger that he was forcing me to tell them. It wouldn't matter anyway. Surely he would sense the tumult of emotions inside me and know the truth.

But he didn't. And from the darkened expression on his face, I soon realized what a mistake it had been to lie. Because without the bulla, he had no reason to tell Radulf I had escaped from the cave. My life was worth nothing to him.

A wicked grin spread across Sal's face. "We can't let the other slaves think there's a way out of the mines. And if they do, they need to know the consequences of trying to leave. It's not enough to brand this boy's forehead. We have to kill him."

EIGHT

Despite my struggles, the guards threw me back into the wagon and held me tight. They wouldn't do it here, in view of the others. Instead, they'd take me back down the hill and leave my body in the weeds for the vultures to find. That terrified me more than anything. To enter the other world without a burial — I'd never be able to rest, not for the eternities.

"No!" Livia screamed. "Let him live, Sal, please. He's the only family I have left!"

"Slaves don't get to have families!" Sal said. "Because of your foul brother, that general almost ordered *my* death yesterday. He's not worth the trouble, not even for you. He's a curse."

"I'm not!" I yelled it with more fire than I'd ever felt before, but even then, I knew it was another lie. Maybe Caesar's ghost wasn't telling me that the bulla was a curse. Maybe he had said that by wearing the bulla, *I* would become the curse.

By then, the second wagon came rolling into camp, with Caela's limbs and wings tied up tighter than could possibly be necessary. Tears filled my eyes when I saw her, such a magnificent animal reduced to bondage. Whatever would become of me, I feared that her fate might be no better.

At least it provided a temporary distraction for Sal and the guards, who wandered over to the wagon to get a closer look. I took advantage of the moment to jump from the wagon and run the other way. With my arms still tied, it wasn't the best way to escape, but it was all I had.

I yelled at Livia to follow me, and at least for a little while, she stayed close. Then her footsteps trailed behind and when I turned to look for her, someone grabbed me around the waist and tackled me to the ground.

Sal.

He wrestled me to my back and knelt on one forearm to hold my arms down, then pulled out his own knife. I saw Livia a few feet away, also on the ground.

"Take this as a warning," I said with as much anger as I felt. "Once you kill me, I'm going to come back as a Shade. I will haunt you every day of your miserable life. And I'll enjoy it too."

Sal's eyes widened at my threat, then he said, "I'll have them toss you into the lake and drown your spirit. I will kill everything that is even a memory of you." He raised the knife and I closed my eyes.

"Sal, I will give you what you want!" Livia yelled. "I will marry you."

My eyes flew open and I struggled again beneath Sal's weight. "No!" I cried. As far as I was concerned, Sal was a roach that had crawled from the underworld and taken on human form. He hadn't done a good job of it either — the resemblance was far too close. If she married him, Livia's life would only grow worse than it already was, and I would never, *never* accept him as part of our family.

But she had Sal's attention now and he lowered the knife. Livia walked to Sal and fell to her knees beside him. "Let my brother live," she said, folding her hand around his arm holding the knife. "And when I come of age next year, I will be yours."

Sal put his hand over hers and my stomach lurched. When they both got to their feet, I could finally breathe again, though the air smelled like Sal, fetid enough to make me retch. The guards who had been with Caela returned and dragged me to my feet, waiting for their orders.

"No!" I said again to Livia. "You must not marry him."

"It'll save your life." Tears filled her eyes. "This is the only way."

Something about Sal's widening smile made me nervous. With a quick glance to Livia, he said, "That bird in the wagon will go to Rome, as my gift to the emperor. Nic will go with it, as part of the games in a few days." Now his eyes fixed on mine. "*I* will not kill you, Nic, but I will come to the games and see what sort of fun the empire has with your life there. I doubt you will last ten minutes in that arena."

Livia cried out and pled for Sal to change his mind, but he had kept his promise by allowing me to live, and would not be persuaded to do anything more. I yelled out in protest and fought with everything I had, but the guards threw me into the wagon and bound me to it with chains.

"Let me talk to him one last time!" Livia was sobbing now. "Mother wanted him to know —"

But by then, the guards had already begun driving me away, and her words were drowned out in the noise. I didn't fight anymore after that. My shoulder throbbed, I was numb with worry for Livia, and I was terrified of what lay ahead for me.

As we rode away in the waning light, I saw a wagon approach the mines, bearing a flag marked with the house of Valerius. Even from here, Crispus's curly blond hair was visible. They had come, just as the senator had promised. But they were too late.

NINE

We rode throughout a warm night, and were greeted in the early morning hours by dark skies that threatened rain. I didn't mind rain, especially in these hot summer months, but I dreaded the idea of the storm growing worse. Perhaps the only thing I ever preferred about living in the mines was it allowed me to stay deep underground during thunderstorms. During the lightning.

Our wagon finally stopped just outside the walls of Rome. The guards had sent a rider ahead to arrange my sale and a meeting place, but I couldn't see who had just bought me until he came around the back of the wagon and ordered me out.

My new owner was a handsome man who had the dark hair and eyes of an Arabian, and he had an intelligence about him that made me wary. I watched him carefully, hoping to get an idea for what kind of a master he would be. I didn't need much. In fact at this point, I'd have been satisfied with anyone who kept me alive, based on Valerius's warning. Once my new owner shook hands with the guard who had arranged my sale, he walked up and looked me over, the way he might examine a newly purchased horse. It was part of the process of acquiring a slave, I knew that, and yet I felt like little more than an animal beneath such coarse treatment. At least he untied the ropes around my wrists. That showed some sign of honor in him.

"My name is Felix," he said. "I will be your master, but I am also a servant to Emperor Tacitus, ruler of the Roman Empire. So anything you do for me will also be a kindness to him."

I didn't care. I had no loyalty to Emperor Tacitus. Nor to Felix, for that matter. But I did understand that my only hope of avoiding the lion's jaws in the arena was to make myself useful to him.

"And you're Nic?"

"Nicolas Calva."

He chuckled. "How did a slave get such a fine name? Will you add a *cognomen* to your title once you're in Rome? Nicolas Calva Magnus perhaps? Are you grand enough for a title like that?"

"No, sir." I glanced up at him with a grin. "Not yet."

"Well, Nicolas Calva, you look hungry."

I was always hungry, but for now, I said, "I'm thirsty." I couldn't remember the last time I'd had something to drink, and my mouth tasted like sand.

"We'll get on the road soon, and I'll have water for you then, all right?"

I nodded. My respect for Felix was growing.

Sal's guards began helping a girl transfer Caela into a caravan wagon. Even though her ropes weren't yet untied, Caela was already squawking with irritation. That concerned me, but for the moment, my attention was more on the girl.

Strange as it may sound, except for Livia, I had rarely seen any girls my own age. Girls who were born into the mines were quickly sold away, and the few women who were kept there to cook and tend to our wounds were usually widows of other miners. Livia only stayed because of Sal's fondness for her. So although I tried not to stare at the girl, I wasn't doing a very good job.

Her light brown hair was worn long and pulled away from her face. Her tunic was simple like mine, though a bit longer and in much better condition. Around her neck was a small *crepundia*, decorated with small wood carvings and trinkets that would have been made for her when she was a baby. I found it odd that she still wore it. She was working for Felix, so she wasn't a patrician, but she had a knife at her belt, so I doubted she was a slave either. She must be a plebian, then. I liked the idea of having her life one day, not bound to any master, but no master of others either.

"Her name's Aurelia and she's as cuddly as a rabid bear," Felix said, following my gaze. "She'll be guarding you on the way into Rome, and you won't want to cross with her."

I'd already crossed with a griffin, and based on the sting in my shoulder, I'd lost that fight. I didn't need to take on anyone who was compared to a bear. As if she had overheard us, Aurelia paused from her work to glare at me. I pretended not to notice, mostly because it would probably annoy her.

Felix continued, "I work in the *venatio*. Do you know what that is?"

It was the animal show that took place in the arena before the gladiator battles. Several of the miners had attended those games before and often described them to me while we worked. Some animals were put on display or taught to do tricks — since Caela was so rare, that's what I figured she'd be asked to do. But most of the animals were made to fight one another, just as the gladiators did. The more brutal the show, and the more blood that was spilled, the louder Rome cheered.

When I nodded, Felix said, "Our next games are in two days, but I'm wondering if I'll be able to keep the griffin for even the next two minutes."

The guards were trying to pull Caela from the wagon, while Aurelia held the caravan door open. Caela was resisting the tugs on her ropes, then suddenly screeched and flared out her wings, breaking her bonds. Aurelia pulled out a knife and ran forward, but Caela swatted her to the ground and leapt from the wagon. Sal's pathetic guards ran in fear and in seconds Caela had already driven them away, but Aurelia was trapped.

I ran forward and waved my arms while moving closer to Caela to calm her. Caela squawked at Aurelia, whose knife was still tight in her grip.

"Put that away!" I said. "You're making her angry!"

"I'm making *her* angry?" Aurelia said. "She attacked me!"

I turned on my heel and yelled, "Then stop looking like someone who expects a fight. Put that knife away! I'll manage the griffin!"

Aurelia opened her mouth to object, then shoved her knife into its sheath and backed away. More gently now, I turned to Caela and pointed to Felix's caravan. "That's for both of us. I'll go in with you."

Caela pawed at the ground, then walked with me up the short ramp and into the caravan. Once we were in, Felix said, "Nic, come back out."

"I'd better stay with the griffin."

"No. Come out *now*."

He was eyeing me suspiciously, which made me nervous. But he had also promised me water, and I wouldn't do anything that interfered with getting some. So I went down the ramp again and stood in front of him.

"I saw a tear in your tunic."

My hand brushed against my side where the bulla was hidden. "There are several tears in it, sir. Perhaps you can get me a new tunic."

"I might have to, because I thought I saw . . ." He put a hand on my shoulder, exactly where the strap of the bulla lay. I lowered my eyes, hoping he wouldn't think anything of it, but knowing full well he would be curious. He reached beneath the tunic, pinched the strap between his thumb and forefinger, frowned at me, and then said, "Turn around."

I didn't want to. Valerius's warning still rang in my ears, of the danger of showing anyone the scratch . . . or the mark. I wasn't sure exactly what was there now.

But refusing a master would only earn me a bare-backed whipping, which would reveal the bulla faster. So I turned, expecting the worst. He widened the tear in the tunic until he could better see what he was looking for and even ran a finger over the scratch. I flinched when he did. Not because it hurt, exactly, but his touch sent a spark into my chest that forced me to move.

"Did the griffin do that?" he asked.

I didn't answer. I didn't want him to think Caela was dangerous, or else she might not be given to the emperor. I knew her fate if the emperor refused her.

He grunted and turned me to face him again. "Your master said I'd have no problem with you, but I'm beginning to doubt that."

"I won't cause any trouble." I meant the words, but they still sounded untrue. Especially with the problem already hanging from a strap around my shoulder, which bore a scratch that people would kill for.

Felix frowned, and then grabbed my arm as a passing merchant jokingly called over to him, "Your new slave is young, Felix. Let's hope this one isn't also eaten by tigers."

Though the man who had spoken laughed loudly, it was hardly a joke. My head shot up. "Also?"

"The tigers are not your biggest problem right now." Felix pushed me back up the ramp and into a corner of the caravan where he clamped a manacle down on one leg. "Stay quiet, if you know what's good for you."

"You said I'd get water!" I called. "Please!"

Felix called for Aurelia to come over. "Don't get close to that boy, but keep an eye on him."

Once she was inside, he closed and locked the door behind us.

"You promised me water!" I yelled. And when he didn't respond, I drove my elbow into the side of the caravan, wanting him to know how angry I was. How desperate my thirst.

Across from me, Aurelia gasped, and then I saw why. My elbow had left a deep dent in the metal wall. I couldn't explain how. I only knew that I had done it.

She pulled out her knife and faced me as the caravan began to drive. "Stay away from me," she muttered. "You're cursed."

"I'm not," I said, but the lie sounded insincere, even to me. Every part of me understood that she was absolutely correct. Maybe I hadn't escaped Caesar's ghost in that cave after all.

TEN

In the caravan, Aurelia had a skin of water sloshing at her side, and outside it had begun to rain. They were painful reminders of my thirst, taunting me. Aurelia hadn't stopped staring at me since we left, except to glance at the dent I'd made with my elbow. Then she'd shudder and darken her glare.

"I need some of your water," I told her.

"Felix put that chain on your leg for a reason," she said. "Maybe you'll tell me why."

Maybe not. Her hand still gripped her knife, and the last thing I needed was trouble from her too. I said, "I don't belong in chains. I'm not dangerous."

"I'm sure you're as harmless as a butterfly. If a butterfly could dent metal, of course."

"It's a warm morning. The metal must've gone soft."

"It could be hotter than Apollo's sun, and that metal still wouldn't have softened."

"Give me that water."

Aurelia pulled the skin from over her shoulder, uncorked the opening, and took a drink.

"Please, Aurelia."

She started to cork it again, but I lurched forward, hoping to somehow reach far enough to grab it from her. The chain on my leg pulled tight, then, with a knocking sound, it gave me two more inches. I glanced back and saw the bolt that had fastened the chain to the floor had come loose. But I still wasn't close enough to Aurelia.

"I was going to give it to you. Now you're threatening me?" she asked.

"Threatening you? No, I just need the water!"

"Then take it!" She tossed it to me and her eyes fell upon the loosened bolt.

I didn't want to think about how it had pulled free so easily. Instead, I swallowed the water in giant gulps and too quickly the water was gone. She stared at me the entire time, her finger stroking the crepundia around her neck. There were at least a dozen carved miniatures on it, all strung together on a leather cord. Several were symbols of the harvest, a bundle of wheat or a bunch of grapes. I also noticed an old Roman coin and a carving of a timepiece, but the largest of all was a sickle crossed with a knife that wasn't much different from the real knife Aurelia carried with her. In the center was a satchel only a little smaller than the bulla. Maybe hers also held gems.

I wondered why she might put so much value on what was only a child's plaything. Then I felt the bulla against my side. It was for children too.

I corked the skin and tossed it back to her. "Thank you."

"Something's not right," she said. "I still don't trust you."

Which was fine, given that I still didn't like her. My fingers traced the outlines of the bulla, and I wished I could take it out and study it closer. Whatever Felix decided to do with me next, he knew about the mark and probably the bulla too. Once he forced me to show it to him, he'd accuse me of having stolen it, which, probably, I had. I'd be immediately killed for that.

Caela rolled in her sleep, which left a talon not far from Aurelia's hand. She reached out to pull the remaining rope free from Caela's leg, but Caela awoke and snapped at her fingers. "Fine!" Aurelia said. "Then I won't help!"

I couldn't help but laugh, which only focused the heat of Aurelia's glare on me. In response, I stretched as far from the wall as the chain allowed and patted Caela instead, mostly to prove that I could.

"That griffin saved your life, you know," Aurelia said.

My first thought was how Aurelia could possibly know about our escape from the cave, and I fumbled around for a response.

But she added, "Felix had intended to put you in the arena tomorrow along with the other criminals, but now he'll need you to manage the griffin."

"I'm not a criminal."

"Yes, and you're not dangerous either, I already know."

A crack of thunder roared above us and I ducked. Now it was Aurelia's turn to laugh. "It's only noise."

"The lightning that goes with it isn't noise."

"We won't get hit by the lightning."

"Tell that to my father."

"Did he —?" She answered her own question. "Oh, that's awful."

When I remained silent, her eyes darted up to the window above my head, and she asked, "Ever been in the city?"

"No."

"Rome is the most amazing place in the world. I sometimes help Felix in the amphitheater. It holds more than fifty thousand Romans, and everyone can attend the games for free, even slaves."

"I won't be a slave forever."

She shrugged that off. "Then what would you do? I doubt you have any skills to make a life in Rome."

"Maybe I'll get a job riding in caravans, guarding things that aren't dangerous." A grin tugged at my mouth. "How hard could that be?"

Her eyes narrowed. "I'm paid to control that griffin! There's not enough gold in the empire to make guarding you worthwhile."

She probably didn't know how much gold was piled in Caesar's cave. If I was more trouble to her than all of that, then that was a compliment.

"Why do you need the pay?" I asked. "Doesn't your family take care of you? They must have given you that crepundia."

"My father gave me the crepundia when I was a baby," Aurelia said. "Before I was exposed."

"Oh." I knew about that. Several of the slaves in the mine had come to us through exposure. If the father of a household didn't want a child, he would put it out on the streets. Maybe the child would be picked up by a loving family willing to adopt it. Very often slavers would take it. I wasn't sure what had happened to Aurelia, but if she still had that crepundia, I knew there must be a part of her hoping to learn who her family once was, and trying to earn her way back to them.

"Sorry," I muttered.

"Just stop talking," she said.

That was fine by me. Caela shook her head as if I should've known better. But what did she know about girls? She'd been in a cave her whole life. Of course, so had I.

I did know one thing for certain, which was that I wanted nothing else to do with Aurelia. Felix had been kind when he compared her to a rabid bear. Given the choice of a traveling companion, I'd have preferred the bear. Because Aurelia and I would never, *never* become friends.

ELEVEN

The storm passed quickly and it wasn't long afterward that the wagon stopped too and our doors opened. I put a hand on Caela to steady her from jumping out at any strangers, but it was only Felix who appeared.

"We're at the gates of Rome," he said. "It should be safe to come out now, if you want to enter the city with me."

My heart leapt at the opportunity. I hadn't expected to be allowed to enter this way, like a freeborn. I told Caela to be good, knowing full well she'd do whatever she wanted anyway, and then scrambled out of the wagon.

Aurelia started to follow, then Felix held up a hand to her. "You're paid to watch that griffin," he reminded her.

She shook her head. "I won't stay in there alone. It doesn't like me."

I smiled, but said nothing. The joke was far too obvious.

He sighed. "Then ride on the back. Nic and I need to talk up front."

My grin widened, and I made sure she saw it. "If the griffin makes a mess in there, be sure to clean it up."

She growled back at me, or something very close to it, which only made me happier. Felix returned to the seat of the wagon and then invited me to sit beside him. I couldn't climb up fast enough. Once I was in place, he handed me a sack of olives. I ate five before realizing that he probably hadn't intended for me to eat them all. There were only a few left. Before I could debate the wisdom of my actions, I ate them too.

Now that we were alone, I wanted to ask Felix about the scratch from Caela, or whatever mark he said was there instead. With Aurelia watching me so carefully from the wagon, I hadn't dared feel for it again, but the mark wasn't my only concern. The bulla still hidden beneath my tunic warmed every time I thought about the mark. It was warming now, in fact. Surely that was no coincidence.

"Thanks for the olives," I said to Felix. It seemed like a safe way to begin the conversation.

"Where did you get the bulla?" Obviously, Felix was more direct than me.

I scratched my head while I considered an answer, and finally came up with, "I found it." It might not be the full story, but it was true enough for his question.

"How long have you had it?"

"Only a couple of days."

"And that mark on your shoulder was a scratch from the griffin?"

"Nothing was there before, not until the scratch. What is the mark?"

Felix sighed. "The shape is unmistakable: a circle of fire, with a trail behind it like smoke. The entire mark is blood-colored."

"And what does it mean?"

"It means you're in a lot more trouble than you know." Felix pointed ahead to a massive brick wall that he said now surrounded the entire city of Rome. "They say it's to keep the barbarians out. But I sometimes wonder if the real barbarians don't already live inside these walls."

The arched wooden gate through which our wagons would enter was large enough for a giant and wide enough for men to walk across it from above. Spaced apart every hundred feet were square turrets to protect Roman soldiers if they had to fight during an invasion. As we came closer, several men blocked the road and held up hands for us to stop. They wore the same red-cloaked uniforms as the soldiers who had come to the mines with Radulf, and that was enough to make me uncomfortable. Were they involved in his treason too?

I pressed a hand against the bulla at my side, then noticed it vibrate beneath my touch.

Felix noticed. "Don't do that," he said. "Put your hands in your lap and try to look relaxed." I obeyed and he added, "I'll want to see that bulla next time we're alone."

Maybe. I didn't really want to show him, but he seemed to know more about it than I did. Besides, if my troubles were as bad as he suggested, then I definitely needed someone's help.

When we drew up to the soldiers, Felix told them who he was and about the griffin he was bringing in.

A soldier eyed me. "You have new slaves too?"

"Just this one." Felix's tone was relaxed, a reminder for me not to look as guilt-ridden as I felt. He brushed his arm toward me, pushing my hand away from the bulla again, and then added, "He isn't worth much, but he'll be of some use with the animals."

"Since when does a worthless slave ride up front with his master?" The soldier drew his sword and used it to point at me. "Climb down here, boy."

What if Radulf had told them to watch for a slave with a bulla? What if they saw the tear in my tunic? My heart pounded as I considered my options, all of which ended with me on Caela's back, attempting to outrace the soldiers' arrows. Or Aurelia's knife — I wasn't sure whose side she'd be on. Either way, Caela would have to break herself out.

As if she had heard my thoughts, there was a sudden banging in the caravan, so fierce it nearly overturned the wagon. The soldiers jumped back and Felix began shouting about letting us pass before his cargo became truly angry. But I was more focused on a sizzling sting in my shoulder that seemed connected to Caela's squawking. She *had* heard my thoughts. Just as the mark was a part of me now, and the bulla, she had become a part of me too.

"Move on," the soldier shouted, waving us on. "Get that

animal into a cage where it belongs!" Felix immediately obeyed, though he brushed my hand away from the bulla yet again as we passed between the gates.

"It's safe now," I communicated to Caela. "Be calm." And as she settled down, the sting in my shoulder eased too.

"Can you explain what just happened?" Felix muttered.

"No." Well, I *could* explain it, but I *wouldn't*. Not until I better understood it myself.

Minutes later, as we crossed the bridge over the Tiber River, I began breathing more evenly, and Felix's knuckles around the horse's reins were no longer white. The river was wide and powerful, though I wasn't sure how deep it went. I only knew that I didn't care to find out. On the opposite side, a small brick arch was dug into the bank with dark water pouring into the river.

"That's the *Cloaca Maxima*," Felix said when I pointed it out to him. "Rome brings in new water from all over the land on great aqueducts above our heads, and then sends the old water out again in the sewers beneath our feet."

The very notion of sewers running below ground was amazing. One of my few memories from Gaul was having sewage accidentally tossed on me while walking down a road. I couldn't imagine a place where water freely came and went, where thirst wasn't a daily problem.

As Rome came into view, my eyes fixed upon the aqueducts, large enough that I doubted anyone but the gods could have built them. Their massive arches towered over tall brick buildings that served as homes, shops, and majestic public forums. Shoddier ones were constructed of wood, many of which had burn scars on them, and I wondered what would happen to this city if a fire ever raged out of control.

Around us, the streets bustled with people and carts and wagons, everyone with someplace to go and a job to do. I'd never seen so many people in my life. I had no idea that so many people even existed.

As we came closer to the center of Rome, the buildings grew finer and so grand they stole my breath away. Each one seemed like a palace, lining the streets with white marble walls and columns, or thick, square-cut granite, all of them trimmed with gold, silver, or copper. These were the very materials I had mined for the last five years, which meant that in some way, I had been part of building Rome all this time, and never known it.

"Is this Elysium?" I whispered to Felix, for it seemed impossible that so much beauty could exist anywhere but in the afterlife.

Felix laughed. "No, my boy. You see this place with your living eyes. It was built over hundreds of years and only grows finer. A million people live in this city, all of them engaged in the promise of what it means to be Roman. You are Roman now as well. You are part of this promise."

My eyes widened as we rounded another corner and a

building rose from the horizon, greater than anything I'd seen before in my life.

"It's stood there for two hundred years and will likely stand for eternity," Felix whispered. "We call it the Flavian Amphitheater."

I already knew the name from the men in the mines, but their description wasn't nearly magnificent enough.

The amphitheater stood four levels tall, higher than any structure I'd ever seen. The bottom three levels were a series of grand arches. The public could come and go through any of them on the ground level, but the arches along the two levels above that were only frames to display marble statues of the gods and the images of emperors who thought they should be immortalized too. The panels of the top tier alternated between bronze shields and rectangular windows. It was breathtaking, in every sense of the word.

As we drew closer to the amphitheater, I also saw a colossal bronze statue planted in front, as tall as twenty grown men. My mouth fell open just to gaze at it.

Felix laughed. "That's Emperor Nero, may he rot in peace. He nearly destroyed the empire during his reign, and then built that statue to celebrate himself for it. It took twenty-four elephants to drag that statue here after Nero's death."

I chuckled at the spectacle that must've been, but then fell silent as I continued to soak in the sights as quickly as we passed them.

Finally, we stopped right in front of the amphitheater. Felix looked over at me. "Well, Nic, what do you think?"

I only smiled back at him. Whatever my opinion of Rome had been before, I knew that I had just entered the greatest city in the world. A part of me felt that I had come home.

TWELVE

The city bustled around us. I would have loved to explore and discover Rome's secrets for myself, but that was not for a slave to do. Instead, once we reached the far side of the amphitheater, Felix immediately turned to me. "The griffin is for you alone. A ramp ahead of you leads to the *hypogeum* beneath the amphitheater. Her cage will be the first one you come to down there."

"She won't go in it," I said.

"She'll race in," Felix countered. "I had the men prepare her cage with a large nugget of gold. Griffins will never leave their gold."

Which explained why Caela had fought so hard over the gold in Caesar's cave. She wasn't protecting it for him; she wanted it for herself. That is, except for the bulla, which would have belonged to Caesar in a far more personal way. Once I put it on, our fight was over. Caela may have loved her gold, but she respected the bulla.

I jumped off the wagon while Felix shooed away some workers trying to open the back doors.

"Nic is the only one who will manage this animal," he told them. "Make sure the others know."

I didn't miss the glares from the men, but they didn't bother me either. I had the feeling that nobody spared much concern for the animals here. They weren't worthy to handle Caela. She was the emperor's gift.

Aurelia hopped off the back of the caravan as soon as she saw me. "Your bird is as dangerous as you are," she said. "Did you hear her reaction when those soldiers tried to take you?"

I grinned. "Oh, I thought that was you making such a fuss over me!"

Her face reddened. "I'd never fuss over you."

Despite knowing it would only make her angrier — or perhaps *because* of that fact — my smile widened. "Isn't that what you're doing right now?"

She grimaced and marched over to Felix to collect her pay for the trip. I watched him place a single coin into her hand. She started to argue back, saying something about needing to feed others too, but he said if she didn't leave, he'd hire someone else next time. She gave me a quick glance before walking away. A sad glance that made me wonder if I'd been wrong about her before.

When I pulled the back doors open, Caela reacted to the bright light with an angry squawk that startled me. I couldn't blame her. If she had lived in Caesar's cave for a long time, then I was sure that like me, she wasn't used to so many other people and the hurry of such a vast and complicated city.

For the most part, it was an easy walk toward the amphitheater. However, there was nearly a problem when a patrician passed us on horseback. Caela reacted by flapping her wings and cawing a warning at the horse. I put myself in front of her body to keep her from charging at the horse, whose rider spurred him away. She squawked in irritation, but let me hold her back. Caela didn't seem bothered by anything else here, but she definitely hated that horse.

"Are you trying to get us both in trouble?" I scowled at Caela, who was still craning her head to see where the horse had gone. Then as we kept walking, I felt her beak brushing through my hair, and I smiled. Caela was preening me. Her attempt at an apology perhaps. And in all fairness, I probably did need a lot of preening.

We entered the amphitheater beneath one of its many massive arches, and then found the ramp leading to the hypogeum, which appeared to be an endless underground maze. I hesitated at first, and so did Caela. I didn't like the idea of going beneath such a massive structure. I had seen cave-ins at the mine when nothing at all weighed down the dirt over our heads, and it seemed impossible that even the gods could keep this behemoth of a building from collapsing on top of us. I already felt the heat rising from below, like a summer day in the underworld. I was used to the constant chill of the mines, not the oven that awaited me now.

The smell assaulted me next. Wherever there is heat, there will be sweat, and most of the hundreds of men around me smelled like something that had died. Worse still were the animals in their stacked cages. I had no idea there would be so many. Where had they all come from? I wondered. Everything down here felt inhuman, including the humans. Now I was one of them.

Caela started to back up, but others were behind us now. "No," I said, placing a hand on her side. "Remember that you're a gift for the emperor. He only wants to see you — nothing bad will happen."

Once we were at the bottom of the ramp, it was obvious which cage had been reserved for Caela. A massive gold nugget lay inside it, chained to the cage's bars. I had heard Caela's power against the metal walls of the caravan. If she wanted that gold, no chain was going to stop her.

Cacla forgot everything else around her and ran into the cage. Two other men near me slammed her door shut and locked it. I followed her to the bars and told her everything would be fine, but her attention was on the gold now. She had forgotten about me.

I felt guilty for locking her in there, as if I had betrayed her somehow. But it had to be done — they would've killed her otherwise. Besides, once the emperor saw her, she would be treated as well as she deserved.

Felix found me sometime later sitting beside Caela's cage. I hadn't gone anywhere else because I wasn't sure where to go, nor would I willingly help with the caging of these animals.

"Are you hungry?" Felix asked, and then shook his head. "From the looks of you, I don't need to ask."

"What about Caela?" I asked. "The griffin — will they feed her?"

Felix frowned. "Not yet. But she will have her chance to eat."

So I got to my feet and followed Felix, who led me up the ramp and back outside. I was so grateful to be away from the fetid heat that it would've been enough just to stay here in the open air, but then, he had also offered me food.

As we walked, Felix gestured to a throng of people gathered on a corner of the road who were holding out sacks of coins and yelling at one another. Felix asked if I knew what they were doing, but I only shrugged.

"Setting up their bets for the games," he said. "Mostly on which gladiator they expect to win. By the end of the day's events, some wealthy men will have lost everything as a lucky plebian walks away with his toga and his home."

I squinted into the sun to look at them. "It looks like a mob."

"It *is* a mob," he said, then stopped and looked down at me. "All of Rome is a mob. The emperor and his senators prance about as rulers do, but they know how fragile Rome really is. Without the Praetors, it would've collapsed already."

"Praetors?" I asked.

Felix motioned around us. "They're the ones who really run this empire. The Praetors are our judges, governors, and administrators. They provide bread for the bellies and distraction with the games. But that's only their public face. In private, they are —" He stopped, as if he couldn't force out the rest of his words.

"Are what?" I asked.

"They are dangerous!" He drew in a sharp breath. "But Rome needs them. Without the Praetors, the mob becomes . . . a mob."

I thought about Radulf's claim back at the mines, that he would crush the empire in his fist. Were the Praetors part of his plan? I wondered.

We walked in silence until Felix pointed to a wide hill in front of us. "Do you know the name of that place?"

I shrugged, but held my tongue. How would I possibly know that?

"It's Palatine Hill, the center of the seven hills of Rome. The emperor has his palace there, but that's not why I'm showing it to you. That, my friend, is the most sacred place in Rome. Do you know why?"

I figured it had something to do with the gods, because as far as I could tell, everything did in the Roman Empire. But I knew nothing else.

"A thousand years ago, the twin sons of the god Mars, Romulus and Remus, decided to form a new city on this very spot. Romulus stood on Palatine Hill. Remus stood on Aventine Hill, behind it. Whichever twin saw the first bird would know he was the rightful king."

I pictured Caela in my mind. More perfect than any bird of the skies, or animal of the land.

"As the story goes, Remus saw the first bird," Felix continued. "But immediately after, Romulus saw a flock of ten birds. Which was the greater sign? Each brother claimed the right to the throne. As Remus and Romulus fought for control of the land, Romulus killed his brother, then founded the city of Rome on that spot." Felix eyed me sideways. "Before you can understand Rome, you must understand where we began. We are a product of our history of violence, betrayal, and blood."

I was still thinking of Caela, the way I had abandoned her in that cage. "I know about the execution of criminals at the games, and the gladiators who battle one another," I said warily. "I know those animals must be sent into the amphitheater as part of the battles, but what will happen to the griffin? Surely she is not part of the venatio. She is a gift to the emperor, right?"

Felix drew in a breath and released it with a sigh. "In two days, the emperor will be watching the games. Then he will see who is stronger, his mighty gladiators or the griffin, animal of the gods."

I closed my eyes and tried to absorb the horror I felt. The venatio was a hunt — Felix had told me that, but I had never thought it included Caela. Inexperienced and too eager to please, I had just led Caela into a cage to await her turn to die. I had only one friend left in this world, and with that betrayal, I was already becoming a part of Rome.

THIRTEEN

Eventually, Felix led me to his home, a small wooden box behind a loud tavern and within perfect view of a much larger, fancier building called the Ludus Magnus, where the gladiators received their training. Felix gazed around the spare furnishings of his home and sighed. "It isn't much, but it's what I've been given."

Maybe it wasn't much to him, but I had trouble believing an entire room had been granted to only one man. One day, I would achieve something like this for myself. I would have my own four walls.

Felix picked up a tunic from his table and handed it to me. It was no fancier than my current one, but it was clean and would hide the mark on my shoulder.

"Thank you," I said, already changing out of my old one. I couldn't wait to be rid of it.

Felix next went to a cupboard and pulled out some drink, which he poured for me, and some bread and cheese. He placed them on a small table and then invited me to sit beside him on the floor. "Please," he said, motioning toward the items. "Have all you want."

All I wanted was everything he had set out, and more. But I didn't reach for any of it. Not yet.

"Why are you helping me?" I tried not to sound as suspicious as I felt. "None of the other slaves are here."

"Is that how you see yourself, Nic, as a slave?"

"Why does it matter how I see myself?" I folded my hands together. "You bought me. You ordered me to cage up a griffin who'll go to her death in two days, and I obeyed, because you own me."

Felix hesitated a moment before cutting a slice of cheese, which he held out to me. I popped a piece into my mouth. It was one of the most delicious things I'd ever eaten, and I quickly ate the rest. He cut me a second slice, thicker than the one before, and offered it, but this one I held in my hand. None of this made any sense. Slaves were never treated so kindly by their masters.

Then it became clear. Felix set down the knife and said, "I want to see that bulla now."

Rather than answer, I ate the second slice of cheese. Not necessarily because I wanted it, but because I needed time to figure out what to do. I couldn't allow him to take the bulla from me. And I wouldn't let him give it to Radulf who seemed to know things about this bulla that I didn't. If Felix intended to take it, how much of a fight would it require to stop him?

But refusing him didn't exactly solve my problems. Maybe I lacked enough good sense to keep from stealing the bulla in the first place, but now that I had, I also had to acknowledge that I'd waded into waters that were far over my head. I needed his help. After a little maneuvering with my arm, I withdrew the bulla from beneath the tunic and held it up for him. I hadn't looked directly at the amulet since hiding it. Now I realized the faint glow that had been there the first time I saw it was still there. I started to remove the bulla, then left it around my neck, just to be clear that it was mine. Which really, it wasn't.

Felix leaned over and held the bulla in his hands. I waited for him to comment on its warmth or the vibration whenever it was touched directly, but he said nothing and didn't even seem to feel the difference between this and any other object. Even the glow seemed to escape his attention. He merely brushed a finger over the initials carved on the front and the griffin on the back, then let it fall back to my chest.

"Do you know who that belonged to?" he asked.

"Caesar," I mumbled. "It was his."

"Did you know that Caesar used to claim he was a descendent of the goddess Venus?"

For some reason, that struck me as funny. "Such a powerful emperor claimed to come from the goddess of love?"

"Also the goddess of military victory. If Caesar was telling the truth about Venus, then he would have been more than a simple human. He may have even had some of her powers. What do you think about that?"

It wasn't up to me to believe or doubt him. Nor could I see how it mattered. Caesar had been dead for almost three hundred years. Unless . . . unless he had become a god, one of the immortals. Unless he was alive enough to whisper warnings from inside a sealed cave. I had not stolen the bulla from Radulf. I had stolen it from Caesar.

I nodded and forced out the words that sat like a lump in my throat. "Yes, I believe that."

"Good, because it's true. Venus is the mother of all Romans. She smiled upon Caesar more favorably than any other Roman before or since. And even when he was young, she gave him a way to draw upon the powers of the gods."

My fingers wrapped around the bulla. I was barely able to comprehend the full meaning of what he was saying. "This came from the gods?"

"Straight from Venus's mighty hand to his. When Caesar was alive, this bulla gave him wealth, brought him military victories, and provided him with the power to unify Rome and become the strongest emperor the world has ever known. But he began to believe too much in himself, rather than in Venus's power. His journals boast of his own abilities, not hers. In his arrogance, he removed the bulla and it became lost. Without the bulla, Venus's protections gradually abandoned him. Soon after, he was murdered by his own senators."

"My mother told me about that, sir. Only a few months after the assassination, a comet appeared in the skies for seven full days, bright enough it could even be seen in daylight. The people said it was Caesar's soul, rising to join the other gods."

"They called it the Divine Star. But its journey did not end with Caesar's death." Felix pointed to my shoulder. "That is the mark on your back."

I leaned forward, certain I had heard him wrong. Was he saying that Caesar himself had marked me? Why?

Felix rested his arms on his legs and looked directly at me. "When I held that bulla, I felt nothing. But your hand is rarely an inch from it, and even now, you can't let it go. Tell me, is there any magic left in the bulla?"

My heart pounded. I wanted to lie to him. A convincing lie would allow me to eat the rest of his food in peace, and then go back to Caela's side. The right lie would end this conversation and any special interest in me. The problem was that I had more questions than ever before, and only the truth would get me any answers.

So I nodded. "There's some magic left, but not much. I can feel it, but that's all. Maybe when Caesar put the bulla aside, Venus's power left it."

"Or maybe the gods have waited three hundred years for someone else to pick it up. Someone with Caesar's mark on his back perhaps. You got that mark from the griffin? She is a creature of the heavens, you know. Only something born of the gods could give you their magic. The magic is stronger than when you first felt it, correct?"

I couldn't deny that. But stronger wasn't necessarily a good thing. I hadn't told Felix about the whispers in the cave, warning of the curse that came with this bulla.

Felix clasped his hands and said, "You come to Rome at a dangerous time. The foundations of our empire are crumbling, and we are so large that if we collapse, the entire world may fall with it. For centuries, the barbarians have run in fear, but now they gaze at our walls and see cracks have formed. We are not as strong as we once were."

I pressed my brows together and tried to absorb everything he was saying. Having seen the greatness of Rome, it seemed impossible that it could ever fall. If it did, I couldn't imagine anything but darkness would replace it.

Felix continued, "Emperor Tacitus can see the cracks in the empire, but he doesn't know how to fix them. If only the gods would help him, but they have been silent. If he had a touch of their power perhaps . . ."

Felix's voice drifted off as his eyes fell to the bulla. I wrapped my fingers around it, letting the vibrations travel up my arm.

"Sir, whatever you think I can do with this bulla, I can't. I certainly can't use it to save an empire."

"Can you use it to save yourself? Because people have been searching for that object since Caesar's death. Some want it to expand this empire, others want to destroy it. And if they know you can use it —"

"But I can't use it! I'm nobody. Just a slave —"

"A slave who happens to be holding the most powerful magic the empire has seen since the days of Julius Caesar! And you're right, Nic. You are nobody to this land. No one will fight a war to save you. No one will care if you fall. And if the enemies of this land surround you, even with that bulla, you will have no chance against them on your own."

I felt dizzy. "No one knows I have it. Or even that it's been found."

"Not yet. But how long can something like this remain a secret? Do you think anyone would hesitate to kill you in order to get that bulla?"

My head was already swimming, but I croaked, "Then I will throw the bulla away. Destroy it!"

"Something created by the gods will not be destroyed by a mere human. Besides, if you are captured by the enemy, how much torture can you endure before you convince them it's truly gone?"

This was what Valerius had warned me about. I was in a great deal more trouble than I realized. Because keeping the bulla would destroy my life. And getting rid of the bulla couldn't save it.

"What should I do, then?" I asked.

Felix smiled. "Give it to Emperor Tacitus. Let him bear this burden for you. He can protect the bulla, and use it to destroy our enemies."

"How? You can't feel the magic. If he can't either, then it'll do him no good."

"He believes the leader of his armies, General Radulf, will know what to do."

"Radulf?" I shook my head. "He's the enemy, Felix. He tried to get this bulla for himself. He would use it against the emperor, against all of Rome!"

Felix leaned forward. "How do you know that?"

"I heard him speaking to one of his men. He intends to destroy the empire!"

Felix waved a hand in the air. "We'd better hope to the gods that you heard wrong. General Radulf is extremely powerful. If he were to turn against Emperor Tacitus, that would be a cause for concern. But so far he has remained loyal."

"He said he would crush this empire in his fist. Does that sound like loyalty to you?"

Felix pressed his lips together and frowned. "This will be our plan, then. Keep that bulla until after the games in two days — I suspect you'll need it to control the griffin. But after the games, I must ask you to present it to the emperor. It will save your life, and save all of Rome."

I clutched the bulla even tighter. I had stolen it from an emperor and no doubt it should be returned to an emperor. But if there was truly magic inside it, then I was starting to suspect it had begun to run through me as well. I couldn't separate myself from the bulla any more than I could divide the two halves of my body.

Felix, however, seemed to consider the matter settled. He glanced out his small window and said, "It's getting late. We'd better get you back to the venatio before anyone begins asking questions."

He returned me to the ramp leading underground and sauntered away as if all was well. As if we didn't just have a conversation that I knew in my heart would change my life, and possibly the fate of the entire Roman Empire.

Somehow, no matter how tired I already was, I doubted I would get any rest that night.

FOURTEEN

As expected, it was a long night. I stayed right outside Caela's cage, talking softly to her whenever she stirred, and assuring her everything would be all right, though by now I knew otherwise. While she slept, I began fitting together an escape plan, a solution for everyone. If I left Rome with the bulla, Radulf would never get it from the emperor, and the emperor could not take it from me. And I would save Caela's life.

Admittedly, a few details still escaped me. I needed a way to go back for Livia, which would be dangerous. Beyond that, how was I to free Caela from her locked cage? Although she had already torn the gold nugget free from its chains, the thick metal bars would be too much even for her.

By morning, my plan was no clearer than it had been the night before. I was put to work feeding Caela and then assigned to feed some of the other animals too. Although I had doubted it was possible, the tunnels smelled worse than they did the day before. I asked about mucking out the animals' cages, but the older workers said it would be easier after the games. I knew what that meant and it made me sick to my stomach.

I spoke to each animal as I fed it and was surprised to find each one looking directly back at me. I'd never seen animals behave this way before. Either that, or they had never behaved this way to *me*. The animals weren't given much food — they were supposed to arrive in the arena hungry, and mean. When nobody was looking, I added to their rations. Especially to Caela's. If I had to handle her, she was the last animal I wanted to be hungry.

After morning chores, Felix appeared and motioned me over, almost like he was in a panic. His face was lit with anger. "How does the Senate know about you?" he sputtered. "I've told nobody but the emperor, and he's told nobody at all. Who did you tell?"

"Nobody!" And I didn't particularly appreciate his accusation, considering that I was the clear loser should anyone find out about the bulla. "What happened?"

Felix exhaled. "The son of Senator Valerius is outside. He asked for you by name."

Crispus? That was unexpected, but still a great relief, considering who else it might have been. "I met him before I left the mines," I said. "He's harmless."

Felix's face twisted. "That's why I'm worried. Because with that thing you carry, no one is harmless. Until you give it to the emperor, you must keep it safe."

"Why bother?" I asked. "Radulf will take it from the emperor, so Rome is finished anyway."

Felix quickly glanced around him to be sure no one had overheard us, and then slammed me against the wall. "You don't want to make the general angry, Nic. No one wants that."

Maybe someone should've told me that before I stole the bulla from him. "You're afraid of him too," I said. His eyes widened, and I knew I was right. "Why?"

"He's powerful," Felix whispered. "More than you know."

"Is there a problem here?"

We both turned and saw Crispus standing at the base of the exit ramp, tall and stern, with both hands on his hips. He wore his authority over us like a cloak, perfectly comfortable with his power.

Felix apologized — to Crispus, not to the person whose air he was choking off with his arm — and then released me. But before he did, he grabbed my shoulder one last time and gave me a look that perfectly communicated his warning about not revealing the bulla. As if I needed such a reminder. Nobody understood the potential consequences better than I did.

I walked up to Crispus and gave him a curt bow, but he waved that aside and said, "You can do that for my father perhaps, but not me."

So I stood up straight, but would not look at him. I felt desperate to ask what he wanted, but we couldn't talk here in the open.

"Come with me." Crispus began walking up the ramp. I

started to follow behind him, but he motioned me forward, to his side. It confused me, rather, even worse, it worried me. He would not treat me like an equal . . . unless I had something he wanted.

"How do you like the venatio?" he asked.

"I haven't been here a full day yet," I reminded him.

"My father was disappointed that he never got the chance to buy you." He waited for a response, but I was biting my tongue to keep from saying something I shouldn't. What did he expect from me? Some sort of apology for not being on the market that day? Crispus didn't even notice my irritation. After another step or two, he continued, "And my father would've liked to come here and talk with you, but he felt that would be unwise. After all, he's a senator, and —"

"And senators don't talk to slaves," I said. "I understand."

I had expected we would leave the amphitheater, but instead, Crispus led me through the inner corridor to where merchants were already setting up their shops in preparation for the next day's games.

"It gets bigger each year," Crispus explained. "Fiercer battles, more blood, more death. Whenever an emperor tries to limit the games, the people become angry. The last thing he needs is an uprising within his walls. So he gives them the show they want."

He walked forward and talked to a man with more varieties of fruit on display than I'd ever seen in my life. The more I saw of Rome, the more I realized how sheltered my existence had been at the mines. Much as I already admired this great city, I knew Livia would love it even more. I couldn't wait to tell her everything I'd seen here.

The fruit seller didn't seem too happy about what Crispus wanted, but again, Crispus was clearly comfortable giving orders, and the man was left with no choice but to bow in obedience. He then ordered everyone else out, leaving us alone.

Crispus motioned me toward him. "Being a senator's son has a few advantages," he said, smiling. That seemed rather obvious. He was educated, wealthy, and likely had all the food he could possibly eat. As far as I was concerned, he had every advantage.

Behind the market display was a small room with only a bed inside. Crispus shut the door and suggested that I sit. I took the floor. He started to object, then let the matter go.

Crispus said, "There's no easy way to open this conversation, so I'll just start. My father wants to know about the mark on your back."

I sat up straighter, pressing the wing of my shoulder into the cement wall, and averting my eyes as if I hadn't heard him. Which was idiotic. Obviously, I could hear him fine.

"You can talk to me," he said. "Remember, it was my father who first told you it was more than a scratch."

"And immediately warned me not to discuss it," I said.

"I know." Crispus left his place on the bed and came to sit beside me. Then he lowered his voice. "But you need to know what it is."

"The Divine Star," I whispered. "Julius Caesar's mark."

He seemed surprised. "Yes! The griffin gave it to you, right? That's how a person gets the mark, when they come into contact with a creature of the gods."

My hand brushed over the hidden bulla. It was also from the gods.

"The Divine Star is very rare." Crispus leaned in. "And also, very dangerous."

"Why?" I asked.

"It's magic, Nic. That griffin gave you magic."

It was all starting to make sense. Caela had fought me in the cave, until I got the bulla around my neck. Once I did, she recognized its power, and then marked my shoulder to give me the ability to use it. To the rest of the world, the bulla I held would never be anything but a trinket left over from Caesar's youth. But to me, and maybe only to me, it held the power of the gods.

"So what I'm here to ask," Crispus continued, "is if I can see that magic. I want to see what you can do."

FIFTEEN

Crispus didn't understand what he was asking. I felt nothing in the Divine Star, and I couldn't tell him about the bulla. So I only shook my head. "I can't do magic!"

He obviously wasn't often told no. His voice took on a tone of irritation. "You can't show me, or you won't?"

Frankly, both were true, but I said, "There's nothing to show." I held out my hand, palm up and fingers bent. "Nothing is happening. Nothing will happen because I can't do magic."

"This only means you haven't yet learned it."

I got up off the floor and moved away from him. "Even if I could do it, why should I show you? If your father was right, then I shouldn't trust anyone, including you and him."

Crispus stood with me. "My father can protect you!"

"From who?"

"General Radulf." Crispus barely spoke above a whisper. "He isn't what everyone in Rome thinks. He's got more power than the emperor, the entire military at his command, and a ruthless ambition that only those who've had to deal with him could understand. Once he knows you have magic, he won't stand for a slave boy challenging him."

"I'm not going to challenge him!" I could admit to being foolish in life, but not stupid. Not *that* stupid anyway.

"You may not have any choice," he said. "Eventually Radulf will find out about that mark, and when he does, nothing will stop him from coming for you. Others have learned that same lesson."

Something about the way he said that made my heart skip a beat. "What does that mean?"

"It means you're not the first person to bear the Divine Star. Radulf has found all of them, sooner or later. He pulls out their magic to make himself more powerful, then sucks out their lives along with it. He's done that to all of them, Nic. He'll do it to you too."

Did Felix know that? Because even if I gave the bulla to the emperor, I couldn't remove the Divine Star from my shoulder. And if Radulf was going to come after me, then I needed to keep the bulla. Figuring out how to use what little magic still remained in it was probably my only chance to survive Radulf's eventual attack.

"How can your father protect me?" I asked Crispus.

"He could train you to harness the power in the mark."

"I told you already, it has no power! You're not marked, so you're only guessing that it's magic. What if it's not?"

"And what if it is? You need our help."

I nodded. "If your father really wants to help me, then

he must free my sister, Livia, from the mines. That's what I need most."

Crispus chewed on his lip while he considered that. "If he does that for you, he will expect something in return."

Of course he would, and I doubted it was anything simple. "What?"

Crispus shrugged. "Let me tell him your request, then see what he says. And for now, you stay out of Radulf's way."

That seemed rather obvious, but I smiled anyway. "I can definitely keep my part of the bargain."

As we walked out, Crispus grabbed an apple from the market stall and gave it to me. I started to hand it back to him, but he said, "They won't charge me for taking it. Just eat."

I bit into it and savored the sweet crunch. "They'd cut off my hand for doing that."

Crispus laughed. "Who will they report it to? The Praetors? They won't arrest the son of a senator."

Yet, according to Felix, the Praetors were dangerous. Did Crispus believe that too?

He bid farewell to me at the top of the ramp. I tossed the apple core aside, then walked down to the end of the ramp, where Felix had worn circles in the dirt with his pacing.

"What did he want?" Felix asked.

"Fashion advice." He grunted, and I said, "He doesn't know about the bulla."

Felix seemed to breathe easier, though it was also obvious he had used the past half hour to put together a plan of his own.

On the other side of the nearest archway was Aurelia, the girl who had ridden with us into Rome. She sneered at me as if the last thing she wanted was to be here. I completely agreed. I had no interest in seeing her either. I folded my arms and angled my body so I could look at Felix, but not have to see her.

"That senator's son was a risk," Felix said. "I want you to have a protector."

"Her?" I felt like he had slapped me. "A kitten could do a better job."

"He couldn't find one foolish enough to do it," Aurelia said. "If I didn't need the money, I wouldn't have agreed to do it either."

I took Felix's arm and turned him to face the wall. "The senator and his son are no threat to me. But if an actual threat comes, do you really think this girl can do anything to help?"

"Well, I can't exactly hire the Praetorian Guard to watch you, can I?" Felix countered. The emperor's personal guards? No, I supposed not. He added, "She's stronger than she looks, and nobody will question her being here. Besides, I trust her."

But did I trust Felix? He had misled me about Caela's role in the games. It was possible he was lying now, maybe even likely. Besides, even if I did need help, I doubted Aurelia was the answer, and I had no intention of making anything easy on her.

I stomped away, and heard her follow behind me. Whatever Felix was paying her to watch over me like a nursemaid, I decided to make her earn every single coin. So I found work that smelled bad enough to curl her nose hairs. I darted from one end of the hypogeum to the other, dodging around corners, or climbing into high places that I was sure she wouldn't be able to reach. I loved the idea of forcing her to go back to Felix and tell him she had given up, but hour after hour, she stayed near me, and climbed even higher than I did, just to prove she could. Never speaking a word, only rolling her eyes when I was close enough to notice.

Finally, I found a quiet corner and announced to her how I intended to use the space.

"That's disgusting," she said. "They've got to have latrines somewhere."

"Not for slaves," I said, grinning. "So do you still want to guard me, keep me safe?"

"Don't you want my help anymore?" she asked.

"I never wanted it in the first place!" I answered. "Obviously, I don't need it either."

"You think because you bent the metal in the caravan that you can defend yourself? Can you fight?"

I'd been in plenty of fights in the mines. Admittedly, I'd lost most of them, but not all, and besides, the other men were much bigger than me. She wouldn't have done any better.

"If a fight starts, I'd sooner beg the crippled widows of Rome for help before asking you," I said.

She leapt forward and shoved me against the wall with her forearm pressed against my neck and her knee jammed into my gut. I would've pushed back but I knew her other hand held a knife, and probably a sharp one. Judging by the glare in her eye, I figured that at the moment, she was the one I most needed protection from.

"They tried to sell me into slavery a few years ago, and I fought them off. Do you know why? Because I could. Because I don't give in. I'm not like you, Nic. I don't take orders in exchange for a crust of food."

"Sure you do," I said. "Why else are you following me around?"

Her face reddened. "I'm doing what I have to."

"So am I!" My temper flared, and it took effort to keep from yelling. "They kill runaways." I tried not to think about last night's decision to escape with Caela.

"At least the runaway is willing to pay the price of freedom. You're not," she answered with equal fierceness.

"My sister is at the mines!" I was yelling now and got control of my temper again. "I wouldn't leave without her."

"Oh." Aurelia released me and turned away. When she looked back, the anger in her eyes had caved into sadness, which she quickly tried to hide. "I have nobody."

That gave me pause. Even though it was like a stab in the heart to think of Livia, at least we had each other. Aurelia only had a crepundia to remind her she had once belonged to a family, and no longer did.

I continued looking into her eyes and watched her fight back tears beneath my gaze. When she wasn't angry, her eyes were sort of pretty. The wall she put up was only her way of hiding the person she really was. Whoever that was, she wasn't the difficult person she pretended so hard to be.

I wanted to ask about her family, but figured it would only start another fight. So instead, I asked, "Did Felix really hire you to protect me, or are you here to make sure I don't run?" Because she was definitely interfering with that plan.

She waited until some other workers had passed us by, then in a low voice said, "Felix does his job here at the venatio, but he reports directly to Emperor Tacitus. Whatever you're hiding, he wants it for the emperor."

I looked down. If Crispus was right, then Radulf would be coming after me. The bulla was my only defense.

Aurelia poked my arm. "Oh, so you haven't agreed to give it to him."

I started walking away but she followed. My own shadow didn't stick this close to me.

"Who do you think you are?" she said. "They'll kill you for refusing the emperor's orders. But . . ." She paused and her eyes narrowed. "Oh, I see."

I turned and folded my arms as I faced her. "What?"

"Even if you give it to the emperor, they're still going to kill you."

"Why? If I don't have it anymore —"

"This thing that you have — it's special, right?"

"Yes . . . maybe . . . I don't know." Silently, I groaned. My lying skills were pathetic.

"Felix said he can't use it. But you can."

"Yes." That was only partially true. I could feel the magic. I couldn't use it.

Aurelia's eyes softened. "This is Rome. Things are different here and you must learn to think the way the empire thinks. They don't want the slaves to have power, and the emperor certainly doesn't want a slave boy out there who can do something that he can't. So tell me, once you give him this . . . thing, why would Tacitus allow you to live?"

Ever since the moment I set foot in the venatio, a weight had been growing in my chest, and right now it was heavier than ever. She was correct. If I refused to give the bulla to the emperor, he would order my death. He would do the same if I gave it to him. And whatever choice I made, once General Radulf found out I had it, he would focus the whole of his power on finding me. Every choice was wrong, which really meant I had no choices at all. No way out. No chance.

Unless I found a way to escape it, this was Caesar's curse.

SIXTEEN

Aurelia left soon after our conversation. She said she had stayed for as long as Felix had paid her and that I seemed determined to ignore her anyway. That might've been true at first, but once she announced she was leaving, things changed. Maybe she was difficult and disagreeable, but so was I at times, and her reasons were every bit as valid as mine. I wished I had a way to ask her to stay. She hated me, obviously, but oddly, that seemed like a good thing. It meant she had no problem with telling me the truth, even if the truth was bad. I needed a friend here. I needed her here.

"I doubt you'll be alive by this time tomorrow," she said as she sauntered away. "So don't let them bury you in the city. I live below ground and don't want your body dropping in unexpectedly."

I would be alive. I just wouldn't be here. Caela and I were going to escape tonight. The only question that remained was how to do it. I was no further in my plan than I'd been the night before.

The problem was that as evening approached, our true work began. Even more animals that had been stored east of the city were now being brought in, which only increased the noise and the stench. "And the danger," added a slave working nearby as he recounted the time a few years ago when several hungry lions had escaped their cage and killed nearly thirty men before they were all recaptured. "But the slaughter down here was nothing to that day's venatio." I shivered at the thought of it, and found somewhere else to work.

In preparation for the games, the arena was being decorated to look like the jungle from which many of the animals had come, and so we spent the entire night hauling trees and grasses into place, and creating sandbars, then filling the low points with water. It spooked some of the other men to see the arena turned into such a foreign setting, but the mines were always creepy, and Caesar's cave worst of all. Compared to that, a fake jungle was nothing.

As we worked above ground, other slaves continued their efforts in the hypogeum below. By the time I got down there, it was so thick with caged animals that there was barely room to move, and nothing but stale, foul air to breathe.

"All of these are intended for the venatio?" I asked one man, who only grunted his way past me. At this rate, I wondered how long until the world ran out of animals, all for Rome's entertainment. It disgusted me.

Dawn rose faster than we were ready for it, and I'd had no chance to get near Caela's cage, much less figure out a way to break the lock. I wasn't even sure she'd agree to leave. She seemed perfectly content with the gold they had given her.

We had barely ended our preparations when Felix sent around orders to allow us each a drink and a bit of food. Nothing was to be given to the animals. The venatio was the first event of the day, and Felix wanted them eager to kill.

I skipped the food and surveyed the various routes Caela and I might take to escape. The obvious choice was the ramp leading to the ground level of the amphitheater, especially since it was the closest to Caela's cage. But Roman soldiers were positioned at the top of the ramp to keep onlookers from coming down, so I doubted we'd get very far. There were other exits too, including some of the larger lifts that went directly into the arena, but unless I stayed behind, there was nobody to raise it. Besides, the exits weren't the biggest problem. It felt like every slave in Rome had been brought here to assist with the games. Even if I got Caela out of her cage, there were too many men for us to fight them all.

Maybe Aurelia was wrong about my death. After all, the emperor needed me alive in order to operate the bulla. Additionally, nobody seemed to be treating me differently than any other slave. Felix had his eye on me a lot, but he still wasn't shy about barking out orders. As had been the case back at the mines, I worked hard, and obeyed every command that made sense. There were good reasons to keep me alive.

And an even better one for the emperor to kill me. The bulla was heavier than ever. The magic in it was growing stronger. I had to get out of this place, and take Caela with me.

I could tell from the noises above that the amphitheater was filling with people. Time was running out. I began looking for anyone who might have keys to Caela's cage. If I got a set and then coaxed her out, maybe I could convince the others that I was moving her into place for the hunt.

But nobody would believe such an obvious lie. Felix himself had said that Caela was intended for the middle show. Besides that, the keys were on ropes hung around the supervisors' necks. How exactly was I supposed to steal them from there?

Once the games got under way, the tunnels beneath the amphitheater flew into action. It was still morning and yet with so many of us, the humid air rose to boiling temperatures. Further dampening my hopes to escape, I was assigned to work on the upper level of a two-story lift to send the animals onto the arena floor. We were to push the bars around a rotating capstan that would gradually raise the animal's cage. Once we got the animal to the right level, another group of slaves pulled the cage door open. The animal would instinctively walk the narrow plank toward the light, with no idea it was heading into a battle arena.

At first I refused to help. It wouldn't stop the venatio, but at least it would allow my conscience to sleep at night. Then I heard a snap and instantly felt a sharp sting on the back of my leg. I collapsed to one knee and turned to see a supervisor below us with a long whip in his hand.

"Get up, you fool!" a nearby slave hissed at me. "Do you think they won't kill you?"

On the contrary, I was certain they would try. Remembering Caela, I stood and took my place on the capstan. Three slaves worked alongside me with another four men turning the same capstan below us. Despite their warnings, the lifting seemed easier than it should have been, and gradually the other men fell away. Without them, it became hard, and I was moving slower than before, but I was doing it.

One of them said to me, "How is a boy your age strong enough to do the work of eight men?"

I didn't have an answer for him. No doubt my years in the mines had made me strong, perhaps stronger than many men. But not eight of them. I felt the warmth of the bulla again, flowing into my back and arms. If it was giving me strength, then it meant I was doing more than just feeling the magic. I was using it. I pushed the bars again, amazed at the surge of energy. Maybe it was only borrowed strength — or stolen strength, since I knew full well the bulla didn't belong to me — but I liked the feel of it.

There were dozens of other lifts, all of them working at the same speed, constantly delivering new animals into the arena to fight. I tried not to listen to the noises above, and hated every second of what I was being forced to do.

I worked solidly until the announcement went out that the venatio was over. The animals still alive were being allowed to remain in the arena for the next event. That was the one in which Caela would participate. We were almost out of time.

I turned to the man next to me. "What happens now?"

"It's lunchtime for the spectators," he answered with a smile. "Execution of the criminals. It's too bad you can't be up top to see the show to follow — we have an elephant trained to walk a tightrope. It —"

I wasn't sure I wanted to know, but I asked anyway. "How are the criminals executed?"

He shrugged. "Various ways, depending on the games. Somctimes they make it quick, like a beheading, but the people always enjoy it more when the criminal's death is part of the entertainment. Today they'll use the jungle setting for more fun. They'll set the criminals loose and unarmed. Some animals up there might find them first, or I saw a *bestiarius* wandering around here too. I imagine he'll go in and hunt for the survivors."

"What about the griffin?" I asked. "What's her role?"

The man smiled. "She'll go in at the very end, as the finest of all animals versus the strongest of all animal hunters. Your griffin will have to lose of course — they'll make sure of it — but it's certain to be a great fight."

No, there wouldn't be any fight at all. I intended to do everything in my power to get her out of here.

Power. On my own, I could do nothing for Caela. But I had the bulla, and it had magic. All I had to do was figure out how to use it. I really was running out of time, though, and didn't know where to begin.

"How many criminals are being executed today?" I asked.

"Not many. In fact, they're bringing 'em in now." The man pointed to the ramp where Roman soldiers were leading a small group forward. I counted two men, then a woman, and then — my jaw fell slack and might've landed on my chest.

The very last man was Sal.

SEVENTEEN

Even from the distance between us, Sal's eyes immediately locked on mine. He started shouting, so loud that from here I could hear every word. He pointed at me with one shackled hand. "I told you I never killed that slave boy!" he yelled. "I sold him to the venatio — he's right over there!"

The soldier closest to him struck his cheek. "You're here because General Radulf wants you punished."

Blood ran down the corner of Sal's mouth. "Radulf can have his boy — go get him, over there!"

By then, I had slipped out of sight. Sal took another hit for lying.

I couldn't let Sal see me again — he'd talk until the soldiers eventually cornered me and it wouldn't be hard for Sal to prove I was the boy Radulf wanted to find. Sal was a roach, and had abused every slave in the mines simply because he could. How many times had I wished to the gods he would get what he deserved?

But not today. Sal could have killed me for trying to escape the mines, but he didn't. I'd certainly given him plenty of reasons to do it before then as well. I had to help him now.

The criminals were unshackled, then quickly sent up into the arena. I heard the hisses from the audience when they appeared, and I knew that one man was almost immediately attacked by an animal because I heard his screams for help right above my head and the cheering that followed. It was horrible, but at least it wasn't Sal's voice.

If Caela and I did not leave in the next few minutes, she'd be taken to the arena and hunted down. Then Felix would come for the bulla, and for me. If we left now, we both had a chance to live, and yet I could not leave knowing I had let Sal go to his death.

Caela would have to help save him. I didn't know how to convince her to help, but I had to try. I started running to Caela's cage, but was blocked by two soldiers on my way. Felix was with them.

"I'm sorry," Felix said. "Please know that I didn't want this."

"What are you talking about?" I asked.

"This!" One soldier grabbed my arms while another knocked the flat end of his sword behind my knees and sent me to the ground. I cursed at him and even threw out a punch until he swatted my mouth and got me in the servile position they wanted.

While they bound my hands in front of me, Felix said, "If it makes you feel better, I'm getting no reward for the bulla. The emperor wants the people to see the bestiarius take it from you after your death and present it to him. He thinks that if Rome has any enemies in the audience, it's the best way for them to know he has the power now."

"I've committed no crime," I said, struggling against the ropes. A soldier behind me took exception to that and hit me in the back, forcing the breath from my chest.

"You committed several crimes," Felix said. "You stole that bulla and tried to escape your master at the mine. And only yesterday, someone spotted you eating a stolen apple."

I was still fighting, though I was quickly losing against the soldiers. "Those are all lies, Felix. You know they are!"

"Not all of them," he said. "A slave who steals from an emperor's treasure has committed treason. If that emperor is also a demigod, then it's heresy. There is nothing I can do to save you."

"What about Caela? She won't cooperate for anyone but me."

"We're counting on that," Felix said.

A fine brown horse was brought in by another slave, and even from her cage quite far from us, I heard Caela already squawking. One of the men at the lifts had explained why griffins hated both horses and men. The men, because they always tried to steal the griffin's gold. And the horses, because they carried the men to their crimes.

Despite my protests, the soldiers lifted me onto the back of the horse and then tied my feet to each foothold of the saddle.

"If you try to slide off, this horse will drag you to your death," Felix said.

The soldier beside me laughed. "And if you don't, that griffin will take care of it for you. She's already angry."

They led me to a larger ramp normally used for raising sets into the arena, and immediately ordered the other slaves to raise me up. When it was halfway there, someone opened Caela's cage.

Caela thundered out of her cage toward the closest open entrance. The noise she made spooked the horse beneath me, and as soon as he was able to run, he rode us into the arena and took off into the jungle setting.

I heard the deafening noise of the audience before I saw them, and once I did, I was amazed to see such a vast crowd all in one place. It was impossible to believe there were so many people in the world, and yet I knew this represented only a fraction of Rome's total numbers. They filled every bend of the arena, row after row of them crowded together, like I had entered a hive of bees. Between us was a wall made of polished marble bordered by ivory rollers that even the best climber could not get over, and elsewhere was a tall metal net. Attendants roamed behind the net to threaten the animals and drive them to the center of the arena, and to kill them if necessary. There were other things happening in the arena too, hidden from my view by the dense jungle foliage, so I didn't know what was causing all the onlookers' cheers and screams and boos. I probably didn't want to know because whether the audience was happy or angry, nothing happening in here was good news for me. Sunlight poured into the arena, filtered through a vast canopy over most of the amphitheater. The red wool cloth kept out some of the heat, but gave the arena a slight reddish tint. So the empire would give the people comfort in their barbarism. If I could've done it, I would've pulled the canopy down and let the people feel the same heat and sweat they had inflicted upon me.

The horse turned again, and I tried to get my bearings from what we had put in place last night, but it had been quiet, and dark, and empty then, like a mine. It was nearly impossible to concentrate in here now.

The brush moved past us in a blur and it took all my strength to hold on to the horse, especially since my hands were still tied. I didn't want to be on this ride, subject to the horse's fears and instincts, but with my feet fastened to the saddle, there was no smart way to leave it.

Or maybe it was foolish to consider leaving. We came to a clearing where a tiger darted out from the underbrush. On my own, it would've gotten me. But instead it nipped at the horse's heels, encouraging him to go faster. The audience reacted to that with a roar that sounded like disappointment. I hoped they'd get used to it, because I wasn't finished with disappointing them. Not even close.

Once we got more into the open, I caught my first glimpse of Caela. She fluttered off the ground like she was trying to fly, but whenever she did, the attendants behind the nets threw rocks that forced her back down. She had the nugget of gold in one of her talons, and sacrificed her body to protect the gold from those stones. Her screeches came out almost like a lion's roars, and further terrified the horse beneath me.

"Bestiarius, bestiarius," the audience chanted. He was the hunter, and I assumed he must've just entered the arena. A knot formed in my throat. My life had been in danger many times before, from the risks I was forced to take at the mines, and from Sal's punishments, but nothing like this. For the first time ever, I was prey.

Along with the attendants, in one area just outside the arena podium, I saw archers crouched with their bows at the ready. I didn't understand that at first — after all, the bestiarius was somewhere in this arena, and I trusted that he was deadly enough. But then I saw the people right behind the archers: senators and Praetors and their wives and children. The archers were there to make sure nothing left the arena alive. Not the animals or criminals, or Caela. Or me. The only one who would walk out of here was the bestiarius, after he removed my bulla and presented it to the emperor.

This was exactly what Aurelia had tried to warn me about. She said I needed to think like a Roman.

That was what I needed to do now. I had to think. Concentrate. Escape.

The bulla had given me strength in raising the pulleys. If I was strong enough for that, maybe I could break the ropes around my wrists. I tried it and they snapped like brittle twigs. That was almost too easy, and I wondered if all magic was like that, as simple as having the thought.

I shook off the rope from my arms, and just in time too, for the horse reared up when a wild boar charged out from the underbrush.

"Turn right!" I yelled. "Now!"

And it did, as if it had understood me.

I rubbed a hand across his neck and leaned into his ear. "I will help you, if I can. But you must be calm."

Not far from us, a horrible scream erupted. The audience roared with delight — another criminal had been attacked. I didn't know who or what had gotten him, but I needed to keep riding as far as possible from that sound. The sweat that had creased my brow dripped into my eyes, stinging them. But I wiped it with the back of my hand and kept riding. I could not stop now.

Caela was still somewhere behind me, hidden within the thick jungle leaves, but her feline instincts seemed to have taken over those of the eagle. I didn't see her trying to fly anymore. She would be somewhere, silently crouching, and waiting for the moment to pounce.

The horse took us into a clearing near the edge of the arena floor. When we emerged, a man in the lower seats stood and his glare bored right through me.

Radulf.

Radulf knew I was alive, and likely guessed that I had the bulla. From the expression on his face, he wasn't particularly happy about either of those facts.

EIGHTEEN

From his seat, Radulf pointed at me and shouted orders at some soldiers in the aisles. They pulled out their swords and began running out the doors. It would only take them a few minutes to get in here. Every passing second threatened any hope I still had to escape. I redirected the horse into denser jungle and glanced back only long enough for a quick look at Radulf. His face was nearly as red as his uniform.

The next face I saw was even more familiar. Sal leapt out from behind a tree — one I had put in place myself only the night before — and tried to jump on the horse, but he missed and fell to the ground instead. If he had caught me, with my feet still attached, he'd have sent me to my death.

So I concentrated again, just as I had before, and as I thought about the strength I needed, it wasn't hard to snap my legs free from the ropes.

I immediately led the horse to where Sal was standing on the ground. He was limping from his failed attempt at taking my horse, and, I noticed, also bleeding from a wound in his shoulder. "The bestiarius has a good spear," he said. "But terrible aim."

I slid off the horse. "Get on, but avoid the griffin. She hates horses, and probably hates you too. So get out into the open — she won't be there. When you have the emperor's attention, tell him I'm alive, right now while he can see me. It's your only chance to prove your innocence."

Sal climbed onto the horse and started to ride away, then said, "Why are you helping me?"

Instead of answering such an impossible question, I asked, "How's my sister?"

"I don't know." Sal's eyes flickered with something that almost passed for regret. "When they arrested me, they took her."

Spurred by a mix of panic and anger, I lunged forward and grabbed the horse's reins. "Who took her? How could you let that happen?"

Sal kicked me away with his foot and I landed on the ground. "*Let* it happen? Do you think I wanted any of this?" He prodded his horse away. "Wherever your sister is, it's your fault, Nic. You started all of this!"

I yelled at him to give me a better answer, but he was already gone. My mind raced to fill in its own explanation. When had she been taken? Because only yesterday morning, Crispus said he would ask his father to get Livia from the mines. The timing was tight, but that had to be where she was, because nobody else would've had any reason to take her. I made myself believe Senator Valerius had her, and she was safe here in Rome, because if he didn't, then she could be anywhere . . . or not. I felt a swell in my emotions, terrified at the possibilities that ran through my mind. Wherever she was, Sal was right about one thing. This was my fault.

Above the jungle leaves, I saw the tip of a spear. The bestiarius had probably heard me yelling at Sal and was following the sound. I immediately ducked behind a tree, causing an audience uproar as they tried to point me out to the hunter. So I sprinted back in the direction I had come, calling Caela's name. The arena seemed so much larger than it had been the night before, and with the heat and the yelling crowds, I could barely hold two thoughts together.

So I let there be only one thought. *Livia.* I had to find my sister. And for that, I needed Caela's help.

I passed the remains of one of the criminals who had been killed and several of the animals that had been sacrificed to the games earlier that morning. It was repulsive to think that this day was only half over. The biggest event still remained for the gladiator battles that afternoon. And the audience cheered on, with an appetite for blood that might never be filled.

On my entry into Rome, I had been able to reach for Caela with my thoughts. Maybe that was the way to find her now.

Where are you? I thought.

I heard nothing in response, and wondered if she was still angry because of the horse. It was a stupid grudge, compared to our much bigger problem. So I called her name, which was even more stupid, considering the bestiarius wasn't far away. Seconds later, his spear missed my head by less than an inch. Above the crowd's noise, I heard its whoosh in the air and I was pretty sure it grazed my cheek because I felt a sting that hadn't been there before.

I turned to see the bestiarius facing me, bare-chested except for a strap to hold his weapons, and with a brass mask designed to look like a bull's head. He was snarling because he had given up his hiding place and gotten no one's death as a reward, something that gave me a small amount of satisfaction. The audience was booing him now, which he deserved, but I wouldn't have minded also hearing some cheering for my escaping such a close call.

"They don't think you're very good at this," I yelled at the bestiarius. "Better you give up now and avoid further embarrassment!" And then I grabbed the thick spear and borrowed enough strength from the bulla to splinter the long handle against the tree. It was useless to him now. The audience definitely reacted to that. Maybe they were cheering me this time. So I gave them an elaborate bow and then continued running.

I finally found Caela in a thicker part of the brush, where she seemed to have created a bed for herself in the jungle foliage. In her claw was the gold nugget. She didn't look happy to see me. No doubt she still smelled the horse on me.

Well, I wasn't happy to see her here either. The bestiarius couldn't be far, and Caela and I were his prime targets.

"This isn't the time for a nap!" I yelled at her. She got to her feet and silently stared at me. Then her eyes darted behind me, to the right.

That was the direction the bestiarius came from when he attacked me. He jumped directly on my back, knocking me down, and my face skidded in the yellow sand. His next punch landed squarely on the Divine Star, hard enough that I nearly passed out then, and I felt his weight change as he reared back for another hit.

But Caela charged directly into the bestiarius. She came at him with both talons spread apart and then used her hind legs to kick him a short distance away. I tried to prop myself up on all fours, but still couldn't draw a complete breath, much less sit up. Caela moved toward me as if to help, then suddenly screeched in pain.

That got me up. The bestiarius must have found a second spear, which was now lodged deep in Caela's side. I stumbled over to her and pulled out the blade, but blood poured from her wound. The bestiarius yelled out some sort of battle cry and came charging toward us, swinging a mace in his hands.

"You first, and then your bird!" he yelled.

"Stay back!" I held out my hands to block him, knowing full well I couldn't do much to enforce my warning. Then the bulla warmed so fast that I felt the burn on my skin. I thrust an arm down to move it, but the sudden action caused the entire ground to shake, as if the gods had pounded their fists into the earth.

Off balance now, the bestiarius's mace slammed to the ground and he crumpled beside it, then slowly stood up again, his eyes wild with confusion. Like us, the audience had gone still, waiting to see what might come next. I couldn't explain what had happened any more than they could. Based on the energy that had flowed from my hands, I knew I had caused the quake. Or maybe it was the bulla, acting through me. Perhaps there was no difference anymore.

I had wanted the quake to happen — or something to stop him. The thought had nestled in the far reaches of my mind, but not too far for the bulla to find it.

Simply as a test, I brought my hands up overhead again and then, with the bulla still burning at my side, I slammed both hands down to my waist. They didn't fall naturally, but rather felt like I was pushing them through a thick mud. Once they came to my sides, I was more tired than I'd ever been from working in the mines or raising the lifts or anything else I'd done in my life.

And I would've tried to rest, except that my actions were already having an effect. Areas of the arena floor were collapsing. The ground upon which the bestiarius stood rumbled a second time, and when he took a step forward, the wooden floor completely gave way beneath him. His body and legs fell, but he held to the edge of the floor and cried out for help. I ran forward to answer his pleas, but somehow my legs had lost all strength and folded before I could get there.

"What have you done?" he cried, and then, even while I lunged for him again, he fell to the level below. I saw his body there, broken and still, and workers around him, pointing up at me and yelling that I would bring down the entire amphitheater.

I stood and looked around, wondering how to stop what I had somehow started. I wrapped a hand around the bulla, but even through the tunic, it burned too hot and I had to let it go. Above me, a great cracking sound was echoing throughout the amphitheater, like rolls of thunder. The wood supports for the enormous canopy were folding like twigs and the ropes had failed. The entire canopy was floating to the ground, a red sky falling. It was what I had wished for earlier. But so much worse.

As the ground continued to shake, and as the canopy came closer, audience members screamed, panicked as they hurried to leave the amphitheater. I yelled for Caela and found her back in the nest she had created, trying to snatch the gold with her wounded claw.

"Enough of this, Caela! You'll suffocate in here to keep that gold!" I grabbed her nugget in my hands and began running, intending for her to follow me.

She squawked with anger at my theft and took off after me. When she reached out with a talon, I stopped running, grabbed her feathers, and swung myself onto her back. Once I was balanced, I yelled, "Fly, Caela. Now!"

She tried to obey, but with only one wing, we quickly tilted back to the ground. I encouraged her again and this time we took off at a better angle.

Below us, I caught a quick glance of Sal, still on the horse. He was close to an exit, and in the pandemonium I had created, I figured he would make it out alive. But I worried that everyone else might not be so lucky. From here, the destruction that had come from a simple swipe of my hand was clear, and it horrified me.

Caela arced higher into the air. I ducked as the falling canopy came closer, but with her other talon she created a long scratch in the cloth, and, as we continued to rise, we tore through it. I looked down and noticed the ground had stopped shaking, but one man stood out from them all. Radulf. Even from this height, I felt his eyes pierce right through me. He would know that I had caused the trouble below. Worse still, he would know how I had done it.

Felix had warned me what might happen if even one person found out I had Caesar's bulla. After what I'd just done, I figured it was safe to assume that I had been found out — by everyone.

NINETEEN

Once we cleared the amphitheater, I had no idea where to direct Caela to fly. She was still bleeding, so I knew she wouldn't get us far, and with that injury, and my weight with the gold, she was on an uneven, downward angle. We might not even make it out of the city.

I pointed to the Tiber River, the same point we had crossed to enter Rome. If she could clear the city wall, then get us across the water, we had some chance of escaping into the hills.

Below us, Roman soldiers had already collected to follow our route. One of them shouted up for us to land at once, or we'd be killed.

By now, I knew better than that. The more correct order was that *after* we landed, *then* we'd be killed. The emperor had already given his orders concerning both of us. Why would I think they had changed now?

I reached down to pat Caela's shoulder. "Stay strong," I told her. "Look at this mighty city, and how you soar over all of it."

We were still higher than even the tallest apartments, and I saw the forum stretched out behind the amphitheater with its mighty temples and buildings. Rome was so much more beautiful than I'd ever imagined. Caela had given me the view of the gods.

Surely there had never been a city like this in all the world. Perhaps nothing so great, or so terrible, would ever match this empire again.

Caela's arc took us toward the Tiber River. Once we crossed it and she was healed, we'd have to search for my sister. Then the three of us would find the ends of the Roman Empire, if such a place still existed in this world.

Suddenly I heard a whoosh past me and saw an arrow fly through the air. Soldiers had taken to the rooftops and were shooting from there.

"Higher, Caela!" I ordered.

Caela started to climb, but she was struggling and couldn't get us beyond the arrows' reach. We were almost to the banks of the river when I turned and saw an arrow coming straight for us. There was no time to think. I stuck out my arm to protect Caela from any further injuries, and instead felt a sting above my elbow, like a thousand furious wasps had targeted that one spot.

With a cry, I instantly lost my grip and fell from Caela's back. Panicked, I clutched at empty air, but there was nothing. Nothing but the hard ground lay below, rising up at me far too quickly.

Then something curled around my chest and slowed my fall. Caela had me wrapped inside her talon and was still speeding toward the earth. I yelled at her to slow down, but she only listened when she wanted to. We were lower than the treetops, and still diving. Then as smoothly as we had dived, we leveled out. I opened my eyes and saw the nugget of gold inside Caela's other claw. I had let it go when I fell.

Just like that, Caela had what she wanted, and she released me from her grip like a wad of garbage. I didn't have far to fall, but it wasn't the softest landing either.

I rolled to my side and tried to draw in some air. My hands sank into mud and I realized I was still on the city side of the Tiber River. On my best day, I couldn't swim across. And the way I felt now, I wouldn't make it three feet into the water before the current carried me straight to the underworld. Soldiers on the nearby bridge gave a call of alarm and began running toward me with their spears raised. Caela, somewhere overhead, had vanished. With her injury, I wondered if that was the last I'd ever see of her.

My arm was still burning, and I rotated it to see how bad it was. The tip of an arrow was stuck in my flesh, though most of the shaft had broken off in my fall. I couldn't run this way, so with my left hand, I grabbed the remaining shaft and yanked.

It hurt enough that I screamed, drawing the soldiers to the very spot where I had fallen. They edged down the steep bank with drawn swords. I had to move.

Dizzy with pain, I ran. My left hand was clasped tightly over the wound but blood still dripped between my fingers. I stumbled forward, with no idea of where I could possibly go now.

Then, in the darkness, I tripped onto a concrete spillway. Water flowed beneath my hands and legs into the river, but the smell was horrible. Felix had already told me what this was, the exit for the Cloaca Maxima. The sewer.

I nearly became sick from the odor, but reminded myself that it wasn't too different from what I had smelled beneath the amphitheater. Maybe the stench was stronger here, but I could manage that — I *had* to. Hopefully, the soldiers could not.

Another arrow whooshed past me when I took my first step into the sewer, but it hit the far wall. I needed to go faster. I had to crawl in on all fours, and duck even lower to squeeze beneath a brick overhang. It was a tight fit, but I was inside.

It was almost as dark in here as Caesar's cave had been. Considering how things had been going since that adventure, it was hardly a comforting thought. Even when I got all the way into the sewer, I couldn't quite stand upright, but I moved faster on my feet.

Outside, I heard the soldiers arguing about whether they should continue to pursue me. Finally, two men were ordered in, chosen because they were smaller than the others.

They had a torch with them, casting distorted shadows along the sewer walls. It didn't give me much light, but it was better than nothing and allowed me to move more quickly.

A narrow walkway lay on one side and the sewage streamed in an equally narrow ditch beside it. To keep from falling in, I kept my weight against the wall, ignoring the rough brick that tore at the knuckles of my left hand, still pressed against the open wound in my right arm.

In some places, the tunnel became even smaller, forcing me into the mucky water. At least I seemed to be handling the smell better than the two soldiers. One in particular had already stopped twice to be sick. His companion said if it happened again, he'd be killed in here.

I hurried faster, until I outran the flickering torch and their echoing voices. Surely there would be an outlet soon. I found a few, but they were covered in bars that kept me as caged in as the animals in the venatio. A few others were open, but so much water poured from them that I'd never reach the top without drowning. The longer I walked, the more my hopes of finding an exit faded.

At one point, the sewer widened and divided into paths, much like the intersection of a road. It was impossible to tell exactly where I was. I didn't know the lines or the outlets to the surface. But I was somewhere beneath Rome and with so many paths, it was probably a busy area. I recalled a large exit opened into the hypogeum, but Felix would be there waiting to hand me over to the emperor. Not exactly the ideal solution to my problems.

I turned right, or left, or right again. I walked in any direction I thought the soldiers wouldn't. If it was dark, or small, or smelled particularly bad, that was my choice. I ran so far and so fast that when I finally stopped to listen, I heard absolutely nothing. I saw even less. I had lost them.

But in doing so, I had also lost my way out. I had become a rat in a never-ending maze without food or light or anywhere to rest. I couldn't survive in here, and I'd never be allowed to live if I tried returning to the surface.

I stumbled on something that squeaked back, and tried not to think about how big it had been. Then, in regaining my footing, I felt the bulla bounce against my waist. It was as heavy as ever, but also cold and lifeless. It had brought so much bad into my life. I couldn't see how anything might get better if I continued to wear it, and yet, I couldn't bring myself to throw it down either. Whether keeping the bulla was a sign of strength or weakness, I didn't know, but I brushed my hand over it and continued on.

I stumbled again, but this time fell to the sewer floor, completely indifferent to how it smelled and without a thought for the filth that surrounded me. Then I removed my hand from my arm and nearly blacked out when my wet fingers dripped into the wound. The pain was beyond anything I'd ever before experienced.

The only reason I didn't scream was that I was too frightened and exhausted to make so much noise. Tears came to my eyes, but not from the pain. The harder I tried to make things better, the worse they got. Only days ago, I was a slave in the mines, a hopeless situation, but at least it was a life I knew.

"Nicolas, you are the head of our family now." After she was sold away from us, my mother had cried those words as she was being led away in chains. "I'm relying on you to protect your sister."

"I will," I had promised her through my tears. "Always."

"Stay together. Because I will see you again," she'd said. "If the gods are willing."

And then she was gone.

Whatever my fate, I had absolutely failed my family.

And that was the worst thought of all.

With little hope, and even less of an idea of what direction to go, I finally forced myself to my feet. Maybe the gods would seal me in here forever and laugh at my failures. But until they did, I had no choice but to continue searching for a way out.

TWENTY

The bleeding in my arm eventually stopped, though the pain erupted every time I stumbled off the narrow pathway and fell into the sewage. My eyes had adjusted a little, but then I'd spot a grate overhead where the sunlight poured in and the darkness beyond it would turn black again.

It had been two full days since I became lost in here and nighttime was approaching again. Except for one grate that had poured in clean water, I hadn't had anything to drink, and nothing at all to eat. Despite that, and the endless ache in my arm, the worst pain came with the realization of how stupid I'd been. Unforgivably foolish.

Sal had been right. From the moment of my birth, I was cursed. Born in poverty to a father who lost a half-second battle with a lightning bolt, and a mother who gave up hope for us too soon. The bulla — a mistake of my own doing — was a second curse. Caela had abandoned me. Radulf knew I was alive and held the bulla. And the empire had turned on me, just as Aurelia had predicted.

Aurelia. Something flashed in my memory from our last fight. Hadn't she said that she lived below ground? I had always pictured her in some sort of mine, but there were no mines in Rome. This was what she had meant. Aurelia had to be here somewhere, in the sewers. We hadn't exactly parted on good terms, but she might be my only chance of survival.

I wandered on farther, trying to convince myself that she was down here and probably knew this maze well enough to walk through it blindfolded. If she used the sewers, then she knew the ways in, and the ways out. She would have food, and perhaps a solution for the growing pain in my injured arm. Whether she would share any of that with me, however, was a question I preferred not to think about.

Despite my hopes, as day faded to night, the sewer walls all became the same again. I didn't dare call her name for fear of someone above hearing me and reporting where I had escaped. It was probably useless anyway. If only I knew where I was. I had gone for miles in infinite loops, likely repeating the same senseless steps that I'd crossed a dozen times already. My injured arm throbbed, and the hunger that had gnawed at me was now becoming a warning of how serious the situation was if I didn't find food and clean water soon.

Eventually, I was forced to rest on the narrow walkway, every part of me feeling shredded apart. I leaned against the brick wall, which was covered in a slimy moss that could only have grown from the underworld. I reached for the bulla, hoping to draw in some of its warmth, but it had slid around to my back, and I didn't have the strength to retrieve it.

I must've fallen asleep that way, and sometime later awoke to a fierce ache in the mark on my shoulder. It froze me in place at first, as I struggled to move my arms and unclench my teeth. In my sleep, I had rolled onto the bulla, which was now sucking strength from the Divine Star into itself. But it was doing more than pulling out my strength. Magic was going with it.

Finally, I was able to shift enough to move the bulla. The ache immediately stopped, though it was several minutes before I was breathing evenly again. Oddly, the bulla then began to replenish my strength, returning to me what it had just stolen.

As I lay there, I began to wonder how Radulf stole magic from others with the Divine Star. He had no bulla, but the effects Crispus had described to me seemed similar to what I'd just experienced. With pain like that, hopefully I never would again.

Once my strength returned, I began to walk again, weighing the few things I already knew about Radulf, and what I understood about magic. There had to be a way to save my life. Once I escaped these sewers, I would find it.

I crossed to a grate overhead, one of hundreds I had seen over the last few days, but every one of them was sealed, or too far above my head to reach, or too small. This one wasn't much better, but at least it seemed to be in a quiet part of the city and I had a way to climb up to it. All I needed was a way to make the opening larger. Perhaps with the bulla's help, I could collapse the rock around it.

That was where I stopped. The memory of what I'd done in the amphitheater was still raw. When he fell, the bestiarius would've been seriously injured, or maybe worse, though I hated to think about that. Clearly I had drawn upon the magic in the bulla, somehow. I still wasn't sure if the magic was good or bad, which meant I could no longer be sure whether *I* was good or bad. But it saved my life before, and I needed it again.

So I raised my hand and tried to summon enough strength to push the grate out of its place. All I needed was to spread the rock farther apart or for a couple of rocks to fall. With the right tools back at the mine, I could've done this in an hour, but here, I felt ridiculous attempting it by only willing it to happen.

And this time, my will was not enough. The bulla had gone cold on me. Maybe because I was afraid to use it. Without even meaning to do anything, I had unleashed a magic in the arena that I did not understand and could not control. There were thousands of people at the games, every one of them endangered because of my recklessness. For all I knew, using magic in these tunnels might bring an entire street down over my head and any number of people with it.

Only the gods were meant to have magic. It was never intended for someone like me. I grabbed the bulla's strap and tried to pull it over my injured arm, but my arm ached too badly to move it. So instead I cursed loud enough for the gods to hear and kicked at the sewer wall with all the strength I had left.

"It's dangerous for any slave to have such a temper," someone said. "It's worse when that slave has the power to use his temper against fifty thousand people."

Aurelia.

I swerved around so fast that I slipped and fell back into the sewage again. With the sting in my arm, I sprang back to my feet with lightning speed and then bumped my head on the curved wall above me. Truly, my grace was no better than my magic.

Aurelia stood in front of me, arms crossed and eyes narrowed like she was staring at a madman. Even in the darkness, I saw that Aurelia was better armed than she had been on the surface. She had a bow slung over one shoulder and a quiver full of arrows on her back. She had all sorts of tiny sachets attached to a belt around her waist, as well as the long knife I had seen before. As far as I knew, she was armed in twenty other ways I couldn't even see.

"It's not a temper, just desperation." I stepped toward her. "I need help."

She took the same number of steps backward and put a hand on her knife. "Don't come any closer, Nic. I'm warning you."

I stopped and, through the little light seeping in from the grate, tried to read her expression. Her eyes were wary and watchful and her jaw was tense. She was afraid of me, probably for good reason. I raised one hand to her, hoping to show I wasn't armed, but she flinched.

"I won't hurt you," I said. "I would never —"

"I was in the amphitheater. I saw what you did. Lots of people got hurt trying to escape. Some people didn't escape at all."

The hand of my injured arm wrapped over the bulla as it warmed again. "I don't know how that happened. I didn't mean for any of that."

My explanation wasn't working. She shook her head, undoubtedly trying to figure out how to get away from me, but I couldn't let that happen. With every passing moment, I felt another piece of my life slipping away. I was dying in here.

"Are you all right?" she asked.

The bulla finally warmed and traveled to the wing of my shoulder. Everything about me felt warm, even hot. I didn't want to feel magic now, not when I was trying to convince her there was no danger in being near me.

"No," I mumbled, not sure if I was responding to her or trying to command the bulla. I fought against the heat inside, but as weak as I was, the magic wanted to take over. Not here, not now. Not ever again. A sudden feeling of dizziness swam through me. I set a hand on the sewer wall to keep myself from falling, and the wall shook, as if something were trying to break out from behind it. It happened only once, but it startled me and I immediately let go.

Aurelia put out both hands as if ready for a fight. "Did you do that?"

"Please help me." I was about to black out. "I'm drowning." I lowered my hand and took another step forward.

Before I had any chance to react, she kicked out a leg and connected directly with the wound in my arm. I cried out with pain and splashed into the rancid water, but this time I couldn't get up again. The bulla tried to help — I felt it trying, but there was nothing left inside me now.

"I'm sorry." She crouched down to help me up. "You scared me, that's all." She grabbed my hand, then touched it with her other hand. "Nic, you're burning with fever." Her hand ran up to the injury in my arm, and through my haze, I heard her draw in a breath. "It's infected."

"I won't hurt you," I said, and then everything faded around me.

TWENTY-ONE

My eyes opened slowly and unwillingly. I would've preferred to remain asleep, but at some point, the need to know where I was overpowered my desire to roll over and let everything vanish again.

Except for a few candles around me, the room was dark. Since there were no windows, I wondered if it was day or night, and how much time had passed since I had last opened my eyes. The room was round with dark bricks stacked as high as I could see, and one doorway leading to an outer room had faint light streaming in from overhead. So we were still underground. It seemed quiet at first, but then I noticed a buzzing sound nearby. No, not buzzing. As I became more awake, I realized it was the sound of voices.

Suddenly a face appeared right in front of mine and I yelped with surprise. It was a little girl, with dark African skin and large eyes. She didn't look half my age, but was already quite pretty.

"He's awake!" she called. "Aurelia, he's awake!"

I sat up on one elbow and saw Aurelia stride across the room toward me. Her mouth was pressed into a tight line. Her whole face looked strained actually, and I wondered if that was because I had slept so long. Or because I was awake.

"How do you feel?" she asked.

"Awful."

She frowned and folded her arms. "You look awful. But that's an improvement from before."

"How long was I out?"

"Two days. The infection in your arm was so bad we almost had to cut it off, but we decided to scrub it and see if it could be saved. It was a good thing you were sleeping so deeply, because the cleaning would've made you faint again anyway."

"I didn't faint," I muttered. Fainting was for weak rich women who had slaves to catch them when they fell.

"Sure. If you want to believe that."

Well, I did. I wasn't weak. Though I did have to lie back down again as dizziness swarmed my head.

"You need food." She twisted behind her and then returned with a bowl in her hands. She thrust it at me and whatever was in there looked gray and mushy, but at least it was warm. "Eat this."

"What is it?"

"Only people with money get to ask such a question. It will do you good. Now eat."

I smelled it first, and happily realized it didn't smell like the sewers, or wherever we were. Not that the stuff in the bowl smelled good — it was some sort of porridge that probably had gone sour. But I began eating anyway. She was right, about the poor not being choosey.

"Before you fainted, you said you were drowning." Aurelia pursed her lips.

"No, I didn't," I said with a mouthful of food. "I wasn't."

"Well, you said it," Amelia insisted. "What did you mean?"

Then I remembered the bulla. I felt for it at my hip, and tried to find the strap at my neck, but it was gone. My temper instantly rose. "Where is it?"

She folded her arms. "I hid it. How did you do the magic in the amphitheater?"

That was none of her business. I put the bowl aside and sat fully up in the bed. "Give me the bulla."

"Not until you explain what happened. Magic belongs to the gods. Not to humans, and certainly not to a slave boy."

"And the bulla doesn't belong to you!" I said. "Give it to me and I'll go."

"Go where? You're lost down here. Besides, I felt the bulla myself. There's nothing different about it than any other trinket. You just want it for the jewels inside. I think the magic is in that mark on your shoulder. We would've cut that off too, if I'd known how."

I'd had enough of her. I threw off the blanket and swung my feet to the floor, but the effort was too much and made me dizzy again, so I had to stop. My arm was wrapped in a tight bandage from my shoulder down to my elbow and was wet with a peculiar smell.

I touched it, then sniffed my fingers. "What'd you put on there?"

"Olive oil and oregano, for the infection." She smiled. "It stings at first but it works. You were worse off than you might've realized."

Seeing her smile softened my own anger. I reached for the bowl and finished the rest of the porridge, then she said, "Let that sit for a while. If you can handle more, then we'll get you some bread."

I would've liked the bread now, but I wanted the bulla even more. Once again, my hand slid to my side where it should have been, and wasn't. I felt its absence as intensely as I would've felt a missing arm or leg, and wished I had enough energy to fight Aurelia for it. "Give me the bulla and directions to get out of here," I said tiredly. "Then I'll go."

Aurelia cocked her head at a couple of young children in the room with us, ordering them to leave. When only she and I were left, she said, "While you were asleep, I went back to the surface and asked around about you. There's nowhere to go, Nic. Nowhere. Everyone is looking for you. The emperor ordered his soldiers to kill you on sight, and they've blocked every gate to this city. The Senate wants you brought before them for questioning. Then yesterday, General Radulf gave a speech in the forum. He promised to drag you back to the amphitheater to answer for your crimes. He said he will over-turn the city to find you. A million people live in Rome, and by now, every single one of them knows there's a reward for turning you in."

I looked down and kicked my foot against the ground. By now I should've been used to bad news, but this was even worse than expected.

Aurelia moved from her chair to sit beside me on the bed then placed a hand on my forearm. "In the forum, Radulf said you stole something from him — the bulla, obviously — and that you want to use it to overthrow the empire."

"That's not true!" I said, and then clicked my tongue. "Well, it's not true about overthrowing the empire. And I didn't plan to steal the bulla — it's just that once I had it, I knew I couldn't give it to him."

"So you admit to being a thief," Aurelia said. "Radulf was telling the truth about that?"

"Yeah," I mumbled. "I guess I am."

I hated the sound of it spoken aloud. One of the last things my mother ever said to me was that no matter what else was lost, I must always keep my honor. That was gone now too.

Aurelia nodded, and then I felt the cold blade of her knife at the back of my neck. Her hand that had brushed across my forearm was now locked around it, and she called for the other children to come back in with a chain. I cursed under my breath. And then cursed a second time, louder, in case she hadn't heard me before.

"This isn't personal," she said as two girls hurried in. They started by locking manacles around my wrists and next moved to my feet. "I've stolen things too — every one of us down here has done it when there's no other choice to live. But you did have a choice with the bulla, and so the crime is different."

"This isn't about what I stole," I said angrily. "You want that reward money."

"I *need* it," she said. "That money is my way back to my family."

But I shook my head, trying to make her understand the stakes that were involved. "If you take me to Radulf, he'll kill me."

"Senator Horatio is offering the biggest reward right now. I'll take you to him."

"What? No!" He was the pompous senator who had wanted to see my teeth. Aside from my personal objections to having to breathe the same air as him, he was no better than Radulf.

"It's for the best," Aurelia said. "The Senate wants to question you."

"And then execute me!"

"They might listen to your explanations."

"What explanation?" I spat back at her. "It isn't my bulla, Aurelia, or it isn't supposed to be. How can I explain that?"

"I don't know!" she said. "But that's not my problem."

No, she was *my* problem. For at least the twentieth time in the last week, I regretted ever having met this girl. Of all the curses in my life, she was proving to be the worst.

Once my legs were manacled, Aurelia removed her knife and replaced it in the sheath. I immediately tried to summon any feeling of strength inside me, but I was still weak from lack of food and my injury, and besides, without the bulla, I was nothing more than I'd ever been before. The mark on my shoulder prickled as if it was trying to respond to my call for help, but that too faded. I pulled against the chains, hoping to find a rusted link that might break or maybe the lock hadn't been securely fastened, but they held fast. Then I kicked at one of the girls who had put them on, just because I could. Aurelia swatted my leg and told the two girls to return to the outer room with the others.

"You said you wouldn't hurt anyone," she said.

"I missed. Anyway, you said you would help me," I countered.

"That was before I knew you were a thief."

"You're a liar," I argued. "That's worse."

Well, it wasn't, but I needed something to say back to her, and she only clamped her mouth closed at that, which was all I wanted anyway.

She stood and pulled me up beside her, keeping a firm grip around my chain.

"You're making a huge mistake," I said. "Radulf cannot get that bulla."

"Radulf is a great man. If Horatio turns you over to him, then it'll be the right thing to do."

"What world do you live in to believe all that?" I said.

Aurelia's mouth moved like she was responding, but I didn't hear the sound. Instead, my ears filled with echoes of footsteps splashing through water. Heavy, marching footsteps, and many of them. It was so clear, I looked around for the source of the noise, but saw nothing to explain it. Aurelia didn't seem to notice the sounds and had simply continued talking. Why could I hear it, and not her?

Something was terribly wrong.

TWENTY-TWO

The sound of footsteps in my head was growing, and the splashing was so distinct I couldn't understand why water didn't leak from my ears. Was I going mad?

Aurelia jabbed my arm, drawing my attention to her while quieting the noises in my head. "Aren't you listening? I asked if —"

"Where are we?" I shuffled forward, pulling on the chains as much as they'd allow. "Is this part of the sewers?"

"It's an old cistern, but we cut the pipes connecting it to the sewers and use the flow for washing. We still come and go through the sewers, though. Why?"

"We've got to get out of here. Soldiers are coming." I started to move, but Aurelia pulled me back.

"Impossible. They never come down here." Her brows pressed together. "How would you know that anyway?"

"I just know!"

She made a face. "I'm not releasing you. If you think I'd fall for such an obvious trick —"

I didn't hear the rest of what she said, because now a voice thundered in my head, so loud that I tried to raise my hands to cover my ears, except the chains were attached to my leg irons and wouldn't reach that far.

"Nicolas Calva!" That was Radulf speaking directly into my head. I didn't know how that was possible, but I couldn't hear anything else, not even my own thoughts.

Aurelia didn't seem to hear it. "What is the matter with you now?"

"Can't you —" I started, but then Radulf's voice continued.

"I found you, Nic. By joining those children, you have chosen them to die with you."

"No!" I fell to my knees, and lowered my head enough to get my hands over my ears. But covering them only made the sound louder.

"If you give yourself up now, I promise to let them live. If you don't, there is no escape for any of you."

I looked up at Aurelia, who was staring back at me as if a horn had sprouted from my head. I pointed to the doorway. "How many exits out of here, into the main sewer line?"

"Only one," she said. "But nobody else —"

The same girl who had manacled me rushed into the room. "Aurelia, I hear sounds in the tunnels. Men's voices. Lots of them."

Her eyes darted back to me, full of alarm. "How far away?"

The girl shrugged.

"They're here for you, right?" Aurelia didn't say it as a question, and didn't need my nod for an answer. She pressed her lips together for only a moment before saying, "I'm sorry, Nic. I have to give you up to them."

"They'll kill me if you do!"

"They'll kill all of us if I don't. Including you!" She tugged on my chains.

But I wasn't going to budge. "I can get us out of here."

She turned around the room. "I told you, there's only one exit, from the outer room. And that will take us directly into the sewers with those men!"

"What's above us?"

She rolled her eyes. "Dirt."

Well, obviously. "No, above that!"

Aurelia shrugged. "An olive orchard, I think." Then her eyes narrowed. "Don't even think about it!"

"Give me the bulla."

"Is that how you did what you did in the amphitheater?"

"Yes. I think so." Somehow.

She shook her head. "I tried using it and nothing happened."

"And when I use it, big things happen, so do you want to debate why or let me have it?"

Then her eyes widened further. "I only *think* it's an open field. What if I'm wrong?"

"What if we do nothing? Do you really believe Radulf will take me and leave the rest of you alone?"

Aurelia reached for a familiar strap that had been hidden beneath her tunic and lifted out the bulla, which she shoved into my hand. It was heavier than before, which meant either I was weaker, or the magic in it was growing. I immediately began to feel its strength flow into me, moving through my chest, down my legs and arms, up my back and into my mind. The magic dug deeper, burning its way through my blood with a power I had never noticed before.

The children who had been in the outer room came running in, far more of them than I had expected. I counted at least a dozen heads, some of them quite young, and all of them looking to Aurelia for answers. "They're here!" one of the younger boys cried.

"Get behind me," I said, only because it seemed safer there. Maybe it wasn't.

I turned until I had a direct view of the doorway into the sewer. Radulf entered the outer room flanked by six large soldiers. I saw the amusement on his face grow as he scanned my shackled arms and legs.

"They got you ready for me," he said, smiling. "How kind of them."

"You saw what I did in the amphitheater," I warned. "Stay back."

"That was an accident." Radulf stepped forward, daring me to act. "You have no idea how you did that."

The bulla was becoming hot in my hands, but with the

manacles, I couldn't get it around my neck. "I do know. And I'll do the same thing here if you don't leave."

It was a badly told lie. I didn't know how I'd used the magic before, or whether I could use it again. I didn't even know if I *should* use it again. Collapsing wooden beams and a fabric canopy was one thing. Several feet of earth and rocks lay above our heads now.

"Right now, you're an untrained boy with a sword, swinging wildly in any direction you want and calling it success if you happen to hit something."

"That's right," I countered. "So get back, or I might happen to hit you."

"Give me that bulla." Radulf's face darkened. "Now."

"No." I kept my body square to him and hoped he couldn't see the way my legs were shaking. "Leave. Before I use the magic."

A wicked smile stretched across Radulf's face. "You're not the only one who can use magic, you know."

Then he raised a hand, and punched it forward. It sent an invisible wave of air toward me. Even if I couldn't see it, I definitely felt it, like he'd thrown a boulder at my chest. I took the hit directly, but it traveled to my shoulder, igniting the Divine Star with pain.

I yelled, but flung out my chained hands as if to empty the pain somewhere else. There was no reaction from him, so for a moment, I thought perhaps I hadn't done anything. He started forward, but then a large cracking sound came from above the doorway between us. Heavy chunks of bricks fell, along with the dirt and rocks they had held back. It was similar to what had happened in Caesar's cave, shortly after I'd first put the bulla around my neck. But that magic hadn't come through me then, or if it did, I was feeling it far more powerfully now. The falling rocks forced Radulf back, but once everything settled, he and his men would be able to climb over the debris to get to me. Radulf ordered the soldiers forward, but then other loosened bricks started falling as well. No one obeyed his order.

"Where's my archer?" Radulf yelled through the dusty air. "Fire into that room!"

"I'm as good as any of them!" Aurelia yanked the bow off her back and fit it with an arrow, which she immediately released. It hit the hand of a man who had been reaching for his own bow, and he yelped with pain.

More rocks continued to fall, until the doorway between the two chambers was completely barricaded. So much brick had come down that the entire cistern looked in danger of collapsing, and escape was impossible now.

With the children huddled around her, Aurelia glared over at me. "That was a great move, Nic! Solve a big problem by creating a bigger one. I should have given you up!"

"You should have listened to my warning!"

"Aurelia!" One of the girls pointed above her head where the end of a large pipe stuck out from the rocks and mortar. The rushing sound of water was easily heard, and growing.

"We disconnected that pipe!" Even as Aurelia cried out the words, water gushed from the pipe. "How is this happening?"

"What a mystery!" I yelled back. "Do you think maybe they reconnected it?"

"Why would he do that?"

"That great man of yours, General Radulf, intends to drown us in here."

"In a room you just sealed off!" she yelled. "I should've turned you in after you FAINTED!"

"Open this doorway," Radulf said, directly into my head. "The water will empty out. You can still save them."

I had no intention of opening that doorway to him. But I would do everything I could to save the others in here with me. All of them were innocent, even Aurelia, I supposed. The water was rising fast. If we were to have any chance of getting out, I needed magic.

TWENTY-THREE

Water poured down on all of us, and seemed to be filling the room faster than it should have. The children were holding one another and scrambling away from the falling water, and I knew from their cries that I wasn't the only one who couldn't swim.

"Everyone stand back!" I yelled above the noise. I had little strength, but plenty of anger at what Aurelia had just said. Out of spite alone, I raised my hands again, imagining my fingers were grabbing the dirt itself, and pulled downward. Large clumps of earth, roots, and rock came with it. They fell into the water, which was already up to my knees, splashing mud all over us. I didn't figure the mud was a problem. Dirt was nothing, especially compared to drowning.

Aurelia pushed the children onto the rocks that had collapsed and out of the direct path of the falling dirt. Over their heads, I noticed a rusty ladder, partially attached to the wall. If they could reach it, and assuming I could create a hole above us, that would be their escape.

I started forward to join them, but another large chunk of earth fell, landing on my back and bringing me down with it. The water level wasn't so deep yet, except that my legs, still chained together, slipped out from beneath me and my head went completely under. I struggled to set my legs upright, but my manacled arms were little help. I tried rolling to my back long enough to take a breath but the weight of the chains fought me.

I finally got one foot braced against a sunken rock, allowing me to come up long enough to look for sky above. Had I broken through? I hoped so, because I didn't know how I'd find the strength to try again. But to my dismay, I saw nothing but more falling dirt before I was thrown back underwater. I hadn't caught a breath this time, so when I breathed in, water came with it, flooding my lungs.

Then a hand grabbed my arm and dragged me to the surface. I began choking for air as I came up again. Aurelia had waded back in and gotten me balanced on my feet. Still holding my arms, she yelled, "I don't have the key. You'll have to break your chains."

The water was past my waist now, creating a swirling current that threatened to pull me under again. But Aurelia kept hold of me while I closed my eyes and focused on the manacles. Because of the magic I'd just emptied into the room and the injury to my arm, it was so much harder than the ropes had been, but I braced my right hand on the wall, and with my left arm, split the chains around my wrists.

"There's a hole above us!" one of the children said. "But we can't get there."

I looked up. The children had climbed as high as the ladder allowed them, but the water would soon reach those on the lower rungs. Nothing other than some dangling roots were there to get them over to the hole in the ground, and we had no way of knowing if they would hold the weight of the children. If they tried to cross and fell, they'd land back down here in the water.

"Help them," I said to Aurelia.

"What about those chains on your legs? They might be harder to break."

She said it as if she didn't have everything to do with that fact. But I bypassed the argument and told her again to help the younger ones get out. Once she left, as carefully as I could, I waded through the water, at my chest now. But I only got a short ways before I gave up. I needed my legs free, but it also took all my concentration to hold my balance. I didn't want to go under again.

"This isn't worth it, Nic." Radulf's voice in my head was so calm that it seemed out of place with the rest of the chaos literally spilling into this room. "The water's pressure will open the doorway anyway, so there's no point in making things harder on all of us."

"There are children in here!" I yelled. "Stop this!"

"He can't hear you out there," Aurelia called down to me. And maybe he couldn't, but I had to say something. She didn't know how his words thundered between my ears, whether I wanted them there or not.

Anger began filling me, crowding out every other sense of fear, guilt, and despair. I was consumed with fury at what Radulf was doing, and a desire to prove Aurelia wrong in every possible way. It was enough that even without concentrating on it, my next step forward broke apart the chains. The pull threw off my balance and I fell sideways into the water.

Or I thought I was sideways. I thrashed my hands through the water, but that sent out more magic, which pulled chunks of dirt and rock down from above. I vaguely heard the children yelling at me to stop what I was doing, but I didn't know how. One large rock fell from above, landing on the dangling chain of my left hand and locking me to the bottom of the room, far below the water.

I struggled to break loose, which cost me the last of my air. My lungs burst apart and I flailed around for my life. Finally, I broke enough of the chain to push up off the ground and spear my way to the top.

I came up long enough to choke out some of the water, and to see the hole had widened, making it easier for the children to climb onto dry earth.

When Aurelia saw me surface, she called my name and started to say something else, but I went under again. So much dirt and rock had fallen that the water was now a thick, blinding soup. At least the ones who were innocent would get out. Unfortunately, the list of innocents did not include me, which was something I would have to accept. Maybe this was what I deserved for my crimes. As I sank to the floor again, I put both hands on the bulla, letting it warm me.

"Why aren't you fighting?" Radulf said to me. "Foolish boy, it is not in you to give up so easily!"

I ignored him. This wasn't giving up. I just needed a rest.

"You will fight!" Radulf said. "Put your feet on the bottom and push yourself up to the air!"

In my years as a slave, I had received thousands of orders, directing my every move. It wasn't up to us to think, only to obey. And though I always bristled against those orders, this time my fight had to be for obedience. I righted my body in the water, then found the cistern floor and pushed hard against it. I shot upward and quickly found air. But this time, as I began sinking again, something went around my neck and one arm. I grabbed hold of it and realized I was caught inside the bow Aurelia had been carrying. I rolled in the water and saw her in the water with me, one arm locked around the ladder, and the other dragging me toward her.

When she was closer, she grabbed my arm and then pulled me with her onto the ladder. She lifted the weapon off my head and then cursed. "That figures. You broke it!"

Still trying to catch my breath, I noticed her bow, which was cracked where I had held it. I should've felt sorry, but I didn't. With a good bow, and her temper, chances were she'd shoot me once we reached the surface. If she handed me her knife, I might try breaking that too.

She dumped the bow back into the water, and then told me to start climbing. It seemed so far to the surface that I couldn't understand how any of the others had already made it. My lungs ached, and my entire body was drained, but she yelled, "I can't get out until you do. So move!"

Forcing myself to climb was a test of willpower rather than strength. But with every rung, I came closer to the hole I'd opened up. At the top, I found some exposed roots poking through the dirt, which slid through my wet hand. I grabbed them again, wrapping the thinner tendrils around my fingers. Useless as my injured arm was, it served me no worse than my other arm, drained by the magic.

Radulf seemed to sense it too. In a warmer voice than I'd heard before, he said, "Magic is like a muscle. The more you use it, the stronger you'll be. You're already stronger than you were. Come with me, Nic. I can teach you everything."

Was this how he had lured others into his web? "Never," I whispered. I had no idea whether he could hear me too, but for that one word, I hoped so.

Finally, I was topside and reached back to help Aurelia climb safely to the top as well. The twelve other children who had been underground now sat around me in the field. It seemed to be very early in the morning, long before even the farming slaves would be awake, so we all lay out to rest.

Aurelia was beside me in the dirt. I caught her sideways glance when she said, "Maybe you were right about Radulf. He's going to be a problem for us."

I heard her sigh, but I was already thinking about the other thing she said, that he was a problem for *us*. My eyes slowly closed, but I couldn't stop thinking about her. Aurelia's fate had suddenly become intertwined with my own. The only question was if that would make things better, or worse.

TWENTY-FOUR

When I next opened my eyes, Aurelia was no longer beside me. As waterlogged as my brain still was, I knew she had lain here and spoken of *our* problem. I couldn't explain that, because although my entire world had turned upside down, one thing I had never doubted was that Aurelia hated me. Stranger still was acknowledging the presence of just the opposite emotion inside me. I disliked Aurelia, of course. But maybe my dislike for her wasn't as intense as I had thought.

More damp now than wet, I rolled to my side, and took in the fresh smell of dirt and the olive trees overhead. Their fruit was still too hard for eating, which was disappointing. I might've braved their bitterness just to have some food to gnaw on once I got up. If I could've gotten up.

My entire body felt like a rag that had been wrung dry. Back at the mines, Sal had once punished me by requiring me to dig through rock for twenty-four hours without sleep or meals. Once I was finally allowed to rest, it had taken an hour for my muscles to stop shaking from pain. It was awful then, but that was nothing to how I felt now. Worst of all was my injured arm, which lay on the ground in front of me like an empty tube that was attached to my shoulder. With the broken manacle cuffed around my wrist, I couldn't lift it, and the limb didn't even seem to be part of me anymore. The bandage over my injury was still knotted at the end, but the rest had come undone and lay in a heap on the dirt. And though I felt its burn, I couldn't see where the infection was. That would require me to rotate the arm, which simply wasn't going to happen. I didn't even care to look.

I flicked my eyes upward at the sound of voices some ways off from me. Aurelia was gathered in a tight circle with the other children, who occasionally leaned back to look at me, but I couldn't hear any of what they said.

Finally, one of the children got up, the African girl with the wide eyes. She walked over to me and said, "Thank you and I'm sorry."

I smiled — even that hurt — and asked, "Why and why?"

"You saved our lives down there."

"What happened was my fault. You don't have to thank me for that." Then I added, "Why are you sorry?"

"For the chains."

"You were only following orders. Maybe you can help me get these manacles off, though."

"That's why I'm sorry. The key got lost when all that water came in."

I rolled my eyes. That was a problem. If I was going to be on the surface with the entire population of Rome after me, I needed a way to blend in. With a little luck, I had some chance of passing as a free person, as Aurelia did, but not with manacles on my wrists and ankles, and lengths of chain dangling from every limb. They were almost as bad as a brand on my forehead.

"Don't worry," I told the girl. "That's not your fault either." Then I smiled up at her. "What's your name?"

She started to answer, until Aurelia appeared behind her. "Don't say your name," she said. "It's time to leave. I'll find you again when I can."

The girl thanked me once more, and then wandered back to the others. I looked past Aurelia to watch the children form into a tight group, check around for anyone else in the area, and walk away.

I squinted at Aurelia. "Why can't she tell me her name?"

"Because I still don't trust you."

"No, of course not. I only saved all of your lives."

"And why do you think they needed saving?"

"When you said the pipe was disconnected, I assumed you'd destroyed it. Not taken two pieces apart."

"Nobody would've cared to fix it unless they were after you!"

"You brought me there!"

"You asked for help. I gave it to you!"

"Right. If your idea of help was to put me in chains that nearly got me drowned!" I changed my mind about her. Again. At the moment, I had every confidence in my dislike for Aurelia.

"Sit up," she said. "It feels ridiculous to argue while you're lying there like a half-dead fish."

"I feel like a half-dead fish." But I gritted my teeth and got to a sitting position. When I did, I found Aurelia's knife at my neck again.

"Tell me how you do the magic," she said. "Also, I want that bulla back. It's safer with me."

This time, her knife was more of an annoyance than a threat, and I pushed the blade aside. "Is that how you make new friends, with a knife at their throats?"

She knew I had called her bluff, and put the knife back in its sheath. "I don't make new friends," she mumbled. "Or keep any."

Hardly a surprise. "What about those children?"

"They're trying to stay out of slavery, and I help them. That's all."

"Where are they going?"

"To other safe havens. But don't ask where because I don't think you should know."

I didn't think so either. Radulf could speak inside my mind, and I worried that he might also have the power to read it. I hoped not, but until I was sure, I wouldn't ask for information I shouldn't have.

"Why do you stay in Rome?" I asked. "If you're as strong as everyone says, then leave."

Aurelia bowed her head and her fingers traveled to the crepundia around her neck. Nothing more needed to be said. I understood now. Her family was here, somewhere. Just as my sister must be here too. Somewhere.

"Listen, I'm sorry that happened below," I said. "I had no idea Radulf knew where I was, or that he could do something like that."

"And I'm sorry I didn't believe you. When I take you to Horatio, we'll convince him of how dangerous Radulf is."

My mouth literally fell open. Either she was evil or completely insane because I was pretty sure I had just proven how difficult it would be to force me to do anything. That said, when I stood, my legs were wobbly and Aurelia came closer to assist me. Before she could, I locked my knees and turned away. Every time she helped me, my situation got worse, which was no small accomplishment since it had started out pretty close to the bottom.

"You walk like you have two broken legs," Aurelia said. "How are you going to run from me if you can't walk?"

"I'm not going to run," I said. "But I won't obey you either. I'll never have a master again."

Aurelia hesitated and then smiled sideways at me. "Finally, you're beginning to make sense."

Well, it wouldn't last long. Because the idea I was about to propose defied any logic. Hopefully, it was worth the risk.

"If you're going to find your family, then you need money, right?"

"I need a lot more than what you could pay me."

"How much is Senator Horatio offering for me?"

"It's not about the money, Nic. I really think he will help you."

I snorted. Maybe he wouldn't try to drown me in a cistern like Radulf had, but . . . actually, maybe Horatio would. According to him, I was only a filthy slave boy.

Aurelia rolled her eyes. "It's five hundred *denarii*. But even if there were no reward, I'd still take you to him, for everyone's safety, including yours. Who knows what damage you'll cause next?"

Certainly, I didn't know, and for that reason, I had a hard time arguing with her. But that didn't mean I would cooperate. Not the way she wanted anyway.

"Maybe we can help each other," I said.

Her brows pressed together. "How?"

"I think Senator Valerius took my sister from the mines, at my request. I don't know my way around Rome, especially with everyone looking for me. I don't know the customs here, and I don't know how to control the magic. I need your help to find Valerius." I drew in a shallow breath, one that chilled my lungs and sent shudders through me. "If you can take me to him, then afterward I will go with you to Horatio. He'll give you your reward money."

She frowned, obviously skeptical. "Just like that?"

"No, not just like that. I have to be sure my sister is safe, and I hope that Valerius will help me get my freedom from the emperor. Then Horatio won't be able to touch me."

"Horatio is the presiding magistrate of the Senate. If anyone can convince the emperor to spare your life, it's him. I'm sure he can help you."

My eyes narrowed. "Don't pretend to care about what happens to me. All you want is the money. Well, you'll get it. But you have to help me first."

Her eyes shifted to the bulla folded in my palm. "What happens to that?"

"I don't know." Radulf would kill me for it, the emperor too, and probably Horatio. Which meant Aurelia might do the same, especially if we ran into any problems on our way to finding Valerius. I shrugged and said, "I'll keep it until I find my sister. I might need it, especially if Radulf tries anything else. But when this is all over, I'll be glad to get rid of it. It's brought me nothing but trouble."

Aurelia bit her lip while she thought about my proposal. "Valerius is a senator, so I can find him. But once we do, getting close to him will be your problem. Runaway slaves can't just walk up to senators. For that matter, neither can plebian girls."

"He'll see me." That part of the plan didn't concern me at all.

"And once your sister is safe, you'll come with me to see Horatio? You promise me that?"

"You'll get your money, Aurelia."

Then her head tilted. "What about Radulf? This could be dangerous."

I barely held back a mischievous smile. "Yeah, I figured you wouldn't have the courage."

She lightly punched my arm — my injured arm, but I probably deserved that much. "I'm in."

TWENTY-FIVE

It turns out that I'd already worn these very manacles once before. Aurelia confessed that this was the same set Felix had made me wear in the caravan. Instead of returning them to Felix, she merely kept them.

"You mean you stole them," I corrected her, only half teasing. "Was this one of those choices you had to make to survive? Or are you also a thief?"

"I'm a girl with a knife, so be careful of your accusations," Aurelia shot back. Not half teasing.

We were hurrying toward the venatio, hoping to get there before it was light enough for many people to be around. She believed Felix would have another key.

"He won't give it to you," I said. "Especially if he knows why you want it."

"Then I'll have to steal it." She caught the playful gleam in my eye and immediately followed that with, "Don't say another word." But this time, I was sure I saw a hint of a smile. Barely, but it was there.

No matter how quiet the city was in the predawn hours, the venatio workers were already hard at work. Other animals were being transported to the amphitheater, which likely meant more games were coming soon. The animals clamored for attention as the workers shouted orders to one another about filling the animals' needs.

Only days ago, I had been one of them. Moving about in a haze of blindness, thinking that even if life in bondage was bad, it was still tolerable. But no more. From behind the copse of cypress trees where we hid and watched, I already felt apart from that world. I repeated in my mind the same vow as before, that I would never again fall into chains. I was my own person now. My own master.

"There he is." Aurelia pointed at Felix, who was crossing from his home to the amphitheater.

We darted out into the street, and then ran up to Felix. He heard us coming and started to yell for help, but Aurelia drew her knife. "None of that," she said firmly. "We need the key for these manacles. My copy was lost."

Felix looked from me back to her. "After what happened in the amphitheater, now you're helping this slave boy? He could've caused thousands of deaths. He's a fugitive of the empire, not to mention a runaway slave. I paid good money —"

"I'm free now," I said. "I don't care what you paid."

Felix shook his head. "Ah. So slaves can declare their own freedom now? Why not make yourself a patrician, or a senator?"

"Because I don't stink as bad as they do," I retorted.

"The key," Aurelia repeated.

Felix produced a ring full of dozens of keys and handed them to me. As I started poking each one into the manacle lock, hoping for a match, he said, "All of Rome knows you performed magic, and those who know how you did it will kill to get that bulla. Do you think Aurelia is any different?"

I glanced sideways at her. The very opposite was true. Despite the fact that I needed her help, nobody seemed more dangerous right now. What if we couldn't find Valerius? Would she become impatient and try turning me over to Horatio early? What if someone else — such as Radulf — offered a greater reward? Would she lead me to him instead? And if she tried, could I stop her? I had a bulla I scarcely knew how to use. She had a knife. At least her bow was gone. Considering the possibility that she'd try using it against me, I was glad I'd broken it.

Still looking for the right key, I said, "Why did the emperor have to make this a fight? I was on his side."

"I warned him you'd find your magic in the arena, but he didn't believe it." Felix clasped his hands together. "You're a threat to him, Nic."

"I'm not!"

"You nearly brought down the amphitheater with a stroke of your arm, while holding a bulla that would be useless in his hands. You frighten him, and for good reason."

"He should be frightened, but not of me. He has an enemy —"

"He has many enemies, and if they get the bulla, they can use it against the entire empire. You proved that in the arena."

"I didn't control any of what happened!"

"Exactly my point!" Felix gestured in the direction of the amphitheater. "If you caused destruction like that without having control of the bulla, imagine what an enemy who controlled it could do."

"The enemy is General Radulf," I said. "Emperor Tacitus must have him arrested."

"On what charge?"

"Illegal sheepherding, for all I care!" I shrugged angrily. "If he made up charges against me, then he can do it for the general."

Felix snorted. "The general cannot be stopped. As I've told you, all the emperor can do is hope Radulf does not turn against him."

"He already has! I've told you what he said!"

"Give me the keys, you're too slow." Aurelia took them and knelt at my feet, working first at the manacles there.

"What if I get evidence against Radulf?" I offered.

Felix's eyes narrowed. "What would you ask in return?"

"For my life. The emperor must forgive all criminal charges against me. And I want my sister's freedom." When I found her. "And I want five hundred denarii."

Still at work with the keys, Aurelia muttered something under her breath. It shouldn't matter to her where she got her money. This way, I could avoid Horatio forever.

"Those are heavy demands," Felix said. "But I might be able to persuade Emperor Tacitus *if* you give him the bulla as part of that agreement."

"I will trade the bulla for my freedom. But until Radulf is defeated, he can still get at me, and I need the bulla for defense."

Curious, Felix tilted his head. "What do you mean Radulf can get at you?"

"He's got magic, Felix." I had seen it, and felt it, and still had the echo of his voice in my head.

Felix's expression changed. It wasn't one of surprise, but rather, as if I had spoken a truth he had refused to acknowledge until now. "Are you sure?" For the first time since we began talking, he sounded as frightened as I felt.

"It's different from whatever I can do with the bulla, but just as strong. And I bet that if he got the bulla, he could use it, maybe worse than me. He'll make what I did in the arena look like a game of knucklebones."

Felix's face went pale. He took the keys from Aurelia, sorted through them until he found the one he wanted, and handed it back. She stuck it in the lock on my manacles and it opened.

While she completed the others, Felix said, "General Radulf wasn't born a Roman. He came from a barbarian tribe up north and was captured thirteen years ago when Rome conquered his land. He became a gladiator here, one of the few to never lose a fight. Radulf became a hero in this city, and through his skills, he earned his freedom, then his citizenship, then his military position."

Aurelia snapped off the last of my manacles and said, "Let's go."

I resisted her tug. "You think he won because he had magic?"

Felix looked around before speaking, as if he thought we might be overheard. "I worked with the animals while Radulf waited for his turn to enter the arena. I saw him up close many times, bare except for his gladiator uniform. Nic, whatever that mark on your back means, Radulf has one exactly like it."

"Nic, now!" Aurelia said. "We've been spotted." Two soldiers talking by the amphitheater glanced at us.

No, this was my chance to get answers. Maybe my only chance. "I heard he killed others who had the mark."

"Every one of them, and now we know why. He'll do the same to you." Felix's eyes darted around again. "If that mark is a source of magic, then you have to worry about more than the bulla. It means there is magic coming from inside you."

Aurelia pulled at my arm, but Felix grabbed my shoulders. "Listen carefully. These are dangerous times, and what you did in the amphitheater proves you will either be the emperor's greatest friend, or his greatest enemy. He will not take the risk of guessing wrong about you. If you go to the emperor or anyone loyal to him right now, they will kill you."

Aurelia only briefly met my eyes. Clearly, Felix's warning

included Horatio, the leader of the emperor's Senate. And I had agreed to go.

Felix continued, "If you want forgiveness from the emperor, you will have to do more than get evidence against Radulf. You will have to defeat him and take his magic, just as he has taken it from others."

I shrank beneath his gaze. "I can't stop him, Felix! Expose him, maybe, but that's all."

"You may be the only one who can."

The thought of that terrified me, but then I remembered when the bulla had pressed against the mark on my back, the way I had felt it pulling out the magic. If I could do that same thing to Radulf, I could win. There was an obvious problem, of course. I would have to get close to Radulf, and I doubted he'd cooperate with my plan.

"We have to go now!" Aurelia grabbed my arm. The two soldiers who had been talking to a slave closer to the amphitheater pointed at us. One of them pulled out his sword.

I started to leave, but turned back long enough to look at Felix. "If it's the only way I can get freedom, then I will do as you ask. But if the emperor doesn't keep his end of the bargain, then yes, I will become his greatest enemy."

Felix only stared as Aurelia and I hurried away.

TWENTY-SIX

This time, Aurelia actually had a good excuse to be angry with me. I had tarried so long with Felix that the Roman soldiers were on our heels now. As far as I was concerned, my reasons were good. Aurelia disagreed.

"Why didn't you listen?" she scolded.

"You could've left, you know. It's only money." I spoke as irritably as she had, though I hoped she wasn't angry enough to actually leave.

"You're worth more than just money," she said, then shifted directions slightly. The soldiers had taken a high road, hoping to cut us off. This bought us a few extra paces. "This way! We'll hide in the forum."

It didn't seem like the best suggestion, and in any other situation, I'd have stopped to make an argument of it. I'd only seen the forum from a distance, but enough to know it was always full of people, going to and from the many temples, markets, and other public buildings. Most of them had probably been in the amphitheater. I figured it was a safe guess that they'd remember the boy who had nearly destroyed it.

We crossed in front of a building with enormous marble columns. My mind filled with the possibilities of what would happen if I accidentally released any magic here. If I toppled one column, or even cracked it, the entire building could collapse.

"I have an idea!" Aurelia grabbed my arm and yanked me midstep toward one of the temples, built up on a ridge of earth higher than many others in the forum. We ran around a speaker's platform to a wide flight of stairs, where, for a moment, we got ahead of the soldiers when they tripped over each other in their race to snatch me. At the top was a second set of stairs, divided by wide marble columns. Behind them, the great doors of a temple were already open. Aurelia ran in, but I stopped at the entrance, my breath caught in my throat.

An imposing statue of Julius Caesar stood inside the entrance, and it stared down at me as if he were alive, warning me I had no right to enter this building. Carved into the statue's forehead was the Divine Star. My hand was around the bulla and I released it at once, ashamed of having stolen it from Caesar's own cave. Although it was still hidden beneath my tunic, I had no doubt that Caesar knew exactly where it was.

"Do you want to stand there and be cut down?" Aurelia scowled and grabbed my hand again, this time dragging me inside the temple with her. Inside Caesar's temple.

As soon as we crossed the doorway, my shoulder started to prickle. I took it as a sign that Caesar was displeased with me, but he would have to get angrier than that before I'd leave. At least so far, no one in here was trying to kill me. The same could not be said if I stayed outside.

The temple was filled with altars for sacrifices, elaborate vases, sculptures, and, of course, the colossal statue of Julius Caesar, still watching me. I stood up taller and gave the statue a nod of respect. I had his magic now, and I intended to use it well. For the record, it didn't nod back, which was a relief. Turning away from Caesar's gaze, I noticed the walls of the temple, decorated in frescoes of other gods and goddesses, all more beautiful than anything I'd ever seen before. But the one that caught my eye was a painting of the Divine Star, the red comet of fire leaving trails of light on its journey through the heavens.

Aurelia touched my arm. "That's the image on your shoulder. Almost exactly alike."

There were a few other patrons inside, but a woman in flowing white robes saw our entrance and put a finger to her lips to remind us of the need for silence here. She was as beautiful as the paintings around us and I lowered my eyes, humbled by the power she seemed to possess.

"She's a *vestalis*," Aurelia whispered. "She is a sacred woman — her job is to care for this temple. Come, we have to speak to her."

"Not me," I whispered, pulling against her. "Not here."

"You're a slave, Nic, not a plague. Come on."

She misunderstood. The bulla was warming again, and I grabbed it, hoping to dispel any magic that might still be there. Whatever they might do to me in here, I would not destroy this temple. I needed a place to calm the bulla. To calm myself.

Aurelia started forward, but the two soldiers who had been chasing us walked through the doorway. Their eyes fell immediately upon me.

"Stop!" one of them called out.

By then, we had come up to the vestalis. I had been wrong before, for she was far more beautiful than the images painted on the walls, with eyes like the sea and a smile that passed with the wind, leaving a stern expression behind. "Yes?" she asked. Her voice was kind, at least.

"We seek asylum." Aurelia's head flipped around to the soldiers, then turned back to the woman. "Please."

One of the soldiers approached her too. He bowed respectfully and said, "My lady, this boy is a criminal and a slave, wanted for crimes against the emperor and against all of Rome. He is dangerous."

She looked at me. "This boy? He doesn't look dangerous."

I tried not to look dangerous, but inside I felt worse than ever. Because I was everything he said, even if I didn't intend to be.

"Even for criminals, Caesar's temple is a place of asylum," she said. "Or do you not feel that this temple should be honored?"

The soldier's eyes darted. "Of course, *Domina.* Which is why I need to remove this boy. He carries powers that should not belong to any human. He defiles Caesar's temple."

"No, my lady, he honors it." Aurelia pulled my tunic down at the shoulder, exposing the mark to the woman. "Grant us asylum. *Please.*"

I heard her draw in a breath as she recognized the Divine Star, then she said to the soldier, "You will leave, sir. It is not I who has granted this boy asylum. Caesar himself has done it."

The soldier grunted a terse "Very well," and gave her another bow, but before he rose back up, he met my eyes and said, "You can't stay in here forever, slave. If you stick even one hand outside this temple, I will cut it off, and catch the rest of you as it falls."

"If you see my hand, be sure it isn't aimed at you," I snarled back before Aurelia kicked me in the shin. Maybe it wasn't the wisest thing to say, given the shocked reaction of the vestalis, but I felt better afterward and that had to be worth something.

Once the soldier left, the woman frowned at me. "I know what happened in the amphitheater. It will not happen here, on sacred ground."

"No, Domina," Aurelia said. "Of course not. We promise."

She seemed to accept that and her tone softened. "This is the place where Caesar's body was burned after his death. At times, his wandering spirit can be felt here. No doubt he will feel the presence of your . . . abilities."

No doubt at all, for though I tried to deny it, I already felt the truth of her words. Yes, he was here. And not at all pleased that I was too.

TWENTY-SEVEN

Caesar's temple was grand, ornate, and very tall, but not particularly large inside. The vestalis told us we were free to remain as long as we wanted, but warned that the Roman soldier had been correct before: Once we left, the laws of asylum no longer protected us. I kept my back to the other patrons, who seemed equally uninterested in me. The last thing I needed was their curiosity.

While we obviously couldn't stay in this temple forever, I wasn't sure I could even last the night — my hunger was becoming desperate. Within another day or two, if I didn't risk my life trying to outrun the soldiers, I'd lose it anyway to starvation. I glanced over at Aurelia, who didn't seem much better off. She eyed the sheath for her knife like it was dried meat, and I wouldn't have been surprised if she gave it a taste, just to be sure.

As. we entered the afternoon hours, the temple seemed less busy, though the forum was as lively as ever. A careful glance outside the doors indicated the soldiers were still there, determined to wait me out. I walked into the *cella*, where Aurelia was on the floor leaning against a wall.

At first, I thought her mind was somewhere much further away, but once I sat, she whispered, "If Radulf has the Divine Star on his shoulder too, then maybe that's how he found you. Maybe you're connected."

"Or maybe his soldiers saw me go into the sewers." That was a better thought than acknowledging any connection between us. I didn't want to think about how his voice got into my head.

"I don't understand what happened in the cistern. There are easier ways to kill you."

I looked over at her. "Well, that's good to know. Thanks, Aurelia."

"I only mean that if he wanted you dead, why go through that elaborate attempt at drowning you?"

"He wanted to scare me into unsealing the room, but I don't think he wanted me to drown." How else could I explain the moment I had almost given up, when he urged me to force myself back to the air? Obviously, it had something to do with the bulla, but too many questions still remained. Although it sent a shiver down my spine, Aurelia was right. There were easier ways for Radulf to get me.

"How are you going to take Radulf's magic?" Aurelia asked. "Is that even possible?"

"I think so." I *hoped* so.

"He'll probably try to do the same to you," Aurelia said. "Before he kills you."

I shook my head at her. "Is this a normal thing for you? Encouraging people right into the grave?"

"I just think you need to be realistic about what you're facing!"

I gestured around us. "We're starving, and trapped in here with soldiers waiting to arrest me! Radulf is probably already on his way here, and I doubt he'll care about the laws of asylum. I perfectly understand the reality of my situation!"

"*Our* situation." More quietly, Aurelia said, "I'll stay with you until we get this figured out. I promise."

I couldn't hold back a grin. "The way my life has gone since I met you, that sounds more like a threat."

She giggled and squeezed my arm. I wished she had not withdrawn her hand as quickly as she did, but at the same time, I wasn't brave enough to reach for it again.

Aurelia should have been as tired as I was, but she spent the next half hour tapping her feet or fidgeting with her nails, maybe out of frustration at being trapped in here. Not me. I was glad for the chance to rest. Aside from the hunger, which was already bad enough, the magic I'd used underground had drained me, and the stinging in my back was growing worse. It felt like hundreds of needles were poking at me all at once, going deeper each time. I shifted around in hopes of relieving the discomfort, but movement only seemed to make it worse. Probably that was Caesar's reminder that he didn't want me here in his temple. As if I wasn't already perfectly clear on that.

By early evening, the temple patrons had grown tired of their worship, and had cleared out, leaving us entirely alone. Aurelia had fallen asleep and I finally dared to take out the bulla and really look at it. The soft glow that had drawn me to it from the very first was still there. When I opened it up, I saw why. The jewels inside were the finest stones I'd ever seen. The largest was a bright green emerald, set between a purple amethyst and a blazing red stone that I didn't recognize. All of them were glowing.

The bulla was cool now, and I was beginning to understand that the magic only worked when it was warm. But I didn't know what caused it to heat, or how it was connected to the mark on my back, or how its power was supposed to be controlled. Maybe it couldn't be controlled, at least by a human. If Venus had abandoned Caesar and withdrawn her powers from the bulla, then someone else was giving it power now. But who? Hopefully it wasn't any of the gods who considered my life their personal game of dice.

I stood and walked over to Caesar's statue, expecting the bulla to warm when it came closer to him. But it didn't. The magic in it was no longer his. For reasons I could not explain, it was mine now.

"Are you sure that Senator Valerius has your sister?"

Unsure of how long Aurelia had been awake, I immediately hung the bulla back around my neck and hid it. "I told his son that before I agreed to talk, Valerius would have to get Livia from the mines. She's got to be with him."

"Why would he do that for you? He must want something big in exchange."

"Of course he does." That gnawed at me. It was something to do with the magic, obviously, but that's what everyone wanted, so I couldn't avoid it forever. At least Valerius was willing to help me too.

"Why do you trust Valerius? You're so opposed to Horatio, but both men are senators, and both are loyal to the emperor."

I moved back to the wall and scuffed my bare foot against the floor. "When Valerius first saw the mark on my back, he tried to protect me." Then I looked up and met her gaze. "He was hiding it from Horatio."

She didn't seem to like that and only turned away. "Well, maybe Valerius seems nice now, but in the end, there'll be a price for it."

I smirked back at her. "Probably, but I already know the price for you being nice to me."

She chuckled. "It's a good theory, Nic, but you and I both know I haven't been at all nice to you."

No, she hadn't. Which made it all the more of a mystery why I hoped she'd stay. To her, I was a pocketful of coins, a ticket to a better life and nothing more. But to me, she was turning into more than a guide back to my sister. Whether I liked it or not, she was becoming my friend.

Aurelia took to pacing again. "We need to escape this temple. The soldiers can outlast us. If one gets tired, they can just change out guards."

"Maybe you should've suggested a better hiding place."

"Maybe you should've chosen different enemies!"

I opened my mouth, but no argument came. She was absolutely right about that.

She leaned beside me against the temple wall. "If you want to bring Radulf down, then you must understand the fight it'll be to get to him. Romans love him. They believe in him, far more than they do the emperor."

"He's a villain, Aurelia! Maybe they don't see what kind of person he really is, but I do. When his voice is in my head, it's so cold it turns my blood to ice. Back at the mines, he told me if I didn't bring him this bulla, he'd leave me to die in the cave."

"Maybe he was saying it for your own good." Aurelia's eyes settled on the bulla, still in my hand. "Maybe he knew that if you tried to keep it, all of this would happen."

I brushed past her, frustrated with the fact that she was actually making sense.

She called after me, "You're not alone, Nic. I'm here to help you."

"You're here to get a reward. I am alone."

"You're not." She walked up and put her hand on my shoulder. "But you have to look at this from the emperor's view. So far, only one person has done anything to threaten Rome. That's you. As presiding magistrate, Horatio could defend you before the emperor."

"Or deliver me to him. Felix said anyone loyal to the empire would kill me."

"Felix should know. He actually tried to do it!"

"And maybe Horatio would succeed." My fists tightened. "You can't possibly expect me to trust him."

"I don't expect you to trust anyone!"

"Even you?"

Aurelia wavered, just for a moment. "All I'm saying is that you can't hide forever."

"That's my problem, not yours." I turned to her. "Once I find my sister, we will vanish."

"No. Once we find your sister, you promised to go to Horatio. I will defend you to him."

"And why would he listen to you?" I asked.

A mischievous smile tugged at the corner of Aurelia's lips. "Surely by now you know that I make people listen when I speak."

I smiled back. "I know that when you speak, it almost always ends in trouble."

"You are the last boy on this earth who should speak about trouble!"

I laughed and moved to brush her aside, but this time she grabbed my arm, playfully twisted it behind me, and then forced me to the ground. I pulled her down with me and she fell at my side, laughing as well.

I stared at her a moment, realizing again how pretty her eyes were when she lowered her guard. No, in this failing light of day, they were beautiful.

Hearing the sound of footsteps in the doorway, we both sat up. Aurelia went for her knife and I hurried to hide the bulla beneath my tunic again.

But there was no need for alarm, or at least, I hoped not. In fact, it was the exact person I had hoped to see again. Crispus. As the son of a senator, he moved in the same circles as other leaders of Rome . . . with Radulf, specifically. I whispered who he was to Aurelia and told her to put away her knife, which she did with obvious reluctance.

Crispus didn't seem to have come to worship. Rather than an offering, in his arms were two folded togas. He smiled and said, "My father spotted you two running in here earlier today. We hoped you'd still be here."

"With those soldiers outside, where else would we have gone?" Aurelia asked.

"Father's out there now, distracting them with some absurd orders, but it won't last long." Crispus grinned. "If you want to escape from this temple, you must come with me right now."

Aurelia started to protest but I muttered that we could sort out whether Crispus should be trusted *after* our escape.

"He might be dangerous to you," she hissed.

I only smiled. "But still not as dangerous as you are." She chuckled, and more important, didn't disagree.

Crispus held out the togas to each of us. "Have you ever considered dressing up like old women?"

My smile widened. To escape this building, I was ready to consider nearly anything.

TWENTY-EIGHT

Crispus gave Aurelia her toga, and since I had never worn one, he helped me with mine. It seemed like a lot of unnecessary cloth, most of which had to be carried over one arm, but he told me since only the wealthy could afford so much cloth, the soldiers would see it from a distance and assume we were patricians.

"Keep your heads covered, like older women do," he said.

"I'm barefoot," I said, holding up one foot. "If they see —"

"Let's hope they don't. And if anyone approaches, let me do the talking."

That was fine with me. Whenever I talked, it only seemed to end in trouble.

Crispus led us through a side door of the temple that exited onto an open-air portico. As warm as it was this evening, at least we felt the breeze now. The afternoon heat inside the temple had been stifling.

"It's getting late, but there should still be some markets open in the basilica ahead," he said. "We'll blend in with the people there. Just don't look back at the soldiers." He glanced at me. "And don't look down. Only slaves do that."

I hadn't realized I was. Raising my head felt unnatural, but he was right, keeping my head down was the attitude of a slave. I had spent too many years with my eyes cast downward and my head and knees ready to bend upon anyone's orders. Well, anyone other than Sal — I had never willingly obeyed him.

"Why are you helping us?" Aurelia asked.

Crispus looked at me as if it had been my question. "Because you need our help. And because Rome needs you."

We made it inside the basilica without drawing anyone's attention. Over the top of the crowd, I saw all three stories of the interior were open and every wall from floor to ceiling was lined with arches. Crispus told Aurelia she could remove the toga from her head, but suggested I stay covered. "At least fifty thousand Romans saw you in the amphitheater five days ago," he said. "It's safe to assume that many of them are here now and will recognize you."

Each shop we passed in the basilica had different wares. I assumed the signs over each one identified their products, and vowed again to one day teach myself to read. But for now, I couldn't take my eyes off the items being sold. There was so much more than I could believe existed in the entire world, much less in this great city. One of the final shops was putting out warm baked bread. Without even thinking of what I was doing, I stopped in front of the loaves, just to take in the glorious scent and hope it filled my stomach enough to dull the ache of hunger.

Crispus walked back and stopped beside me. When he spoke, his voice was kind. "When did you last eat?"

It had been the half bowl of sour porridge from yesterday morning, and I'd had nothing in four days before that. But I couldn't bring myself to say the words. I only lowered my eyes and hoped he'd just walk on so we could go.

"Head up," Crispus reminded me. He reached into a bag he carried and withdrew some coins for the shop owner. "A large loaf," he said, pointing. "That one."

I took a step back, unsure of what to do. I was almost delirious with hunger, and whatever strength I might have had was constantly drained by trying to control the magic of the bulla. Yet I couldn't accept this from him.

Crispus took the loaf and broke it in half, then gave one portion to Aurelia, who immediately dug into it. He held out the other half to me. "Take it," he said. "You're so thin, a feather could knock you over."

My eyes moistened and I shook my head. "No, I can't."

"Just like the apple," he said, smiling. "You can pay me for it later."

"I have nothing."

"Take it." Crispus pressed the loaf into my hands. "Please, Nic."

I immediately ripped pieces from it, as large as I could fit in my mouth without choking. The bread we got at the mines was little more than a baked paste of coarsely ground flour and dirty water. This was soft and fragrant and slightly sweet. It filled my stomach and warmed my body, and for the first time since I had eaten all those strawberries, I didn't feel completely hollow inside.

Once I was finished, we left the basilica. "Don't look around at the sights," Crispus corrected me. "The wealthy have been here a thousand times. There's nothing they haven't already seen."

I turned away, but it wasn't easy. As impressive as my first glimpses of Rome had been, nothing equaled the beauty of the forum. It seemed to have been made for the gods themselves, and yet even the lowest Roman was freely given this place for work, play, or worship. The sun was setting, and from our direction, Caesar's temple left us in shadow. That seemed an apt description for my life at the moment. Wearing Caesar's bulla, a bulla I had stolen, I was now seeking a way to survive beneath his shadow.

Aurelia fell in step beside me. "Where is he taking us?"

"To my home," Crispus said. "My father will meet us there."

"And my sister is there too?" I had so much to tell her.

Crispus stopped and his brows pressed together when he looked at me. "Nic, I'm sorry. My father did send someone to the mines to get her, but she had already been taken away. We don't know who took her, or where she is."

My heart thudded like a cold stone against my chest. I could barely comprehend his words. From the moment Sal had told me Livia was taken from the mines, it had seemed obvious that Valerius would've had her, safe and well cared for. But if it wasn't him, then who?

Radulf.

It was his way of getting to me.

Maybe I had whispered his name, because at my side, Aurelia shook her head and leaned in to me. "That doesn't make sense. You told me that Radulf thought you died in the cave. Livia was taken from the mines before he saw you alive in the arena. So Radulf wouldn't have had any reason to take her."

I threw out a hand in frustration. "Who else would it be?" Heads turned our way and I lowered my voice. "All I can tell you is she's innocent in this. And he certainly knows I'm alive now, so if that wasn't his plan before, it will be now."

Crispus stepped toward me, with his tall shoulders hunched. "We'll find her. I can't imagine Radulf would've had any use for her, but she must be somewhere."

"I agree," Aurelia said. "If she's still alive —"

"Don't say that like it's a question."

"Ignoring reality doesn't change it. Listen, she probably is alive. I'm only saying that Radulf is a military man. He doesn't need girl slaves. He might've sold her off ten minutes after taking her from the mines. She could be anywhere by now."

That didn't make me feel better, and if I was angry with Aurelia for saying it, that was only because she was right.

Crispus cleared his throat. "I know this is a bad time to be getting such news, but we need to keep moving. People are watching us."

Aurelia looked around. "Who?"

Crispus nudged his head to where we had just been in the shops. My heart sank. Only one man was watching me, but his mouth was curled in disgust. It was Sal, lurking in the corners like a Shade escaped from the underworld. Despite Crispus and Aurelia surrounding me, and the toga over my head, he clearly knew exactly who I was. All he needed to do was say my name, and we'd be surrounded. But for reasons I couldn't explain, he didn't.

I lowered my eyes, lifted the toga higher on my head, and followed behind Crispus, hoping that was the last I'd see of Sal for the evening. Or better yet, for the rest of my life.

Aurelia remained at my side. She grabbed my arm to weigh down my pace, and once Crispus was a little farther ahead of us, she said, "Are you sure we should go with him? If he doesn't have Livia —"

"I'm not going to Horatio. Not yet!"

"That's our bargain!"

"What bargain? Crispus is taking me to Valerius, not you." My irritation wasn't entirely her fault. I was terrified for my sister, nervous about what Valerius might want from me, and, delicious as it was, the bread had only barely filled the deep well of my hunger. But on top of all of that, I didn't need to hear her constant pleadings for me to turn myself in to a pompous senator who would most likely pass me straight on to the executioner. "If you're so eager, go run and tell Horatio where he can find me. Maybe he'll still give you that precious reward money."

"Do you think money is all I care about?"

"That's exactly what I think! Why can't you see there is more going on than who will have the pleasure of hauling me in chains before the emperor?"

Her mouth opened in protest, then closed, and she said, "Since we met, I've been shot at, threatened, chased, and nearly drowned. If all I cared about was the money, I'd have disappeared long ago."

"Then what do you care about?" I asked. "It's not finding my sister. You don't even know her."

"But I know you, and . . . and I don't hate you, Nic, no matter what you believe. Maybe we disagree about Horatio, but that doesn't mean I'm trying to hurt you."

I glanced sideways at her. "I don't hate you either. But until I find my sister, we'll continue to disagree."

Her mouth opened again, but this time she said nothing and only mumbled that we should catch up to Crispus before he got away from us.

I adjusted the toga over my head again before joining them. When I did, I noticed her hand at her neck, as attached to that crepundia as I always was to the bulla. With enough reward money, she could make herself into a respectable young woman of Rome, and that might give her access to her family again.

And therein was the problem.

It was becoming increasingly obvious how flawed our bargain was. The only way she succeeded with her goals was to get the reward money from Horatio. But even if I defeated Radulf, there was no guarantee Horatio would persuade the emperor to let me go free. In fact, Horatio might not even deliver me to the emperor. For all I knew, he wanted the bulla for himself, and would kill me to keep it.

Aurelia and I were careening toward an impasse. For her to succeed in what she wanted most, I would almost certainly have to fail.

TWENTY-NINE

Crispus's home was on the outskirts of the city, on a gently sloping hill with vineyards as far as the eye could see. "They're not all ours," he explained when he caught both Aurelia and I gaping at them. "There are many people in Rome far wealthier than us."

"How many people?" Aurelia quipped. "Three?"

Once we entered his home, I doubted it was even that many. The exterior wasn't so grand — on either side of the entrance were ordinary shops, selling food and wine produced here on this land. The inside, however, was anything but ordinary.

The wide entry was tiled with precious jewels similar to those I had once mined. For all I knew, my hands had pulled them from the earth. They created a colorful mosaic pattern of a griffin. I saw it and immediately thought of Caela, wondering if she had survived the injury to her side. I missed her and wondered whether I'd ever see her again. Beside me, Aurelia seemed to sense what I was feeling. She took my hand and gave it a squeeze. I released it as quickly as she had taken mine. It still bothered me to realize only one of us was going to succeed in our bargain, and that it probably wasn't me.

Looking up, large paintings hung on either side of the entry corridor. One was of Senator Valerius, and the second one Crispus said was of his grandfather, who had died only a few years earlier.

"He was a great man." Crispus turned to me. "Did you ever know your grandfather?"

"I never even knew my father," I said. "He died when I was very young." Though he shouldn't have. Why didn't he get inside during the thunderstorm, like any reasonable person would?

It was Crispus's turn to go silent. "Oh," he finally said. "I'm sorry, Nic."

I didn't answer. Not because I was angry, but because I was very aware of Aurelia beside me, who had even less of a claim to family than I did. Crispus never bothered to ask about her. I figured she preferred it that way.

By then, we walked into a large atrium where moonlight poured through an open roof. It reflected down on the surface of a small and shallow pool with another mosaic beneath it, depicting the same griffin as I had seen at the entrance. Bright flowers grew around the pool and their scent carried on the breeze. The full moon and large candles added enough light that I saw the dark orange paint on the walls, elaborate fresco paintings of nature and beautiful women and illustrations of stories that I was sure every Roman over the age of three would understand. Impressive as they were, to me, they were only random pictures.

"This is really where you live?" I asked. "It's not another temple?"

"It's home." Crispus pointed to rooms at the sides of the atrium. "These are our bedrooms. Behind them are rooms where my mother does her weaving, and where the work is assigned to our slaves."

His eyes suddenly darted across to me but I tried to ignore that. It was no surprise that his wealthy family would have slaves, but I still felt a pinch to hear it. I refused to think of myself that way anymore, and yet it was also painfully clear that I did not belong in Crispus's world either.

To ease the tension, Aurelia pointed ahead to a room with a large desk I could see from here. "What's in there?"

Again, he faced me to answer her question. "The *tablinum*, where my father works when he's home. When he comes, he will talk to you in there." Then for the first time, he really seemed to see Aurelia. "We have private baths, here in the home. I can assign a woman to attend to you there."

Aurelia shook her head. "I'll stay with Nic."

"You should go to the baths," I said.

She frowned at me, and I knew she had misunderstood. I wasn't implying that she smelled bad, or, at least, no worse than me. I only meant that I didn't expect any trouble from Senator Valerius. Just the opposite in fact. Though I wasn't sure exactly what he wanted from me, I knew he would help with my problem. Valerius had no love for Radulf either.

But Aurelia wouldn't budge. "I'll stay with Nic."

Crispus sighed, took the bulky togas from us, and led us into his father's office. He gave us seats, then said he would call for someone to bring us more food, and left.

Aurelia immediately leaned toward me. "I don't like it here. I think we should leave."

"Why? Do you object to being somewhere safe? Somewhere I'm going to be fed for a second time in the same evening?"

"You only think about food," she said.

"And you only think about running," I replied. "All I'm asking for is enough time to hear what Valerius has to say. If we don't like it, then we leave. No problem."

We fell silent when a servant entered from a second door behind the senator's desk. He set a tray on the desk filled with more bread and cheese and a soft white fruit that tasted as sweet as the strawberries had been.

"It's a pear." Aurelia took a bite, and then handed it to me. "Honestly, it's like your whole life has been lived in a cave."

"It was," I answered with my mouth already full.

I couldn't eat everything fast enough, and by the time the tray was empty, my stomach ached with satisfaction. But although I had to slouch in my chair and try not to move, I wasn't about to complain. If a second tray were brought in, I'd find a way to eat everything on it too.

Aurelia turned to me and lowered her voice. "Valerius will ask about the bulla. You know that, right?"

My fingers were already tracing the curve where it attached to the strap. "Yes."

"What will you tell him?"

"Nothing, until he tells me something about Livia."

"She's a lost slave girl. Valerius won't care about her."

"But I do!" I sat up straight and stared at Aurelia. "And if he wants my help, then he needs to help me first."

"I'm helping you, Nic. Maybe not for reasons you like, but I am helping you." Then Aurelia shrugged. "Wherever my family is, I wish they cared as much about finding me as you care about your sister."

"Can I see your crepundia?" I asked.

She paused a moment before lifting it over her head and handing it to me. The miniatures were far more intricate than I had realized at first. Someone had put a great deal of work into this, and unfortunately, it was probably valued more than the daughter.

I opened the small satchel in the center of the crepundia and saw inside it poor man's gems. They were so close to the real thing that most people wouldn't know the difference. However, my eye was practiced from the mines. Sal wouldn't have considered these fakes worth our time.

Realizing I knew the difference, Aurelia snatched the crepundia from my grip. "I sold the originals a long time ago. One day, I'll get them back again."

"Why is it so important to find this family who already exposed you?" I asked. "Why do you think they'll take you back now?"

Staring at the crepundia, she said, "I think about them every day. Whether my mother wanted to keep me, and what might have gone wrong for my father to have rejected me so harshly. I hope it's a reason that he regrets now. Maybe there was something sad associated with my birth and he couldn't deal with it then. Maybe our family was having hard times and he had no choice."

"If money is the only reason they'd accept you, then you shouldn't go back to them," I said.

Tears welled in her eyes and she put the crepundia back around her neck. "You don't understand."

"That's right, I don't! You're my friend, Aurelia. Not because of money or anything you can do for me, but because you're a good person, just as you are. Your family should feel the same way."

I noticed her fidget with her fingers. She lowered her eyes and whispered, "I need to tell you something."

But before she could, we both leapt to our feet at the fierce barking of two dogs. Coming our way.

Aurelia and I dashed out of the office as two black dogs raced in from the doorway behind the desk and went straight for us. Once in the atrium, Aurelia darted around as if to go to the rear of the home, but I ran forward. I turned long enough to see them still coming and then tripped and fell into the small pool in the center of the atrium.

The dogs came upon me and I raised a hand to protect myself from the worst of their attack. "Stop!" I shouted at them.

To my surprise, both dogs immediately stopped their barking and only stared at me. Just as the animals of the venatio had done. So I got to my feet, slowly, and told the dogs, "Sit."

They obeyed as quickly as I spoke the words. But that wasn't a fair test. They were probably well-trained dogs, which I'd expect in a household like this. They needed a more unusual command.

Aurelia walked up to us, cautiously, but her eyes were on me, not the dogs. "Nic —"

"Watch this." With a smile, I said, "Tell me if Aurelia thinks I'm the handsomest boy in all of Rome."

Both dogs immediately started barking. Happy, playful barks. They were participating in a joke they couldn't possibly have understood . . . unless they could.

Aurelia wasn't laughing, but her eyes had grown wider. She only said my name again to get my attention, and then pointed. Still in the pool, I was standing directly within the beam of moonlight pouring in from overhead. And when I realized where she was pointing — to the bulla beneath my tunic — I saw why she was so alarmed.

It was glowing, as brightly as if the bulla itself was a moon.

I pulled off the bulla to see it better and then its full glow became apparent. Beneath the moonlight, it nearly lit the room to a daytime light.

Crispus ran into the room. "I'm sorry about — oh!"

Aurelia walked forward until she stood in the pool with me. Staring into my eyes the entire time, she took the bulla from me and hung it back around my neck, on the outside of my tunic.

"I know which of the gods supplies this bulla's power," she said. "No wonder it's given you so much trouble."

THIRTY

Forgetting about the dogs, Crispus walked forward, his attention fixed on the bulla. "We knew you must have it," he breathed. "Nothing else could've caused such damage in the amphitheater. I'll never forget that day."

Nor would I, much as I had already tried to do it.

Crispus reached out a hand toward the bulla, then paused and lowered it again. "How are you making it glow?"

"It isn't Nic," Aurelia said. "The bulla is responding to the moonlight. Watch this." She stepped out of the pool and then motioned for me to come with her. Once I got back onto the tile floor, the glow began fading. After only a minute, its glow was no brighter than before, and I was fairly certain neither Aurelia or Crispus could see that soft glow anyway.

"It's the power of the gods," Crispus whispered.

"No, just one of them." Aurelia turned to me. "You can communicate with animals, and when the bulla is working, you are unnaturally strong. I knew about those, but the moonlight makes it obvious which god gives this bulla its power."

"Diana," I whispered. "Goddess of the hunt and of the moon."

"She speaks with animals and has great strength," Crispus added. "And so now you have her powers?"

"He can command a griffin too," Aurelia said. "That one who was in the amphitheater."

"It's not like that," I said. "She just . . . listens to me."

"Same thing," Aurelia said. "Maybe it was your griffin who pulled the chariot of Diana's twin brother, Apollo. But unlike her brother, Diana isn't known as the kindest of the gods."

I already understood that. The bulla had shown me a great deal of its power, but none of its mercy.

The door to the home opened. Crispus whispered to me, "That's my father. For now, say nothing of this new discovery. Let him talk first."

I nodded, and Senator Valerius came into the atrium. Crispus dipped his head toward his father, and Aurelia did the same. I wasn't sure what to do, but I figured I should probably show the same respect. Once I looked up again, Valerius eyed me suspiciously. "Why are you all wet?"

"The dogs chased him into the pool," Crispus said.

Valerius grunted as if I was some great fool for having fallen in the water which I probably was. But I reminded myself that he had risked a lot to bring me here, so I had already impressed him somehow. I didn't need to do more.

"What about your arm? It's wrapped, and badly done."

Aurelia grimaced, but it wasn't her fault. I had rewrapped the wound myself after we escaped from the cistern. Whatever oils she had put on the cloth to heal the wound were long washed away.

Aurelia spoke up for me and her tone was cool. "There are people who will do a lot worse to Nic if they have the chance. Can we be sure you aren't one of them?"

He didn't answer, and instead turned to me. "Let's talk in private." His eye wandered from Crispus to Aurelia. "While you two are waiting, Crispus, get that girl something proper to wear. She doesn't talk like a servant. Let's not have her looking like one."

Crispus bowed again and with a backward look at Aurelia, I followed Valerius into his office. He asked me to sit, which I did, and then he took his chair behind the desk, clasped his hands, and stared at me. I felt uncomfortable beneath his gaze, but recalled Crispus's reminder that only slaves kept their heads down. I forced myself to look back at him and tried to appear calm.

Finally, he said, "I've been asking questions about you. You call yourself Nicolas Calva — a rather fine name considering you've come from the slave mines. You were known to be a hard worker, and a brave miner, though not the most obedient."

"I obeyed every order that wasn't stupid."

He arched an eyebrow. "As a slave, you took it upon yourself to decide which orders were good and which were bad?"

"You get to decide that. Why not me?"

"I'm a senator!"

"You're a person, just as I am. And I want to live my life."

Valerius leaned forward. "And is that your goal now, to live? I saw the way you fought for your life in the amphitheater. With that magic you threw out, you could've killed thousands of people."

"But I didn't."

"But you could have!" He gestured toward the bulla. "What do you know about magic?"

I hesitated at first, but finally decided that I had made an agreement with Felix, and Valerius was the only one who truly seemed interested in helping me keep it. So after a quick, nervous breath, I said, "I think the Divine Star is the reason I can do magic. Without it, this bulla would be as useless to me as it is to anyone else."

"That's right. But the Divine Star is more than the reason you can do magic. It *is* the magic."

"I don't feel any magic there. It prickles sometimes, but that's all."

"I think you would feel it, except for the other magic that is pressing in on you." He nodded at the bulla, still in my hand. "There is so much power in that object, I would guess you feel like you were tossed in the sea when you only asked for a cup of water."

The comparison fit. The bulla's magic crashed into me in waves, not droplets, always so much more than I could absorb. And I always felt its weight, even when the bulla was cold.

"This used to belong to Caesar," I said.

"Until he abandoned it, and eventually, Venus withdrew her powers from it as well. But Caesar chose a most interesting place to bury it."

"In a cave near Lake Nemi," I said. "In the shadow of Diana's temple."

"Where I first met you." Valerius frowned. "We heard Caesar's treasure had been discovered and went to search for that bulla. Though once I saw the mark on your back, I suspected the bulla had already been found."

"Why do you want the bulla, sir? Without magic —"

"Better I have it than the person who wishes to destroy Rome." Valerius stood and walked closer to me, then sat on the corner of his desk. "Nic, you hold the first of three amulets. Each will make the powers of the Divine Star stronger, and each will give you additional powers. This one, for example, allows you to talk to animals and gives you great strength."

"Because that's what Diana could do," I mumbled. "She powers this amulet now."

"You may yet discover other powers, though if you lose the bulla, you will lose its powers too."

I paused while the warning in my gut battled with my desire to know more. Finally, with a question in my tone, I said. "There are two other amulets . . ."

"The Malice of Mars, which gives its bearer victory in battle. And a third amulet, the Jupiter Stone, which carries rewards so powerful that many men have given their lives hoping to obtain it. So far, none have succeeded. But it all starts with that amulet you wear. The emperor wants it. He's afraid of you, Nic."

"He shouldn't be."

"He'd be a fool not to fear you. Rome hasn't seen magic like that in nearly three hundred years."

I shifted in my seat. "But I've made a bargain with the emperor. If I can deliver Radulf to him, stripped of his magic, then he will grant my freedom and I'll be able to walk away from here forever."

"Radulf is no easy target." Valerius began pacing beside me. "When he first came to Rome, Radulf was such a good fighter, Emperor Gallienus thought he would entertain the people well. So they made him a gladiator. It was a fatal mistake. Radulf's only fear in the arena was the lions, but he defeated them, and won the hearts of the people. Eventually, he gained enough influence to have Gallienus murdered. He was the first of many emperors Radulf has removed from power."

"Does Emperor Tacitus know that Radulf has magic?"

"He knows, but what can he do about it?" Valerius fingered the purple edging on his toga. "Radulf commands the entire military. He also controls the Praetorian Guard, which protects the emperor's life. Or takes it."

"Then it's just a matter of time," I said. "If Radulf wants the throne, it's his."

"That isn't what Radulf wants. A war is coming, Nic, and it is for the control of those three amulets. On one side is Radulf, who will use them to destroy the empire, and then build it up again in his own image. With no Senate, and no government other than himself. He wishes to be worshipped, like the gods. Nobody can stop him" — his eyes drifted over to me — "except for someone else with magic."

Hearing those words sent shivers down my spine. I straightened my back, hoping to hold my courage together. Or at least, I pretended courage worked that way. I said, "And so I am on the other side of this war? No! All I want is to fulfill my bargain with the emperor and walk free!"

"And I will help you do it, but hiding you here is dangerous. So if you want to stay, then it's only fair that you help me too!"

I looked back at him steadily. "You want me to find the other amulets."

Valerius folded his arms and stared at me. "I cannot allow Radulf to get them first."

My hand stroked the bulla's face. By now, I knew every ridge of its delicate carvings. "Do you know where they are?"

"I do. But the answer isn't good." Valerius began pacing again. "The secret for creating a Jupiter Stone is guarded by the Praetors of Rome. They are . . ."

"Dangerous," I finished, grateful for what Felix had already told me about them.

He smiled. "They could be, if they decide to follow Radulf. They guard enough secrets to collapse the world beneath the emperor's feet."

"Surely the Praetors are already loyal to the empire?"

"Not necessarily. They will obey the presiding magistrate of the Senate."

"Senator Horatio," I breathed. His name was sour on my tongue.

"Horatio has no loyalty to the emperor. If he throws his public support behind Radulf, then the Praetors will follow him, and the war — the Praetor War — begins."

"Senator Horatio has the Malice of Mars?"

Valerius shook his head, and only then could I breathe again. But he said, "Not yet. But because of his position in the Senate, Horatio is the keeper of the key that unlocks the Malice. If Horatio knew where the Malice is, I believe he would have already given the key to Radulf."

I asked, "So how do I get the key from Horatio?" Because I'd sooner cozy up to a skunk. Which, as I considered it, didn't seem all too different.

Valerius wasn't ready to share that yet. He only said, "I can find a way for both of us to succeed. But while I work on that idea, you must work on your magic."

I grinned with anticipation at that. "It could be dangerous. You saw what happened in the amphitheater."

"Then I will help you learn. You must do this, Nic. To save the Senate, to save the empire. And to save yourself."

THIRTY-ONE

It was the third bargain I had made today, and all of them had been necessary. By the end of this, Rome would be safe, my magic would be strong, and Livia and I would walk away as free persons. Or I would be dead. None of it would be easy, and maybe it wasn't even possible. But I was committed now.

Valerius put a hand on my shoulder. Instinctively, I jumped away from it, and he raised both arms to show me he wasn't posing a threat. "I can see how tired you are, how much the bulla is weighing you down," he said. "Sleep tonight, and we'll talk more in the morning."

I let him lead me from his office, but stopped in the doorway and said, "Does Radulf know Horatio supports him?"

"There are only two kinds of Romans," Valerius said. "Those who support Radulf, and those he intends to destroy. For that reason, Radulf assumes everyone supports him." He nodded toward the bulla on my chest. "In you, we finally have an answer to Radulf's powers. Trust me, Nic, if I could use the magic, I would grant your freedom myself. But that bulla is useless in my hands. At least in yours, the empire has a chance."

The way he said it, my task seemed so big. No, it *was* so big. I had proposed a plan to move mountains, when I still lacked the ability to move a fistful of dirt.

"Things will look brighter tomorrow. You need sleep."

I needed practice. Radulf had told me that magic was a muscle, and it was true that I was feeling it more every day. But learning to control it was an entirely different matter.

"What about Aurelia?" I asked. "The girl who came with me?"

"She'll have her own room. She will be treated as a lady here. I promise you that."

After a moment's hesitation, I followed him to a bedroom directly across from the atrium. Once he'd left, I examined the room more carefully. There was a table in one corner with a bowl of olives that I immediately ate, despite not being particularly hungry. An actual book lay on the table too, though the words were too difficult for me. More important, a real bed stretched along the far wall. Even before the mines, when my mother kept Livia and me in hiding from the slavers, we never had beds. For months, we traveled anywhere that seemed safe, away from Gaul, and certainly away from Rome. We slept in the woods, sheltered by trees, or in the corners of barns. If I'd ever had a real bed, I didn't remember it. Now I walked closer and stroked the mattress. It was so thick with feathers that I wondered if it might swallow me up once I lay upon it. So I didn't. I grabbed the light blanket from on top of the mattress, and then lay down on the hard floor, where I felt more comfortable. With my cheek on the cool concrete, I faced out the doorway, staring at the moonlight, which still poured into the atrium through the overhead window.

Radulf and I both had the Divine Star, which made me think we had the same magic. The difference was that he understood his better. Or, more accurately, understood it at all, and that gave him a huge advantage over me. On the other hand, I had the bulla, which contained magic Radulf did not have. If I learned to use its powers, Radulf would have no answer to them.

So it was up to me to figure out the magic I already had, and for that, I had to know if Valerius was right, if there was magic in me apart from the bulla.

After listening to be sure the home was quiet, I removed the bulla and set it on the mattress, then stood and concentrated on the mark of the Divine Star. As I made myself conscious of it, the tingling was so sharp that I could almost define its shape just from which parts of my shoulder had come alive.

I focused on what I felt there, letting the mark smolder like a tired fire. Then I willed it to travel down my right arm, which still bore the injury from the soldier's arrow. I felt the magic gather around the wound, but rather than create heat, as the bulla did, it felt more like water passing over and under my skin, soothing the sting there.

But the magic wasn't finished. It breezed down my forearm and finally collected in my fingers and palm, so much that when I tried squeezing my hand into a fist, I felt resistance from the magic. It was similar to the feeling from the bulla, but this magic was waiting for me to act, rather than trying to escape without my permission. I felt the desire to release it from my fingers, but when I did, all that came was a brief snap of air, like an exhaled breath, and then it was gone.

The disappointment tasted bitter in my mouth. A casual whistle produced more power than I had created with the whole of my concentration. There was magic in me, but it was completely useless. If the bulla gave me far too much power, then the Divine Star offered too little.

Except that Radulf's voice slithered into my head again. "So you're experimenting with Caesar's mark. I felt the shift in the air, you know, such as it was. And I will use it to find you."

"I hope you do." My voice shook when I spoke, not from fear, but from the fierce ache his presence created. "But you'll regret the day you find me."

He laughed, which rattled into my bones. "I doubt that very much. You see, I won't come to reconnect a few mossy pipes. I will come with real power that you cannot fight, even with that bulla."

I snatched the bulla and quickly put it back around my neck. Maybe Radulf wasn't here, and didn't have any way of getting at the bulla right now, but maybe he was. I wouldn't take the risk.

Radulf had only one thing more to say. "Or you could join me, Nic. Help me build a new empire, one in which your life matters. That's what your sister wants you to do."

"Do you have her?" I cried. I raised my hands, ready for a

fight if that was what he wanted. But how was I to fight someone who wasn't even here? And how could I pretend to have any chance of winning?

Aurelia appeared in the doorway. "Who are you talking to?" At first, I barely looked at her. Radulf's words still thundered inside my head, confirming my worst fears about Livia, and every suspicion I had about his evil nature.

"I have her," he said. "But for how long? Don't fight me, Nic."

"Nic!" Aurelia called my name, her voice now filled with more obvious concern. I turned to her and drew in a breath of surprise. Aurelia had been given a long tunic made of fine linen, and her hair was freshly washed and fell in loose waves over her shoulders. She cleaned up even better than I would've guessed. "You've gone pale," she said. "Are you all right?"

I wasn't. Though my breathing was beginning to slow, my heart still pounded against my chest. Radulf wasn't there any longer, but he'd left an echo of himself behind, like the chill that lingers after a storm.

Aurelia stepped even closer and put her hands on my face. "You're in a cold sweat. Tell me what's wrong."

"No," I said, backing away. "Tell me if I can trust you. Please, make me believe that I can, because every time I try, I think of our bargain, and I remember that all you care about is the reward you'll get from Horatio."

"That bargain is over." The disappointment in her tone was obvious. "While you were talking with Valerius, he had Crispus pay me six hundred denarii, as his reward for bringing you here.

He said they'd help you find your sister too, so I could leave if I wanted."

I hardly dared asked the question. "And is that what you want?"

She shrugged and even smiled a little. "I should leave. If Rome were invaded tomorrow by barbarians carrying the plague, they'd still be less of a catastrophe than you are. Anyone who comes within a mile of you must be insane."

I grinned. "If it helps to know, I've always thought you were insane."

Despite her teasing, Aurelia's tone turned serious. "To succeed, you'll need a lot more insane friends than just me. Until you find them, how can I help?"

"I need to learn how to use the magic. And I need to know how to fight Radulf, because it's going to come to that." That thought sent shudders through me.

"Then I'll stay. I'll teach you everything I know, at least about fighting."

"He could bring the entire forum down upon me. Can your knife stop that?" The corner of my mouth turned up a little.

She met my challenge with a spark in her eyes. "Until you control your magic as well as I control my knife, you shouldn't complain. Now get some rest. It'll be a big day tomorrow." She glanced at the blanket I had used, still in a heap on the floor, and the undisturbed bed beside me. Her brows pressed together. "I hope you're not sleeping on the floor."

"Of course not." Then I shrugged. "Maybe I was."

She picked up the blanket and handed it to me. "That isn't your life anymore. The world will judge you based on what you think of yourself. If you want to fight Radulf as an equal, then you had better think of yourself that way."

"Do you think of us as equals?" I asked her.

"You and Radulf? He's a general —"

"No. You and me."

"Oh." Aurelia's eyes darted to the side, and her left hand was clenching her dress too tightly. "I, um —"

That was more than enough of an answer. I lay down on the bed, turning away from her. "Good night, Aurelia."

She said my name, but I didn't answer. Nearly a minute of silence passed before her footsteps padded out.

THIRTY-TWO

The following morning, Valerius had plans for me before I began any training. He sent a servant to scrub me, trim my hair, and, in his words, try to make me look like a "presentable Roman." I wasn't sure what that meant, but the haircut was definitely necessary, and the bath was a luxury beyond any I'd ever imagined possible. I had never had a bath before, but I was given the entire area of the senator's *tepidarium* to use. It filled almost one whole room, with inlaid patterns of tile on the floor and walls, and marble seats built into the sides for people who wished to visit while they bathed. I stayed in it until my skin wrinkled, and even then I might never have left, except the servant told me the women of the household may be using the baths soon. That hurried me out.

Afterward, I was given a tunic almost as fine as Crispus's toga. I ran my fingers along the smooth creases of neatly woven fabric, tracing the blue edging, and noting how odd it was to wear something that didn't scratch my skin.

Crispus came in afterward, with a pair of sandals in his

hands. Even after he held them out, it still took a moment to realize they were for me.

At first, I only stared, unsure of what to say or do. "I won't know how to walk in them," I finally said.

Crispus handed them to his servant who fit them on my feet and began lacing them up my calves. "You'll learn," Crispus said. "If you want to be free, then you must walk in the shoes of a free man."

When the first sandal was finished, I wiggled my foot and smiled. "It feels so different."

Crispus shrugged. "The leather will relax after a while."

"No," I quickly added. "Different is a good thing. Different is an amazing thing." I stood and tested both sandals on the floor. It was odd to feel something beneath my bare foot other than rocks or sand. I looked over at Crispus. "Thank you." The words weren't nearly enough, but they were all I had.

After that, the servant set me in front of a polished brass mirror so I could see my reflection. I'd seen pieces of myself at times, my face in the waters of a mud pond following a rainstorm, or the corner of my eye reflected on a metal jar, but never so much of me all at once. I stared at my own image. With the way they had cleaned me up, I didn't look like a slave, nor did I feel like one. For the first time in my life, I felt that I deserved my name. I *was* Nicolas Calva.

Which inevitably brought my thoughts back to the way last night had ended with Aurelia. I wondered how she would respond to seeing me this way. Probably it wouldn't matter at all. Her opinion of me had nothing to do with outer appearances. Whatever I wore, she would always see me as less than her.

Once I did see her, Aurelia was back to her normal self. A little subdued perhaps, but then, so was I. She was at breakfast with Crispus, who excused his father, saying he had early business in the forum. The table was full of fruit and fresh bread and a white fish to be dipped with honey. While they reclined to eat, I sat as close to the table as possible, unable to eat fast enough. At one point, I caught Crispus staring at me, probably horrified at how much I was consuming, but I didn't care. My time here wouldn't last much longer — it couldn't — so I wanted to eat everything while I had the chance.

When I reached for some cheese, Aurelia caught my arm and unwrapped the bandage from it. She gasped loud enough to get everyone's attention and said, "This wound is so much worse! Why didn't you say something?"

I rotated it to see it better. I knew it was getting bad, but so many other issues had pressed harder on my mind that I'd nearly forgotten it. I couldn't see the entire wound, but what I could see wasn't good. No wonder it hurt the way it did.

Crispus sat forward, obviously concerned. "I'll inform my father," he said. "We need to get that examined right away."

While Aurelia rewrapped it, she said, "No, I've taken care of things like this before, and I can do it again."

But I pulled my arm away. "If your treatment stings as bad as you said before, I'll lose a whole day of practice just recovering."

"You could lose that arm!"

"And I'll lose my life if I don't learn this magic!" It sounded brave, but the truth was far more cowardly. Aurelia's treatments sounded like the kind of thing I wanted to avoid for as long as possible. Even the thought of her scrubbing that deep wound made me cringe. "We'll do it tonight, before bed."

Aurelia objected, but my mind was made up. Crispus quickly agreed with me, not because he cared about the pain her treatment would cause, but because he wanted the practice time as much as I did.

So he reclined again to eat, and slowly his eye wandered from me to Aurelia. "We could probably find out who your father was," he said to her. "Surely there are records kept of exposed children. Then it would be a matter of narrowing down the possibilities."

"Please don't," she said.

"Why not?" I asked. "If he can help —"

"It wouldn't help." Aurelia looked from me to Crispus, then her eyelashes fluttered and she returned to her food.

Not for the first time, I wondered who her family was. Were they poor, like my mother, and so exposure had offered her some hope of a better life? Or wealthy, like Crispus? If so, then my friendship with her was forbidden. Maybe that's why she had paused last night, when I'd asked if we were equals. Because she already knew the answer.

Crispus had gone back to eating. He'd probably only offered as a matter of good manners anyway. Unless Aurelia suddenly announced she was his sister, I doubted he'd give the matter a second thought.

"And what about you, Nic?" he said. "You told me your mother was Roman, but had fallen into slavery. Did she have skills to become a household slave?"

"Maybe." I had been so young when Sal sold her away from us, I really didn't know. "Five years ago, she brought my sister and me to the mines and told me it'd be safer if she lived elsewhere. I think she came to Rome, but I could be wrong about that."

"Wait," Aurelia said. "What did your mother mean that it was safer?"

I shrugged. "It was long ago. I was too young to ask such questions."

Crispus seemed to consider that settled. He got to his feet and said his father had suggested I begin practicing magic as soon as possible.

"Deep within the vineyards is a tract of land cleared for replanting," he said. "That would be a good place to practice, when you're ready."

I stood as well. "I'm ready now." Despite the worries that lingered inside me, I had to admit I was excited to finally learn how to control the magic. Every day it flowed with more strength, moving deeper inside me. At last I would have the chance to learn everything I could do with it.

The three of us walked side by side to the vineyards. Aurelia had somehow acquired a new bow and a quiver of arrows, and had already threatened me twice if I broke them. I told her I wouldn't break them if she agreed not to shoot me.

As we walked, Crispus explained that the origins of his family's vines could be traced back hundreds of years, much like his family's history.

"For a patrician in Rome, your family name is everything," he explained. "With a good name, you cannot fail here. With no name, you cannot succeed."

I glanced at Aurelia, who was making a serious effort to pretend she hadn't heard the talk of families, and wondered then about mine. From what I understood of my father, claiming his name wouldn't have helped me in life anyway. Maybe when Livia and I left Rome, I would offer to bring Aurelia with us. Then she wouldn't have to care so much about her name either.

"Is Valerius a good name, then?" Aurelia asked.

"It's a very fine name," Crispus said. "My family boasts of military leaders, senators, and other high officials. My father has hoped that I might one day become emperor myself."

Walking between Aurelia and Crispus, I couldn't help but notice the way she smiled when he said that. Aurelia got her reward money last night, so maybe she considered Crispus her equal now. And why shouldn't she? In comparison to Crispus, I had nothing to offer her. Then I snorted quietly. In comparison to anyone at all, I had nothing. The unfortunate man who plucked the emperor's armpit hair could give her a better life than I could.

"But my becoming emperor is only a fantasy for my father, it could never become a reality," Crispus said sadly. "Much as I want to please him, I don't enjoy politics, so he rarely discusses it with me. I know I disappoint him."

"It doesn't seem that way," I said.

Crispus shrugged. "Things are rarely what they seem."

I didn't reply, mostly because I knew he was right.

We reached the open field, which was larger than I had expected, but also as private as Crispus had described. He said all the workers had been dismissed from this part of the vineyard for the day, so if anything happened, as long as the damage wasn't too massive, it was probably acceptable.

I understood what that meant. If I accidentally set a fire or created an earthquake that destroyed centuries-old vineyards and forever ruined his family name, that would be bad. Anything short of that should be fine.

I rubbed my hands together and smiled with satisfaction, then asked, "How about it? Shall we learn some magic?"

THIRTY-THREE

The vineyards were different from anything I'd known at the mines. There, the world was gray and dusty, and the people weren't much better. But though I always knew I'd find a more beautiful world one day, I had never expected anything like this vineyard. The rolling hills carried row after row of green vines. Here, where I stood with Crispus and Aurelia, we were surrounded by tall trees that must have been there since the first breath of man. At the far end of the field was a pile of ruins that looked as if they had been decaying for hundreds of years. It seemed odd to find rubbish in an otherwise fine field, and I asked Crispus about it.

He shrugged. "I don't know much. My father said it's the ruins of an old temple that used to be on this land. The temple once held the body of a vestalis who was punished for violating her oath, probably buried alive. A few years ago, I tried to get closer and see it, but a large wolf appeared so I ran away. There wasn't anything to see anyway, just broken rocks." Then he clasped his hands. "Shall we begin?"

Aurelia and I stood in the shade of one of the tallest trees with blank expressions. Neither of us knew where to start. Such as it was, I was the only one here who'd actually used magic, and since most of those experiences had been disasters, I suddenly felt nervous about practicing.

"My father believes the magic responds to your emotions," Crispus said. "It comes on strongest when your emotions are most intense. You were terrified in that arena."

"That's ridiculous." I forced out a laugh and eyed Aurelia to see if she would think worse of me. "Terrified isn't the right word at all." Which was a perfectly true thing to say, though admittedly, this was only because what I had felt then was far beyond terror.

Aurelia didn't seem to care. She only said, "Crispus is right. When you bent the metal in the caravan, you were angry with Felix. And what about when Radulf attacked us underground?"

Crispus's jaw dropped. Obviously he didn't know that story. "Wait a minute," he said. "You've already fought Radulf once?"

I shook my head. "No. And if it was a fight, then I lost. But you are right about my emotions being connected to the magic."

"Which is what makes this magic so dangerous," Aurelia said. "Emotions can be unpredictable and hard to control. I don't decide to get angry or sad or even happy. I just feel the way I do."

Inwardly, I smiled. Maybe she didn't decide to become sad or happy, but I'd certainly seen her get angry.

"Then that's what I have to learn," I said. "I have to let myself feel enough to generate the magic, but then control the emotion."

Crispus seemed ready for that. "My father had servants working down here throughout the night." By then, he had grabbed a rope with a wooden handle at the end. The rest of it was strung up high into the tree, though the rising sun made it impossible to see where it was tied. "Here, Nic. Take this."

I grinned. "Why?" My hands were already on the handle, so I hoped it wasn't anything too risky.

"Just hold on." He started to walk away, then turned back to me. "Seriously, hold on."

I redoubled my grip and by the time I looked back at him, he was already midway through releasing another knot around the tree. Before he was entirely finished, the rope pulled violently from his hands and flew into the air. At the same time, I noticed a stack of bricks almost above my head plummeting to the earth, mortared together and attached by the same rope. I was at the other end, and as they came down, the rope flew through a pulley above us and yanked me high into the air.

"Nic!" Aurelia yelled. It had happened so fast, I wasn't sure that she had seen what happened. Beside her, Crispus was laughing harder than someone ought to, given that I was now dangling nearly thirty feet above the earth. With the pulley above me, I was too low to reach the nearest branch and too high to jump. Another branch was below me, but a ways behind me as well, and I didn't trust that I could reach it from here.

"I bet that bulla is warming now!" Crispus said, regaining some seriousness.

"Are you joking?" I scowled down at him. "Get me down!"

"Is the bulla warming?"

I closed my eyes and felt for it at my chest. At first there was nothing, but then the bricks settled and the rope punched me even higher. I gasped as I almost lost my hold. The bulla definitely reacted to that.

"It's warm," I said. And with that acknowledgment, magic flooded in through my chest, so fast that it nearly suffocated me. "I'm going to fall!" I yelled. The heat alone was making my hands sweat. "This is too much!"

"Not if you control it!" Crispus pointed to the bricks, now in a pile on the ground. "Lift them and you'll come down. But not too fast. Control it."

I gritted my teeth, forcing myself to breathe, and feeling the flow of magic. Last night's experiment with the Divine Star had been like cool water through my veins, but the bulla was warmth, closer to the way sunlight feels after a cold night. It might respond to my strongest emotions, but magic was so much bigger than a simple emotion. It was strength, and power, and raw energy. And with each use, *I* was becoming those things too.

Using that strength now, holding on to the rope became easy, so I focused on the stack of bricks. A quick test from my fingers rustled them.

"You're doing it!" Aurelia said.

With some effort, I allowed more magic into my hand. When I first sent it to the bricks, they rose in the air by a few inches. Then as I started to descend back to the ground, more magic emptied than I had intended. It shot from my hand with far too much force and hit the bricks like an explosion. The bricks flew into the air and I worried they'd come back down on Crispus and Aurelia, so I used another nudge of magic to push them farther away. That sent the bricks spiraling around one of the branches where they quickly became tangled in the thicket of leaves. I lost my grip on the rope, and would've fallen except the force of pushing the bricks had also blown me backward. Suddenly I found myself clutching the tree branch that had been behind me.

"This is a terrific plan you came up with!" I yelled to Crispus. "I'm having a great time!"

Now it was Aurelia who was laughing, so hard that tears were streaming down her cheeks. "You should've seen your face!"

"If it's so funny, then come up here and describe it to me!" I swung my body to the top of the branch but it was already groaning beneath my weight.

Below me, Aurelia removed the bow from over her shoulder and nocked it with an arrow. "I can help you," she said. "I'll shoot the arrow into the tree. Tie your rope to it and then you can slide down."

It was a terrible plan. But better than what I had now, which was no plan at all, so I scooted aside to make room for her arrow. She shot it, but instead of hitting the tree, it arced to the right, heading straight for me.

I ducked as it flew past me, grazing my hair. "I forgot how not helpful you can be!"

She glared at Crispus. "He shoved me!"

Crispus only shrugged. "You're up there to learn magic, not to be rescued by a girl."

"You're right." Then I leaned down as far as I dared. "Aurelia, do that again."

"Are you insane? No!"

"A day ago, I wouldn't have had to ask you to shoot me."

"A day ago, you deserved it."

I shook my head. "Listen, I felt something when the arrow went by. If you want to help, then shoot me."

Aurelia began muttering under her breath. I couldn't hear the words, but Crispus was chuckling, so I was pretty sure it was a string of insults about me. She drew another arrow, aimed directly at me, and let it fly. The arrow whooshed past me. I heard it move through the air and even watched its spin. Every feather on the shaft was as clear as if I were studying it up close. The arrow wasn't moving any slower than usual, but I saw it that way as it flew past me. As soon as that one passed, she sent another one. This time when the arrow approached, I reached out for it. I felt it brush through my fingers, but then it was gone.

In the attempt, I lost my balance and my hold on the rope and began falling. Air rushed through my hair and I was pretty sure Aurelia and Crispus were yelling at each other to help me, though there would be nothing they could do. I crashed through some lower branches as the ground came ever closer, ripping away the remnants of the bandage on my arm. I sent out all the magic in me, with no thought in my mind except to slow my fall. But when the magic hit the tree above me, all I heard was a terrible cracking sound.

I landed hard on my back, and directly on my wounded arm, which exploded with pain. But there wasn't a moment to waste, for the tree was already beginning to tip.

"Run!" Aurelia yelled.

"Nic!" Crispus sounded panicked, but kept running. I got to my feet just in time to see the trunk of the tree and its load of tangled bricks coming directly at me.

THIRTY-FOUR

"Nic! Nic!" Aurelia was screaming my name. She and Crispus were pushing at the tree, trying to move it off me, but it was as large as a ship and they were having no luck. Then she shushed Crispus. "What is that sound? Nic, are you laughing?"

I couldn't help it. Nor could I remember a time in years when I'd laughed so hard. This entire situation was so completely ridiculous, what else was there to do? Of course I was laughing.

Finally, I squirmed around until I was in a better position, then with my back braced against the ground, I pushed up on the trunk with my legs. The bulla was doing the work, I knew that, but it was still amazing to feel the weight shift. I rotated my hips to get the thickest branches off me, and then pushed at them with my arms.

Once he saw me, Crispus twisted his body between the smaller branches until he could offer a hand to help me up.

"How did you survive that?" His eyes were wide with amazement. "You should've been crushed."

"I just stopped it." Which was all the explanation I could offer. "When the trunk fell, I grabbed hold and pushed back."

Crispus grinned. "It's exactly what we thought last night. You have the powers of the goddess Diana, her strength, her ability to communicate with animals. She can heal people." His eye traveled to my injured arm. "Nic, she can heal herself."

By now, the wound felt hotter than the bulla ever did, and I held out my arm to show him. "Does this look like I can heal myself?"

"Maybe you haven't tried." Aurelia's eyes brightened.

"I don't know how!"

"Then I'll have to treat it tonight. I'll be scrubbing that arm for hours, and hours" — her grin turned wicked — "and hours."

That was motivation enough. I closed my eyes and thought about the wound, the way it constantly burned and ached. For a moment, nothing happened, but I focused my thoughts even further, and connected them to the warmth of the bulla. Once I did, the feeling of magic rushed through me, wrapping itself around the entire arm like a stiff wool blanket.

"You're doing it!" Aurelia whispered.

I cheated enough to peek at the wound with one eye. A glow no brighter than the bulla's had surrounded the wound and was carrying the infectious heat away. But it wasn't only the bulla's magic. I felt the mark on my shoulder at work and knew Radulf could sense it too. He said nothing, but I felt he was pleased. That bothered me, and I had to break from those thoughts to keep focused on my arm. When I looked again, I saw the skin closing back together, leaving only a thin red scar.

Beside me, both Crispus and Aurelia gasped. For my part, I couldn't believe what had happened. I shook my arm, expecting the wound to somehow reveal itself again, but not only was the limb as good as ever before, I was certain that it felt stronger.

Aurelia grabbed my arm to examine it for herself. When she looked up at me again, her smile was wide. "You didn't need the emotion this time. You just did the magic!"

"You have more power than you think," Crispus said proudly. "That's why you'll defeat Radulf, when the time comes."

"He knows the magic in the Divine Star much better than I do."

"But you have that same mark," Aurelia said. "You can learn the same magic."

"Let's test it," Crispus said. "Take off the bulla. We'll concentrate on only using that mark."

"I won't do that." Radulf's presence in my mind had vanished the moment my arm had healed, and I wasn't about to invite him back again. "Radulf knows when I use the mark, but not when I use the bulla. I'll practice using the bulla, but I won't do anything with the Divine Star unless I have to."

Aurelia and Crispus shrugged at each other, then Crispus said, "All right, but I don't want to risk being crushed by any more trees. Let's work on a smaller scale."

So for the rest of the afternoon, we did. They had me try to start a fire, which after two hours of concentration only produced a whiff of smoke. I mentioned that it was better than me exploding something, and although Crispus agreed, I did wonder if he'd rather have seen the explosion. Aurelia suggested a different tactic, and had me try to move the fallen tree without touching it. I tried, pouring every ounce of strength I had into making it move the slightest inch, but nothing happened. Nor could I throw a rock when they asked me to, or even raise it into the air.

"It seems that we can have either total destruction or nothing." Crispus sounded as discouraged as I felt.

Or rather, I was having trouble feeling much of anything at all. I was exhausted. Through slurred words, I said, "Releasing the whole of my magic is like sending a boulder down a hill. But controlling it is like keeping the boulder from rolling. Much harder."

"We can't keep pushing him like this," Aurelia said.

"The magic makes him stronger," Crispus argued.

"Yes, but it also pulls strength from me!" I said. "You might not see me working, but I am."

"Then let's rest," Crispus said. "We won't make progress otherwise."

Rustling sounds startled all of us to attention. Aurelia pulled out her knife, but quickly put it away when Valerius appeared in the field, accompanied by a host of servants with food and drink.

"I thought you might want some refreshment," he said.

Aurelia walked forward before it occurred to me that he had intended the food for all of us. So after a short hesitation I joined her, but noticed the senator motion for Crispus to stand aside with him for a private conversation. His servants offered us trays of hard-boiled eggs, figs, and some dried fish. I was eager to eat all of it, but my attention was distracted by Crispus and his father. The lines in Valerius's face seemed deeper than usual and I didn't like the way Crispus was nodding. The conversation obviously involved me, and I hated being kept out of it.

"What do you suppose Crispus is saying?" Aurelia whispered.

"That at best, my magic is uncontrollable, and at worst it's completely useless. They're having doubts about me, and rightly so."

Aurelia smiled grimly. "I know you're trying."

"Trying isn't good enough," I said. "Not for what's coming. That's what Crispus is telling his father."

Valerius put a hand on Crispus's shoulder, told him one more thing at which Crispus only shrugged, then Valerius turned to me. "Let's take a short walk. Crispus and Aurelia can rest here."

I wanted to point out that if anyone deserved a rest, it was me. But maybe that wasn't fair. Crispus and Aurelia were doing their best to help me produce magic, and running from it whenever I succeeded. They had to be exhausted too.

I walked with Valerius into the main part of his vineyard. The vines were thick with ripening grapes, creating a sweet perfume in the air that I loved to inhale and hold inside until I drew my next breath.

Valerius obviously had more serious matters on his mind. Once we were far from any listening ears, he said, "I'm sorry I was called away this morning. I had hoped to be here to help in your training."

"I just need more time. It might take years for me to learn this."

"Nonsense. Crispus tells me you healed that wound in your arm. I can see for myself that it's even better than I would have thought possible."

"Healing a wound isn't the same as fighting with magic! When I try to fight, the bulla does nothing. And when I simply react out of fear or anger, then it does far more than I intend. Either way is dangerous."

"Doing nothing is equally dangerous. Have you considered that? The Roman Empire is at stake. Either we get the key, or Horatio will hand it over to Radulf. We need your magic. Whether you have too much, or not enough, you are the only chance the empire has."

If that speech was supposed to make me feel better, it failed in every possible way. Even if I was the only chance, that still didn't mean I had any chance at all. If today had proved anything, it's that I wasn't strong enough to stop Radulf, or save an empire. No, I was the person who, only hours earlier, had toppled a tree on himself.

Valerius sighed. "The reason I was called away this morning was for a Senate meeting, and I'm sure you can guess at the conversation. Senator Horatio is very eager to find you. He's doubled the reward for anyone who brings you in, and made his intentions for you clear. My spies tell me Horatio wants to announce his loyalties in public, so that all of Rome hears of it. We believe he'll do it at the games in two days."

I caught a worried glance from Aurelia and turned away from her and asked, "Two days! No, I need more time!"

"We'll have to go to the games and stop him there. If you can defeat Radulf on the arena floor, Horatio won't have the chance to make his announcement."

"Which would be a wonderful idea, *if* I could control the magic!"

"You will learn to master it." The frown on Valerius's face deepened. "But remember, even if you don't succeed against Radulf, you must stop Horatio. At any price."

I stepped back and shook my head. No, my freedom would not come at *any* price. Even saving Rome would not happen if it meant I had to blur the shades of right and wrong. And it bothered me that Valerius saw things differently.

Either Valerius didn't notice my objection, or he didn't care. "I can feel success coming closer," he said. "Nic, once you do this, you will stand at my side as a hero of Rome."

"No, sir. Once I do this, I will find my sister and leave Rome. But to do what I must, I need the griffin. I wouldn't have escaped last time without her, and I need her again now."

Valerius lowered his eyes. "That's not possible."

"I can talk to her. I'll convince her to come and help me. All I have to do is figure out where she is now."

"We know where she is." Valerius hesitated a moment — far too long — before he continued. "She's taken over the baths near the Appian Way. Nobody will go in there because she's still dangerous, but they say it doesn't matter anyway because of the wound in her wing. She can't fly, and she can't hunt. Your griffin is dying."

THIRTY-FIVE

Valerius took me back to Crispus and Aurelia, insisting I spend the rest of the afternoon practicing. Knowing how little time was left now, I gave it the best I had, but my thoughts were too much on Caela. I had often wondered about her since she last flew away, but in my mind I had always seen her nestled atop a pile of gold or flying over the skies of Rome or swooping in for a hunt. She was a creation of the gods. So I had thought it only natural that she could have healed that wound herself.

"What did Valerius say to you back there?" Aurelia had asked me at least ten times since I'd returned. I had told them my battle with Radulf would happen soon, but nothing about Horatio's role in it, or about Caela. Aurelia placed a hand on my arm, right where the infected wound had been only hours ago. "You don't have to fight Radulf. Just run. Leave Rome on your own."

"I agree," Crispus said. "My father is persuasive, but he can't force you to do this."

"The empire knows what I can do. Do you really think

they'll just let me go? I don't want to be hunted the rest of my life."

"At least you'll be alive!" Aurelia's face fell. "If you lose —"

"Or if I win." I shrugged. "Either way, I get Radulf's voice out of my head."

Crispus nodded as a smile spread across his face. I wasn't sure if he was encouraged by my words, or trying to be the one who encouraged me. "If you win, the emperor will reward you with freedom."

"And your father will find my sister," I finished. "He promised me that."

Aurelia clapped her hands together. "Then let's get back to work. Good things are coming for you, Nic. I can feel that."

I was glad she could, because once we returned to practice, I still felt nothing except for concern for Caela. Even though we worked into the evening, my progress was barely noticeable. I could get the bulla to warm simply by thinking about the proper emotion, but not enough to produce any magic. And nothing Crispus or Aurelia did or said brought up any actual emotions. Nothing was stronger than my worry for Caela, and no amount of magic would change that.

Unless it could.

As we trekked back to Crispus's home, I casually asked him where the Appian Way was. He didn't know about Caela, so the question shouldn't have aroused any suspicion.

"Why are you asking?" Aurelia wanted to know. Of course she would be the suspicious one.

"Valerius simply mentioned it in passing. I was only curious."

Crispus pointed out the direction, then, as we continued walking, he said, "Almost three hundred years ago, there was a rebellion by a slave named Spartacus, who had once been a gladiator. At the time, a third of this city was slaves, so the rebellion was obviously a considerable problem. The fighting lasted for two years, and Spartacus had many victories . . . until he brought his armies to the Appian Way. Rome called in its armies from outside the city and advanced those that were here. Spartacus was trapped. Shortly after his final defeat, six thousand slaves were executed along that road. If you ask me, they got what they deserved."

"That's a terrible thing to say!" Aurelia scolded. "And did you even think about who Nic is?"

Crispus stopped and faced me. "I'm sorry. No, I didn't. I guess I don't think of you as a slave."

"That's because I'm not one anymore." I eyed Aurelia with irritation. "It's who I was. Not who I am." Then I walked on ahead of both of them.

She tried to apologize that evening at supper, but my mind was elsewhere, so our conversation didn't get very far. There was a fine spread of food, but I barely ate any of it, and excused myself early, pleading exhaustion. I was beyond tired, but I had no intention of sleeping. Once the house quieted down, I was going to find Caela.

Since the others believed me to already be asleep, I was left alone for the night. I waited until there were no more footsteps outside, and then carefully opened my door. I crept through the atrium toward the entrance hall. Because of its weight, the main door made little noise when I opened it, and then, without a sound, I stepped out onto the road.

Having been so cautious, it was foolish of me to yelp so loudly when Crispus darted at me from one side and Aurelia from the other. Truthfully, I did more than yelp. I nearly fainted from surprise.

Once I recovered, I scowled, "What are you two doing out here?"

"A fine question, coming from the person sneaking out!" Aurelia retorted.

I started walking away. "I wasn't sneaking out. Just leaving, which I have every right to do. I'll be back by morning."

They caught up to me and continued walking on either side. "We're coming with you," Crispus said.

"You don't even know where I'm going."

"It's not the hardest thing to figure out." Aurelia shrugged. "Valerius told us about Caela. He said you seemed upset. Why didn't you tell us, Nic?"

I stopped and drew in a deep breath. "I don't know. Maybe I should have."

"Come this way." Crispus turned off the road back to his property. "We have a wagon waiting."

My knees locked. I wasn't willing to follow him just yet. "To go to the baths on the Appian Way? Nowhere else?"

Crispus smiled. "You assume everything I say is either a trick or a trap. What kind of life have you led?"

"Let's just say there's a reason I think that way." Then I paused and started walking again. "Thank you for this. I don't know if I could've found it in the dark."

We climbed into the back of a wagon and the driver steered the horse away. Crispus pointed to some sacks inside the wagon. "It's meat," he said. "I had them filled with as much as we had available. Your griffin might need to eat something."

"Thank you again." The more Crispus and his father did for me, the greater my debt to them. I figured they must know more than I did about how hard it would be to defeat Radulf. They wanted to build up that debt while they could.

At my side, Aurelia took my hand and gave it a squeeze. "I understand why you have to do this," she said. "That griffin saved your life. You want to say good-bye."

"Her name is Caela," I said. "And I'm not coming to say good-bye."

THIRTY-SIX

The drive to the baths was longer than I had anticipated. On foot, it would've taken more than half the night to get there, and that didn't even include the likelihood I would've gotten lost. For that alone, I was grateful to Crispus.

Once the baths came into sight, I warned Crispus to have his driver let us off at a distance. "From what I understand, Caela hasn't eaten for several days. In an ordinary meeting, she'd have no love for your horses, but especially not tonight."

He nodded and ordered the driver to stop where we were. That left us each hauling a sack of meat the rest of the way to the baths. With the bright moon above us, I was able to clearly see the red brick building, and the sight was astonishing. The entire structure was so wide that I had to crane my head to see it from one end to the other, and every side seemed to be lined with long rows of arches. Crispus said these were his mother's favorite baths, and that sometimes she would spend entire days here.

"Just bathing?" I asked.

"No, of course not." The smile on his face revealed his constant astonishment at how little I knew. It would've been insulting, except I was just as ignorant of the world as he suspected. Maybe more. "There are places to exercise, socialize in the gardens, or get a massage, and there are places to shop in the daytime. This one even has two libraries."

I chuckled. "I never thought about the baths as places to read."

"Well, she still spends most of her time in the water. My mother might be the cleanest woman ever to roam the earth."

We all laughed, and yet a part of me wondered about that kind of life. I hadn't been above ground for this long since I was sold to the mines, and even watching the sun from first light to sunset was a strange luxury. The idea that a person could spend an entire day doing nothing but lounging beside a pool, with nothing required of them, was completely foreign.

Crispus nudged my side. "If I can judge by your expression, you don't seem to want a life like my mother has."

I grinned. "Actually, I was thinking I should try it for a while, just to see how I bear the burden of wealth."

Once we went inside, beneath an open sky we found well-tended gardens that stretched from one wall to the other. I couldn't see Caela anywhere, but I sensed her, and picked up my pace. We walked along the corridor until I saw the entry doors.

"One side for the men, the other for the women," Crispus said.

"Which side are we going in?" Aurelia asked.

"The men's, of course."

Aurelia teasingly punched his arm and he joked, "If you fight like a boy, and carry weapons like a boy, then I don't see why you can't learn to use the boys' entrance."

"No, I fight and carry weapons like a girl, and I'll use the girls' entrance! See you on the other side!" Then she skipped through the other doors.

Crispus and I walked through a spacious dressing area to find Aurelia already waiting on the other end. Then he pointed out the directions to each of the four baths. "The *caldarium* at the rear of the building is the hottest of them all, and most bathers begin there. Then the tepidarium is in front of it. Maybe your griffin would've gone there."

I shrugged, hoping not. Crispus's tepidarium had been so perfectly comfortable, I'd never have left if women hadn't been coming to bathe. If Caela was in this one, I'd have no easier time getting her out.

"She wouldn't want the *frigidarium,* it's too cold." Crispus shivered to make his point and Aurelia giggled and poked his arm, which I didn't think was particularly funny at all. "But I think she'll be in the *natatio,*" he added. "It's for open-air swimming, and your griffin would like that best."

We entered from the dressing room, but even before we did, I recognized the sound of Caela's breathing, though it seemed raspier than the breaths I had heard in Caesar's cave.

I held up one hand. "Let me go in alone. If she's injured, she might be calm and easy to manage, but she also might want to fight. Stay back until we know for sure."

"We rode in the caravan into Rome," Aurelia said. "She knows me already."

"Yes, but that doesn't mean she likes you." My smile was mischievous. "Don't feel bad. I'm not even sure she likes me."

Once inside, I spotted Caela in the far corner, nestled behind two large columns. I called her name, and saw one of her long, triangular ears perk up, but she didn't raise her head. Not a good sign.

Because of the large pool between us, it was necessary to walk the long way around to get to her. I went to the right, and about halfway there, noticed the nugget of gold she had taken with her from the venatio, dropped on the marble floor like cheap fill rock. If she had abandoned this so casually, then things were more serious than I had thought.

I called to her again, and this time she cawed softly, painfully. She was trying to move enough to greet me, but not succeeding.

"I'm so sorry," I said once I was closer. "I didn't know you were hurt this bad." I lowered the sack of meat right in front of her, but after a sniff, she showed no interest in it. So I ran my fingers across her feathers the way she had seemed to enjoy it before. Once I reached her wing, I understood how bad things were.

The spear from the bestiarius had broken the wing. Either that, or it had injured the wing, and once I had forced her to fly us out of the amphitheater, that had finished breaking it. I would've apologized again, but it seemed senseless at this point.

I knelt beside her and removed the bulla from around my neck to place against her wing. It glowed brighter in the moonlight, and felt heavier too. I hoped if the bulla connected me to her, it would transfer the healing powers better. Because of the seriousness of Caela's wound, I would have to rely even more upon the Divine Star, which Radulf could detect, and it made my heart pound. But this had to be done. All that mattered was Caela.

Pushing aside the nerves that were stirring inside me, I set the bulla directly over her wound. She flinched from the pressure, but had no strength to move away. I whispered another apology for the pain it caused, but I would likely have only one opportunity and I wanted every chance to do it right.

Just as I had done earlier that day, I focused on the magic to heal. It came easier this time, wrapping itself around both Caela and me, and I thought about Radulf's words, that magic was a muscle and using it made it stronger. Having practiced all day in the vineyards, I definitely felt the added strength, and knew I would need it now. I concentrated on the flow of magic, letting it fill every pore in me, giving it more life with every breath I drew in, and pushing it deeper into my core with every exhale.

When it had built up inside me, I willed it to move from my hand, through the bulla, and into Caela's wing. If it healed the infection in my arm, it could heal her as well. I only needed enough strength to outlast her injury.

Caela trilled nervously as she felt the magic, and even shuffled a bit, but my hand stayed in its place. With my other, I stroked her neck, hoping to keep her calm.

"This is too big for you, Nic." There had never been any doubt that Radulf's voice would come again, only how long it would take him to find me. It drizzled through my veins like ice, and I shivered.

"Go away," I muttered. "Live while you can. I'll come for you soon."

He chuckled, which diverted my attention until Caela shifted again. I poured more of myself into her, not only magic, but my gratitude for having twice saved my life, and my sorrow that all I had done in return was endanger hers. For the first time, I began to understand the magic, not just use it. Magic itself was an emotion, and like the strongest emotions, it could build or destroy. Right now, it was doing both. Building her, destroying me.

My arm began shaking and I leaned my weight into her to support it. Even as she was gaining strength, I was losing it, and it was becoming harder to keep her wing from fluttering out of my hands.

"Not yet," I whispered to her. "Not yet, Caela."

"You save the beast that gave you the mark," Radulf said in my head. "How interesting. I wasn't so kind to the unicorn that scratched me." He laughed. "Actually, it gave me the scratch while I was killing it. I don't think it ever intended to share its magic."

I tried to ignore that, tried to shut out from my mind the thought of how Radulf could possibly have harmed a creature of the gods.

My body was feeling heavier, as if my limbs had turned to lead. The magic continued stirring inside me, but I didn't think I was generating anything new. Breathing was harder, thinking was slower. And I couldn't feel the mark on my shoulder any longer. Actually, I couldn't feel much of anything. I was a fading sunset.

Caela cawed, a stronger cry now, and this time when she fluttered her wing, she pushed my hand out of her way and rose up to her feet. Whether she intended it or not, she knocked me to the ground, and I was in no condition to get up again.

"Nic!"

Aurelia's footsteps pounded across the cement, and then she grabbed me beneath my shoulders and dragged me farther from Caela. I wasn't worried about that. Caela wouldn't step on me, or at least, not deliberately.

Once we were clear, Aurelia knelt beside me and asked how I was. I heard her, but not really. It sounded like she was in another room. Without answering, I closed my eyes and tried to find myself again. It felt as if everything I was had vanished, like rainwater into a thirsty earth.

"Healing her cost too much," Radulf said. "Your body can't hold such powerful magic."

"He's shaking!" Aurelia brushed my hair back from my forehead. "Nic, look at me!"

"This girl is special to you," Radulf said. "I feel the beat of your heart when she is near."

"For the last time, get out of my head!" I yelled. Then I forced myself to sit up, to put some distance between Aurelia and me. Waves of dizziness enveloped me, but through that fog, I heard Caela eating the meat I had brought her. Whatever was happening to me didn't matter. She would be all right.

"Those baths are some of the finest in all of Rome," Radulf said. "You've done the empire a service by ridding them of a dangerous griffin. I will tell the emperor of your kindness."

"Do that," I muttered. "Then I'll tell him about your plans for the empire."

"What's going on?" Aurelia asked. "It's Radulf, isn't it?"

"I do have great plans, after I get that bulla," he said. "You took what was mine, Nic."

"It was Caesar's. Never yours!"

Crispus appeared in my line of sight and said something to Aurelia, but all I heard was Radulf saying, "I'll trade for it right now. Go out to the gardens. Livia is there."

I sat up even straighter and felt for the bulla around my neck. No, it wasn't there. I had taken it off to heal Caela. I looked to Crispus, who seemed to understand what I wanted, even without words.

"Stay here with Caela," I said to Aurelia. "Just stay here, please, where it's safe."

"Where are you going?"

"Livia is outside. She's here."

Aurelia grabbed my arm. "Radulf's lying. You must know that."

I pulled my arm away and turned to her. "Of course he is. But I still have to find out for sure, don't I?"

Aurelia sighed. "Be safe, Nic. I'm not wrong about this."

THIRTY-SEVEN

It took everything I had to get to my feet. There was little left in me but the desire to see my sister, and that would have to be enough. Crispus ran back with the bulla in his hands. He hung it around my neck, and it immediately began to supplement my energy.

"I'll come with you." Crispus's offer was stupid, but brave. Two words that accurately described me at the moment as well.

"It won't be safe," I said. "Please don't."

"Better hurry," Radulf said, for only me to hear. "I won't allow Livia to remain there for long."

I did hurry, leaving the same way I had come. Once I was outside, I wasn't sure which way to go, but then saw a strange light, pulsing and floating midair, beckoning me out of the gardens and back to the road beyond the bath walls.

With every step, the bulla continued adding to my strength. I only hoped it would be enough for when I found Livia — *if* I found Livia. Radulf wouldn't make it easy.

But once I got farther out, I saw her from a distance, lit by starlight. She stood on a narrow road between lines of small, thatched-roof homes, dressed in a long, pale yellow tunic, and with her hair pulled back in braids. Never before had I seen her in such fine clothes. She seemed to be looking around, as if trying to find someone. Maybe me.

"Livia!" I called as I ran toward her. "How did you get here?"

But she didn't answer. And then I came to the right angle to understand why. She was a trick of light, Radulf's plan to pull me outside. Exactly what I had feared, and what Aurelia had warned me about.

"Where is the real Livia?" I yelled. "Why did you take her?"

The trick of light that had been Livia shifted. Her image dissolved, which almost felt like losing her again. But worse still, as she faded, Radulf appeared in her place.

He wasn't really here either, or at least, I didn't think he was. But some part of his consciousness was standing directly in front of me.

"How did you do that?" I asked.

"A trick like this isn't even complicated magic. Wait until you see everything I can do."

"Try it, and then you'll see everything I can do too," I muttered. "Mine is worse." That last part was a lie, one neither of us believed.

He frowned at me. "Why must we fight? It doesn't have to be this way."

"I disagree. I think this is exactly the way things must be."

"Livia is a part of my household now. She says I am like Halden, the father she never knew."

My brows furrowed at the mention of my father. Even if Livia had known his name, he would've been nothing like Radulf. Surely she didn't believe that.

"Your mother could come here as well. You'd have your family back, Nic."

"Nobody knows where my mother is," I said.

"Are you sure? What if I am the only one who does know? What would you trade for that information?" He laughed and reached out one hand. "I see the bulla responding to the moonlight. Give it to me. Now."

It was glowing as brightly as when it had first shone in Crispus's atrium. I wrapped a hand around the bulla and felt its growing burn. "You're not here. You couldn't take it even if I tried to give it to you."

"I'm here enough."

"Nic, who are you talking to?" Aurelia ran up behind me. Crispus was with her.

"Go away!" I shouted back to them. "Please!"

Aurelia pulled out her knife. "Tell me who's here. Is it Radulf?"

So she couldn't see him? Only me. In his arrogance, Radulf smiled and said, "Ah, so you have another friend now? Are you sure you can trust them?"

"More than I'll ever trust you," I shouted.

He only laughed at that. "You're probably right. Though if you can't protect yourself from me, how can you protect them?"

I turned back to Aurelia and Crispus. "Get back inside. Now!"

"Nobody's here, Nic. This is only happening inside your head." Aurelia stepped forward and grabbed my arm, but I shook it off.

Worse still, I noticed that families from the thatch homes had heard the noise and begun to wander outside. If Crispus and Aurelia couldn't see Radulf, then neither could they. All they would see was the boy from the amphitheater, wearing a glowing bulla worth years of their income, yelling at an empty road. Now I was not only dangerous and valuable; I was a madman as well.

"Let's go home." Crispus spoke gently, like I was a child. "All of us together. C'mon, Nic."

But my attention flew back to Radulf, who said, "Two hundred years ago, while Nero was emperor, a great fire destroyed nearly all of Rome. It burned for six days and nights. Some think that Nero started the fire himself, to clear away old homes and make room for his new palace." He paused and looked at the thatch homes around him. Not everyone had come outside. But those who had were pointing at me, no doubt thinking about the reward my capture could give them.

"Do you think that story's true, Nic? Would a leader of Rome, even their hero, really harm his own people to get something he wanted?"

"No." Panic rose inside me. "Don't do this!"

But he raised his hands together and a ball of fire formed between them. He threw it at the home closest to him, which immediately lit with flame. The people around it screamed and went running. More people emptied from their homes as Radulf formed a second ball of fire, and then a third. Within seconds, homes on both sides of the road were engulfed in flame, and it was spreading.

I looked around, unsure of my capabilities, but certain I had to do something. I glanced up at the skies, wondering if it was possible to create a rainstorm. If it was, I had no idea how to make it happen. Maybe that was a good thing anyway — I didn't dare stay out here if the storm also created lightning. I had to think of something else. Aurelia was yelling at me from behind, and Crispus was likely doing the same, but I couldn't hear either of them. Why couldn't they have stayed in the baths when I asked them to?

The baths!

I turned my focus there, on the open-air pool. Could I do that, pull at something so formless and vast as all that water? I had to try.

I gathered the bulla's magic in my arms and then used it to call to the water. I didn't need much — just enough to put out the fires. For a few moments, I wasn't sure if anything would happen, but then above the noise of burning and the people's cries, I heard the splashing of water. It traveled as if through an invisible tube, and with each hand, I sent half to each row of homes, letting it rain down on them like waterfalls. But, as with everything I attempted, there was so much more water than I had intended. It came down like an ocean had overturned on us, creating a river in the streets that forced the people still there to run behind me, away from the deluge.

I hoped that at least it would carry Radulf away in its current, but it didn't. He wasn't truly here, so the water passed through him like he was made of air.

"You are stronger than I thought." For the first time, Radulf sounded worried. Then his voice turned icy. "But only because of that bulla. No matter how much power it has, you will always be weaker than me. Because I don't care about any of those people behind you. I will sacrifice them all to get that bulla!"

"Everyone get out of here!" I yelled to the crowd.

"Why?" a man yelled back. "So you can finish destroying our homes? Get him!"

I threw a hand toward them, intending to create some sort of invisible barrier between us. Instead, it threw the people back, like they had been pushed by giants. Where they had stood, a vast ditch opened up in the ground, too wide for them to jump and too deep for them to climb through. One man fell in while trying to lunge at me, and I yelled for the others to help him get out, then to stay back.

Ahead of me, Radulf snarled and drew in a deep breath so forceful that it pulled in dirt from the higher grounds, which writhed and swirled around him like a horde of angry snakes. Once it had collected, he threw everything forward. It came at me like a storm, full of violent wind, dust, and rocks that hit me head-on.

I held up both hands, hoping to contain enough of the storm to protect Crispus and Aurelia, and the others behind me. They might not be able to see Radulf, and for all I knew, they couldn't see this storm either, but surely they'd be able to feel it.

Radulf continued sending anything his fierce wind could pick up, rocks and downed branches and parts of the homes that were shredding apart. I didn't dare let it fly past me and hit someone else, so I took all of it, absorbing the blows as best as I could.

"What is he doing?" I vaguely heard Aurelia shouting behind me. "Crispus, help me across! We have to grab him."

I didn't know how she intended to get across the ditch, or if Crispus was helping her, but I couldn't pay attention to them now. Instead, I pulled my hands together and tried to gather the storm, letting it build in my hands the same way it had done for Radulf.

Before I'd finished, Aurelia's hands were on my shoulders and she was saying something. Radulf smiled. "You know the truth about her, don't you?"

That caught me off guard, but only for a moment before I threw what I had gathered back to Radulf. The storm left my hands with the strength of the bulla, making it far worse than what he had done to me. It knocked him backward, and when he sat up again, a long scratch was on his cheek.

"Thank you, Nic," he said calmly. "Now I know exactly what you're capable of. I will be ready when we meet in person, and I promise to bring the whole of my powers against you."

And then he disappeared.

I lowered my arms and only then turned to Crispus and Aurelia. Their faces registered horror when they saw me. Behind them, the families stood in clumps, frightened by what I'd done, maybe angry too. A fallen plank of wood was lying across the ditch, which they must have used to get across. With the wind Radulf had created, it could never have remained in place . . . unless the storm was invisible too. Nobody felt it, or saw anything other than my standing in front of them, fighting something they could not perceive.

"Your face!" Crispus said.

I felt with my fingers the cuts and bruises I already knew were there. But I tried to smile through it and said, "I've looked worse before."

Aurelia shook her head. "No, you haven't. The corpses of Pompeii look better than you do." But then she smiled too, a little.

I put my hand on the bulla, which was beginning to cool, and though we remained in the moonlight, its glow was fading. Perhaps because I had faded too.

Crispus offered me his arm for support and said, "Whatever that was, Nic, it looked like you were attacking those homes, all of these people."

"I wasn't," I whispered.

"We know." Aurelia drew out her knife and yelled to the crowd, "Everyone get back. Let him pass through!"

They did. With me leaning on Crispus, we waded past them through the muddy waters. His wagon was waiting near the baths, which, thankfully, wasn't far away.

"Where's Caela?" I wanted to bring her to Valerius's home. For her sake, and mine.

"She flew away." Aurelia's voice was gentle now. "We couldn't stop her. I'm sorry."

I pressed my lips together and gazed over the skies, hoping to see her. It would've been nice if she cared for me as much as I did for her.

"Let's go," Crispus said. "When people get a good look at their homes, they'll be angry with you."

"I made things worse. For all of us."

"At least we know what your magic can do," he said.

So did Radulf.

He had promised to come back at me with the whole of his magic. Tonight's display only came from a shadow of who he really was. I lowered my head and let Crispus help me into the back of the wagon. Before getting in, I said, "Radulf knows my limits now, while I only know a piece of what he can do. What I have won't be enough to defeat him."

THIRTY-EIGHT

After returning to the senator's home, I went directly into my room, so tired that in my final moments before falling asleep, I wasn't entirely sure whether I'd chosen the bed or the floor. I slept for a while, but the night was so warm, I eventually gave up and wandered outside to practice again, alone.

Shortly after sunrise, I returned for the morning meal, but hesitated in the doorway, not sure how Valerius would greet me. I was prepared for anything from a sharp scolding to full arrest.

Actually, the arrest seemed most likely. So really, I was prepared to run.

But when he saw me coming, Valerius stood and greeted me warmly, and invited me to sit beside him. Certain it must be some sort of trick, I glanced behind me for the closest escape, but then I saw Crispus and Aurelia already reclined comfortably around the table, and figured everything must be safe.

"Your face looks better than I expected," Valerius said. So he knew.

I touched my cheek. The tenderness of bruising had disappeared and I only felt one remaining scratch along my forehead. Even that wasn't as bad as it ought to have been. "I think I heal faster . . . than usual." Looking over the group in front of me, I said, "If I've put any of you in danger —"

For a moment, Valerius's eyes seemed to redden, but then he shook it off and said, "You're a good person, Nic. Too good for this net you're caught up in, and I'm sorry for that. Now come and eat."

I sat between Valerius and Aurelia. As a kindness, she already had piled my plate with food and set it down in front of me. I dug into it immediately.

"I explained everything to Father," Crispus said.

"And I believe it's good news," Valerius added. "Your magic is growing in strength and in control. You directed the water over those fires, and it obeyed."

"More than I wanted. I might've put out the fires, but I also flooded their homes."

"Who cares about their homes?"

"I care! And you're a senator, you should care too!"

"Nic, my only concern right now is what you can do, and you showed progress last night."

"Radulf wasn't really there, only a whisper of him. It will be different once we come face-to-face."

Valerius stared directly into my eyes. "But I believe in you. I believe your strength will grow to match his. After all, you have the bulla, and he does not."

"You're asking too much of Nic," Aurelia said. "Learning magic takes more than a few hours in a field."

Valerius's features hardened when he faced her. "But it's better to fight Radulf on our timing, not his."

"Not if this is your timing. And not if Nic has to go back into the arena. It's not an equal match."

"When would it ever be equal? Besides, fighting Radulf is Nic's plan, not mine. He knows what he's up against better than anyone." Valerius shook his head. "I want him to win, Aurelia, just as you do."

"Do you?" she asked. "Because there are other ways —"

"If there were an easier way, I would've found it already. But no fears, I have a plan. Crispus, show us the banner."

Crispus reached behind him, then stood and unrolled the large maroon banner of Rome. In vertical gold letters across the top were the letters *SPQR*, standing for *Senatus Populusque Romanus*. The Senate and People of Rome. A picture of a sickle and pruning knife had been emblazoned in the center of it, and the family name, Gens Horatius, was stitched along the bottom.

"For generations, this banner has represented the house of Senator Horatio," Valerius said. "At tomorrow's games in the amphitheater, I will hold this banner high and ask the people to cheer Horatio for his support of the empire. Once he sees the people on the emperor's side, he won't dare join Radulf."

"Join Radulf?" Aurelia sniffed angrily. "Horatio is no traitor. He's the presiding magistrate of the Senate. Second only to the emperor."

"Which is why he must be stopped!" I turned back to Valerius. "Do you think this will keep Horatio from acting?"

"I hope so, though I'm afraid it won't stop Radulf. Once he sees you in the arena, he will attack."

"And then the people will understand what a monster he really is." I shrugged, ignoring the growing pit in my gut. "It sounds simple enough."

"Which is reason to doubt this plan," Aurelia said. "Please forgive me, Senator Valerius. I know you are older and wiser than me, but you are wrong about Horatio's loyalties, and it's a foolish plan."

"I *am* older and wiser," Valerius said indignantly. "My plan will work."

Aurelia stiffened at that. "You didn't see Nic last night! He didn't win. Nic barely held his own, and that was only because Radulf was testing his limits. Now Radulf knows exactly what Nic can do. How can we be sure you're not trying to get Nic killed?"

"How dare you?" Valerius raised his voice, both angry and offended. "Nic is condemned by the emperor himself. Do you know what could happen to me if he's discovered here? Why would I risk myself and my family if I wanted him dead?"

She shrank against the force of his anger, then gathered her courage enough to say, "You don't understand —"

"And you do?" Valerius asked. "Who are you? A girl of the streets, of the sewers even? You have no education, no family name, and yet you question my plans to save the empire? All you have is that crepundia, proof that you were unacceptable to the family who gave you life!"

Tears welled in Aurelia's eyes, then she pulled the crepundia over her head and threw it on the table. She gave me one last look before getting to her feet and running from the room.

"Father, you shouldn't have said all that," Crispus whispered.

"I know. That was cruel of me." Valerius sighed, then he looked at me. "It's not a perfect plan, and I know it doesn't avoid a fight with Radulf, but I sincerely believe it's our only hope. More important, I am certain it is the only chance you and your sister have."

I nodded absently, but my attention was on the crepundia. Crispus still stood right behind it, holding up the banner with the sickle and the knife. Similar images were on the crepundia. I picked it up and felt a stab of realization. No, the images were identical.

Aurelia's father was Senator Horatio.

I grabbed the crepundia and ran after her. She was in the atrium, arms tightly wrapped around herself, and staring at the rainwater falling into the pool. When she heard my footsteps, she turned to me. "What was I thinking, to yell at someone with his station in life? I know he's shown us so much kindness, even saved our lives, and I'm grateful for that. But I don't like his plan for you, Nic. I just don't."

I ignored that and instead held the crepundia out to her. I was so angry that it shook in my hand. "How long have you known Horatio is your father?"

Her mouth fell open and she seemed to be struggling for words. "How did you —"

"How long, Aurelia? Did you know at the beginning, when you threatened to bring me to him? Have you known all this time?"

She nodded, slowly. "That's why it was so important to go to him. Once I proved who I was, I figured I could protect you."

"You *figured*? But you didn't know, did you. You weren't trying to help me, or even to help Rome. I was only your ticket to getting close to him."

Tears filled her eyes. "Yes, I did need you. How else could a sewer girl get the attention of the Senate's presiding magistrate? But I wasn't doing it only for me. Horatio can't be as bad as Valerius says, and maybe he'd even help you. The best chance you have is if we face him together."

"You're wrong!" I spat the words back at her. "Valerius might have a dangerous plan, but it's my only chance at freedom. The best I'd get from Horatio is a return to the mines, and probably something much worse. You know that, Aurelia!"

The tears overflowed onto her cheeks, painting wet lines wherever they fell. "I should've told you who my father was. I almost did, but each time I started to, I grew afraid of what you'd think."

"Here's what I think," I said. "I think you lied to me. I think you used me. And I think you should leave. You have your reward money from Valerius. That will buy you enough status to get your audience with Horatio. Go and beg him to bring you home again. Because you won't find a home anywhere near me!"

"Nic, I'm your friend!"

That was oil to the fire I already felt inside, and I nearly exploded. "A friend would've done what was best for me, not used me for her own purposes. A friend would've told me the truth!"

"Nic, please —"

"You would have sacrificed my life to get what you most want. So from now on, I fight for me. Not for your father's sake, or Rome's, and especially not for yours. Good-bye, Aurelia." I bowed low to her. "Or shall I call you Aurelia, of the house of Quintus Horatio?" When I rose up again, I dropped the crepundia at her feet.

I started to walk away, but immediately there came a pounding at the entry. "Senator Valerius!" a voice announced. "Open up for the presiding magistrate of the Roman Senate. We have information that you are harboring a fugitive of the empire. We want the escaped slave, Nicolas Calva."

THIRTY-NINE

Aurelia breathed my name, but I wouldn't look at her. "Nic," she said again. "That's Horatio. We can talk to him together."

There was more pounding on the door, and Valerius and Crispus hurried into the atrium. Crispus's face was tense with worry, but I couldn't read Valerius as well. Either he was terrified, or else his heart had stopped working. Possibly both.

"You turned Nic in to him?" Crispus asked Aurelia. "How dare you?"

Her eyes pled with me to believe her. "I didn't, Nic. I swear —"

"Don't!" I shook my head. "Don't say anything else."

"Run out the back," Valerius said.

I wasn't going to run, and it would've been futile if I'd tried. The door opened and in poured Horatio's personal guard, looking similar to Roman soldiers except for Horatio's banner worn on their uniforms. They pushed Aurelia aside, and walked directly toward me.

My hand curled around the bulla, which was currently beneath my tunic. The heat in it worried me. Magic flowed in through my fingers, and up my arm. It wanted a fight.

Horatio glared down at me and no doubt was weighing the odds of how many of his men I could take out before one of them got the bulla. The correct answer: all of them. And I would've released the magic already except I wouldn't put Crispus or Valerius at risk. Or even Aurelia, who stood off to the side with her eyes wide and still full of tears.

Horatio's face twisted as he prepared to speak. "Nicolas Calva, Emperor Tacitus has ordered your execution. I am here to arrest you."

"No," I said.

"No?" He arched an eyebrow. "I'm not asking your permission, slave."

"And I'm not giving it. The emperor and I made an agreement. Once I fulfill it, I will go to him. On my own."

Valerius pushed past me. "Senator Horatio, Nic's magic is stronger than you can imagine. He plans to take the key to the Malice of Mars. If you want to live, you will give it to him."

"Stop this!" Aurelia darted forward. "Nic has not threatened his life, not once." Then she turned to Horatio. "And you will not threaten Nic's life either. He's my friend."

Horatio laughed. "And why should I take orders from a street girl?"

Aurelia bit down on her lip, then held up the crepundia,

still in her hand. Visibly trembling, Horatio took it from her and examined the miniatures. When he looked back at Aurelia, there were tears in his eyes.

"Where did you get this?" he asked.

"From you. On the day you exposed me."

He made a sound in his throat and stepped closer to her. "My daughter," he whispered. "I had no idea you were still alive."

"We have much to discuss," Aurelia said. "But first, you must not arrest Nic. He's done nothing wrong."

"Hasn't he?" Any of the sentimentality he'd felt toward Aurelia vanished by the time he remembered me. "Tell me, slave, how did you get the bulla?"

"It doesn't matter how I got it." The magic flared in me again, and I clenched my fists to contain it. "What matters is how I use it."

Horatio nodded his head at Aurelia. "Wait outside, daughter. I wish to bring you home, so we can talk." Aurelia tried to say something to me, but one of his soldiers was already escorting her outside, and I still wouldn't look at her. When she had left, Horatio waved a hand forward for his men. "Burn this house, so other senators may know what happens when they ignore the orders of the emperor. Then arrest anyone who survives."

"No, you won't!" I raised a hand at Horatio. My intention had only been to warn him, but magic burst from me instead and shot him against the wall. Immediately I felt a sting across my back where one of the soldiers struck me with his sword.

His cut went deep, too deep. It might've been worse if I hadn't been moving already, but the injury still dropped me flat on the ground.

"Nic!" Crispus ran to my side and rolled me to my back. I gasped with the pain of moving, but he clutched my hand.

"What have you done?" Valerius cried.

Horatio seemed equally horrified. He shoved his soldier away from us. "You fool! General Radulf wants him alive!"

If anyone answered, I didn't hear them. My breath was locked in my throat and I felt warm blood pooling beneath me.

"Heal this," Crispus whispered. "Nic, I know you can."

So much had happened to my body over the last few days, I didn't have the same confidence. Even with magic, there were limits to what I could take. I closed my eyes anyway and tried to find the Divine Star, or even the bulla, but the pain was so fierce it made any concentration difficult.

Crispus pulled the bulla out from beneath my tunic and pressed it into my hand. Instantly it began to work, though as I called upon the Star, Radulf crept into my head too. He was angry. He hadn't wanted Horatio to injure me. And I understood then that he didn't like Horatio. Finally, we had something in common.

"He should've done worse," I muttered, hoping Radulf could hear me. "This won't stop me from fighting you tomorrow."

"I hope not." Radulf laughed, sending a chill through my bones. "Because if you fail to show up in that arena, I will punish Livia for your cowardice."

His words were like a second wound. "Don't hurt her!" I cried. "I will be there!"

"Who is the boy talking to?" Horatio asked.

Crispus seemed to understand. "Ignore what you're hearing, Nic. Just heal that wound."

"Take the boy," Horatio said. "He's in no condition to stop us now."

That was true enough. The sting wasn't so bad now, so I knew I was beginning to heal, but it had also taken strength from me. While one soldier kicked Crispus away from me and then kept a sword on him and his father, the other picked me up.

"Put him in the wagon." Horatio then turned to Valerius. "There will be consequences for hiding the boy here. Until then, may I remind you that I am the sponsor for tomorrow's games in the amphitheater? As a fellow senator, I expect you to be there to show your support. We must not let the people think there are . . . differences between us."

Valerius responded with a frown. "Tomorrow, you will make yourself a traitor to Rome. Trust me, there are differences between us."

Horatio laughed. "Are you sure about that?" He stepped closer. "If you could use the bulla, would this boy still be alive?"

If Valerius answered, I didn't hear it. The soldier had carried me out by then and dumped me in the back of the wagon.

"Nic? Are you all right?" Aurelia jumped from a carriage, which her father must have arrived in, but a third soldier quickly forced her back inside. Horatio came out immediately after and got into the carriage with them. Once it left, ours followed behind it. Chains lay in a pile near my legs and despite my weakness, I kicked them away.

"We should put them on the boy," one of the guards said.

My eyes narrowed. "Try it and the only parts of this wagon that'll be seen again will be splinters on this road."

One man leaned forward with a sneer on his face and breath so rancid it actually made me remember Sal's more kindly. "I was in the arena that day. I saw what you did, and trust me when I say that there's plenty we'd have done to you already, except that Radulf made us promise not to touch you."

"So Horatio has already given his loyalty to Radulf?" I asked.

"Not yet." The sneer turned into a smile of genuine pleasure. "He's going to announce that in the arena tomorrow, after your execution."

FORTY

Horatio had a large apartment very near the amphitheater, though when we arrived I was immediately locked in an underground room. They warned me not to use magic in this tight space, but it wasn't necessary. I wasn't sure how many families lived above where I stood, and I wouldn't endanger them.

Besides, I had bigger issues pressing in on me. The revelation from Aurelia shouldn't have surprised me, and once I found out, I never should've been so harsh. I was still angry with her, but I also missed her, somehow. Whatever friendship we'd had was in ruins now.

Weighing even heavier on my mind was the question of who had turned me in to Horatio. As I considered it, the answer came like a lump in my throat. Sal.

Of course it had been Sal, who saw me leave the forum with Crispus. Even his crusty brain could figure out who Crispus's father was.

That suspicion was confirmed almost immediately when the door opened and Sal's face was on the other side. He'd been cleaned up and was now dressed in a long white toga. Despite that, he still reeked of the mines.

"Try anything and there's a dozen armed soldiers behind me waiting to take their shot at you," he said.

I didn't even blink. "Are you sure? Getting rid of you would do them a favor."

"I'm part of Horatio's house now, managing servants for the Senate's presiding magistrate. So you can see how much my life has improved from the filthy mines."

"Horatio is filthy too," I said. "Just in a different way."

"The senator pardoned me, after I told him where you were hiding. But to be honest, I'd have told him even without the pardon."

I turned from him and sat down on the single chair in the room. "Go away, Sal. Crawl back underground with the other worms."

He chuckled. "If you knew what Horatio has planned, you would beg the gods to take you right now."

"If I begged the gods to take any life, it wouldn't be mine." With my growing anger, magic coursed through every vein in my body, so much of it that I was terrified of what might happen in this tight space. "I could bring the entire apartment down on our heads right now. I might survive it. You won't."

"Your mother warned me about you!" he said. "I should have believed her."

"Warned you about what?" It had been almost five years since Sal sold my mother, while I'd had this magic for only a few days. She couldn't have warned him about this. When Sal failed to answer, I threw some magic at the wall beside us. A large chunk of concrete tumbled to the ground, not much, but enough to frighten him. "What did she say?" I yelled.

"I hate you," he snarled. "And even more, I hate having a debt to you. You never should've saved me in last week's games."

"And you didn't have to spare my life at the mines. So why are you here now? Not to free me."

"No, of course not." He shrugged. "But since you'll probably die in the arena tomorrow, I thought I owed you an explanation. The day I sent you away from the mines, Livia tried to tell you something about your mother."

"What was that?"

The fingers of his hands pressed together, and then he asked, "Why do you think your mother made you promise to stay together? It wasn't so that you could protect Livia. Nic, she has always been there to protect *you*."

My mind skipped through the last five years, all the times Livia begged me to not to defy Sal, when she hurried me away if Roman soldiers came through the mines, and how she refused to share any of her memories of our parents. I always thought I needed to keep her safe. It had never occurred to me that I was the one who needed saving.

Seeing my confusion, Sal added, "Your mother never sold you to the mines. She paid me the last of everything she had to take you. After the way your father died, she knew the empire would try to find you."

"Why? It was a lightning storm — that had nothing to do with the empire."

"During one of Rome's battles with Gaul, your father saw his people were about to be destroyed. He tried to create something known as a Jupiter Stone, which he could've used to defeat Rome."

Valerius had told me about the Jupiter Stone, the most powerful of all the magical amulets. He had also told me that many men had gone to their deaths in the attempt to create one.

"My father had magic?" I asked.

"Not enough, apparently. Done correctly, the Stone is activated in a lightning storm, but your father failed and Rome had its victory in Gaul. Your mother fled with you and your sister, but she knew Rome would come after you too, just as they tried to destroy all of your family. Magic runs strong in some families, and Rome would not rest until they knew you could not become a threat." He grinned. "Which you are."

I wondered if Livia knew all of this. Probably not, but it bothered me that my mother would've held that one secret back from us. If Rome was determined to destroy my family, how could she have believed they wouldn't one day come looking for me?

"We hid for almost two years," I said. "But I thought it was from slavers, not the empire itself. We would've stayed in hiding, but Livia was getting sick."

Sal grimaced, as if having to look at me made him ill. "All I know is that your mother believed you and Livia were safer in the mines. Then she asked me to sell her far enough away that Rome would ignore you. And look what you've done — made yourself known to the entire empire! It's the last thing she would've wanted."

My breath came in shallow bursts, and the magic swelled again within me. "Where is my mother?" I asked. "Is she still alive?"

He shrugged dismissively. "Whatever happened, it was all her choice. For you, Nic."

"Thank you, then." I hated to force out those words, but they had to be said. Even to him. "Thank you for taking in Livia and me."

"Not a day has passed when I don't regret it." Sal frowned at me. "Well, when I don't regret taking *you*."

I used enough magic to raise the fallen chunk of concrete, although it turned out to be much heavier than it looked. I stepped forward, trying to hide the strain within me to keep that rock held in midair.

"So this is your magic? Lifting rocks?" He laughed. "That would've been useful at the mines. I am still your master, you know."

Grinning, I said, "Let's test that. Command me not to drop this on you and see if I obey."

I lifted it higher so that it came to rest directly over his head. One hiccup from me, and Sal would be finished. He knew it too. Sal backed against the wall and made a cry for mercy.

"Wherever you go, you will never threaten me again," I told him. "And you will never again approach my sister. Never look at her, never think of her!"

"Even if I wanted to, I couldn't." He blinked. "I saw her only yesterday in the forum. She was with General Radulf."

"Why?" Reflecting my anger, the ground shook beneath us. "Was she in chains, or hurt? What possible reason would he have to drag her through the forum?"

"There were no chains, Nic. She walked beside him, clean and well dressed, and she looked happier than I've ever seen her."

I shook my head, more bothered than confused. My emotions were a turmoil inside me, and this new knowledge was yet another weight on my chest. To have any chance of breathing again, I had to let it explode.

But that would be a disaster. If I refused to have any master, then that must include the bulla. I would control *it,* and not the other way around. Nor would I give Sal the satisfaction of seeing me fail here. I was still angry and confused — after everything Sal had said, how could I feel otherwise? But I was also in control, and I let the magic dissipate within me. As it drained out, I was left feeling stronger than before. The magic wasn't gone; it was learning to weave itself through my body where I could manage it better. With more time and practice, I would learn to control it entirely.

"Get out!" I hissed at Sal. "Now!"

The door slammed behind me and locked again. It didn't bother me, though. He may not have understood it yet, but I was glad for his visit. Because Sal had given me hope of coming through this. I would return to the arena in control of my magic.

FORTY-ONE

It was evening before Horatio came to visit me. I hadn't eaten all day, so my hope was that he'd bring food along with him, but it wasn't a great surprise either to see his empty hands. Even if he had left his table with a tray of food, I had no doubt he'd have satisfied his round belly before ever reaching me.

I stood when Horatio walked into the small room. He surveyed me from head to toe, then sat in the chair where I had previously been. My eyes darted to the open door. It was just him and me in here, and as far as I could tell, we were alone. He was unarmed, and I still had the bulla.

"You could run, of course," he said. "But I don't think you will."

"Not until I get an apology for what your men did to me this morning."

He brushed that aside with a wave of his hand. "For someone of your abilities, that wasn't even a scratch. And I know that if you had wanted to stop the arrest, you could have done it." Now he folded his arms across his bloated chest. "Why are you still here, Nic?"

Because going into the arena was now about more than taking Radulf's magic. He had threatened Livia if I failed to appear. But there was more . . .

"We needed to talk alone." I paused to draw in a breath. "When I go into the arena tomorrow, you must not be there."

He smirked. "Yes, that would work out well for you."

"It's better for you too. I think Senator Valerius intends to have you killed in there."

His eyes widened, briefly, before he got control of himself and the greasy smile returned. "Oh? Why do you think that?"

"He wants the key to the Malice of Mars. Before you give it to General Radulf."

"I'll give it to Radulf, after he defeats you." Now the smile curled into a sneer. "Valerius cannot believe you have any chance of winning tomorrow."

"That's exactly my point! He's only using me as a lure to bring Radulf into the arena, which means he must have another plan." I took a breath. "More than that, with your death, he becomes presiding magistrate — he will lead the Praetors and control their loyalty. By tomorrow, Valerius intends to possess all three amulets."

"Whatever his plan is, it will fail!" Horatio said. "When I give Radulf the key tomorrow, I will do it in front of the mob, so they will know the Senate and all its Praetors bow to Radulf now. They will see his power, and see me standing at his side. Once I give Radulf the key, Valerius can do nothing to stop us. Valerius will bow to us too, or the Praetor War will begin!"

"He won't bow," I said. "And if war begins, Rome will be destroyed!"

Horatio grinned. "Yes, destruction is my price for the key."

"You want Rome to fall?" I asked. "You are head of the Senate, second in power only to the emperor. Why destroy your own world?"

"My world was already destroyed, many years ago." His eyes fell, and when he looked at me again, they were full of sadness. In that moment, I saw the resemblance between him and Aurelia, more alike than I had realized before.

Horatio said, "Aurelia is your friend, correct?"

I didn't respond. Not because I refused, but because I wasn't sure how to answer that question. Was she still my friend? Had she ever been?

Ignoring my silence, he said, "She's a remarkably stubborn girl, just like her mother. Maybe you noticed."

I smiled a little. "Yes, I might've noticed that."

"I loved her mother more than I've loved anyone or anything. But she died giving birth to Aurelia, and that released a poison inside me. I was a senator, in the greatest empire the world had ever known. But it was not great enough to save her."

"That's why you exposed Aurelia?"

"She was a thorn in the wound opened by losing her mother. And I thought that by giving Aurelia away, the wound would heal. But all these years later, it's only worse. I will give Radulf the key because I want him to destroy the empire that could not save my family."

"Valerius will stop you," I said. "He will kill you before that happens."

"Valerius has no such power." Horatio reached over and patted my cheek. "You seem like a smart boy, for a slave, but not smart enough. I have the key with me at all times, and tomorrow, it will belong to Radulf. Once he finds the Malice of Mars, all of Rome will be his. What can Valerius do about that?" He motioned toward the door. "Run now, if you wish. I know that I can't stop you."

I shook my head. "Tomorrow you're taking me into the arena to fight Radulf. Well, that's what I intend to do."

He stood to leave and brushed off his clothes from the dirt in this room. "You have the heart of a gladiator. It will be a glorious fight. I'm almost sad that you won't survive it."

Very late in the night, I received one other visitor. I had been asleep on the floor, grateful for the warmth of the bulla against this cold concrete, when the door opened. I sat up and glared into candlelight.

It was set on the floor, allowing me to see Aurelia's face behind it. "Why are you still here?" She never wasted time in becoming angry with me. "There are no guards here, and your door isn't locked. I thought I was coming to free you, but now I see you won't even free yourself!"

"Go back to your father," I said tiredly.

"I've been talking with him all night. Here." She handed me a thick slice of bread, which I gladly took. Then she added, "He said he had often watched for me, and wanted to bring me back home, but never knew where to look. He never remarried, or had any other children. Lately, he'd begun to worry about dying without an heir."

An interesting worry, considering the warning I had given him only hours ago. "Congratulations," I mumbled. A part of me meant that. Even if she had lied about him, I knew that getting back to her family was as important to her as Livia was to me. Would I have lied to Aurelia if it meant I could recover my sister? Yes, I probably would have.

She leaned against the wall with slumped shoulders. "However, he's not who I thought he would be."

Her tone was blank, not quite disappointed, or angry, or even sad. It was just stating a fact, I supposed. I stared back at her, completely unsure of what to say. Finally, I came up with a question. "Why?" It seemed safe enough.

"He told me that a war is coming between those who support the empire, and those who support Radulf. He called it the Praetor War." She sighed. "Then he said that if I am to be part of his household, I must support Radulf."

"What did you expect? Valerius already told you all of that."

"But I didn't believe him. I never really trusted Valerius, so I thought he was lying to you."

I paused, and then said. "He told plenty of lies. Just not about that."

She pushed the door back. "Come with me, Nic, but we have to hurry. We'll leave Rome tonight. Go anywhere else that we want."

"What about my sister? I'm supposed to leave her in Radulf's control?"

Aurelia brushed a hand through her hair, obviously frustrated. "Do you know what Horatio has planned for tomorrow? It would be awful to leave Rome without your sister, I agree, but at least you'll leave alive."

"I have a bargain with the emperor. Tomorrow in the arena, I will take Radulf's magic, and when I do, he will grant Livia and me our freedom."

"It won't work."

"When I leave Rome, I want to go as a free person, not a fugitive."

"Nic, you're not listening —"

"Neither are you!"

"They intend to kill you in the arena!"

"And I intend to live!" I exhaled a slow breath. "There's no other choice for me now. Either you'll stand by me and support what I have to do, or you'll get out of my way."

She turned toward me, as her face slowly pinched into something resembling pain. "I can't help you destroy yourself."

"Then this is good-bye."

She tried again. "I was wrong to lie to you about my father, and wrong to want to bring you to him before. I will admit to both of those. But this time, you are wrong. If you go into that arena tomorrow, something terrible is going to happen."

I didn't look at her to ask, "How do you know that?"

"Because I can feel it. Because we're friends, Nic. So you have to believe me now."

I scoffed. "Well, that's the question, then. Whether I still believe that we are friends."

"Do you?"

I held out my hands to her, remembering several days ago when she had slapped chains on them. "Are we equals, you and I? Or do you see me as a slave?"

I must've turned enough for her to see the dried blood on my tunic from where I'd been cut. She gasped and cried, "What happened to you? They told me you weren't hurt!"

My eyes darted behind her as Horatio filled the frame. "Ask him what happened."

Horatio eyed Aurelia cautiously, and said, "It's time, Nic."

"Don't go into that arena," Aurelia said.

Horatio pushed her aside. "If you are living in my home, you must obey my orders."

Aurelia's eyes went from me to him, and she said, "Then I will not live in your home." She removed the crepundia and hung it over my shoulders instead. "Maybe Nic should've been your child. He seems perfectly willing to obey you." Then she pushed past Horatio's guards and was gone.

Horatio briefly stared at where she'd been before his face hardened again. He turned to me. "I expected you'd have run in the night. Surely you were warned about the arena today."

"Many times," I said as I walked out of the room. "But my bigger worry is that you weren't warned enough."

FORTY-TWO

As I had done days earlier, we entered the amphitheater beneath a tall arch and walked down the ramp that would take us into the hypogeum. The smell assaulted me far worse than it had the first time. Had I already come so far from the pits of slavery that I could see this place as a free person? Because although I had disliked it before, I had also felt like a part of its filth, used to being chained like an animal. But now I wasn't that slave boy anymore. I remembered freedom again and could never go back to this.

We passed Caela's former cage, now occupied by animals with black and white stripes. Horatio called them tiger horses. I thought of how enraged Caela would be to know they were here, and wished she were here with me again. There were several lions today and one very large black cat that paced anxiously in his cage. I understood his restlessness, which filled my veins as well. I paused long enough to whisper that there would be no death in the arena today. He watched me, and even dipped his head as I passed by. If that cat were a human, it would've been a bow, a thought that amazed me.

Horatio told a passing slave to fetch Felix, then turned to me. "I don't know if it's bravery that leads you into the arena today, or foolishness."

"Bravery on my part, foolishness on yours." I stared back at him. "Let me go in alone to fight Radulf. If you enter the arena, you will not come out again."

"I am the sponsor of these games," he said. "The mob will expect to see me, and I will give them the show of their lives."

"Don't give Radulf the key," I said. "Don't start this war."

He sighed. "If you were right to warn me about today, then I do owe you some thanks for trying." He stared off and his eyes glazed over. "*A caelo usque ad centrum*. Do you understand those words, boy?"

From heaven to the center of earth. I knew the words, not their meaning, and told him so.

Still staring away, he smiled. "You will. If you survive the arena today, then you will soon understand everything." Then he saw Felix coming and pulled me forward.

It was obvious from Felix's expression that he was not happy to see me. But he bowed to Horatio and said, "I will get him ready."

As Felix led me away, I asked, "Get me ready? What does that mean?"

"Do you understand the position you've put me in?" Felix scowled. "Horatio is the presiding magistrate *and* the sponsor of today's games. If anything goes wrong, he'll have my head. But then last night I had a visit from Senator Valerius, who believes that Horatio's games are a threat to the emperor. He insists you can stop it."

I clicked my tongue. "Just do as Horatio asked. I don't want you in any trouble. If I can stop Horatio in the arena, then I will."

"And if you can't?"

"Then Rome will go to war against itself." We walked on farther and I asked, "Is the emperor at the games today?"

"No." Felix glanced over at me. "When I found out you'd be here, I sent messengers warning him to remain at his palace. It's for his own safety. I hope you understand."

I did, and if anything, I was relieved. If things went well, the emperor would hear about it. But if things got out of control here, and they probably would, I didn't want to feel responsible for his life.

"Is Valerius at the games, then?" I asked.

"He'll be in the imperial box at the north end. When I bring you up in the lift, you'll be directly in front of him."

"Will there be animals?"

Felix sighed. "That was the original plan — we even have them all in place. But last night, Senator Horatio suggested a reenactment might fit better than a venatio."

"A reenactment? Like theater?"

"Everything in the arena is theater."

I stopped and stared up at him. "Felix, how bad will it be up there?"

His face remained as solemn as mine. "If it was bad, would you leave?"

I should. A person would have to be an utter fool to walk into a situation designed to destroy him. But since the moment my life had crossed with the bulla, it was hardly the only foolish thing I'd done. Besides that, Radulf had my sister.

"I have to fight Radulf, as we agreed," I said. "This is my chance."

His smile back at me was grim. "Well, it is bad. Just . . . be smart up there. You'll need your wits more than your magic."

By then, we had arrived at the lift, the very one Felix had forced me into when I was tied to the horse. "Here." He handed me a tunic I recognized very well. It was the one from when I had been a slave, complete with all its rips and holes. It felt like grit in my hands.

"He wants me to wear this?" I asked.

"There's dried blood on yours. Even with that, you look like a patrician now," he said. "Horatio doesn't want the mob to think he's executing one of his own."

"Fine. I wouldn't want anyone confusing me with his kind anyway." I pulled off the nicer tunic Valerius had given me and tossed it aside, then put on my old one. The smell of it shocked me. I'd never realized it before, but the odor was more animal than human, and more dead than alive. And against my skin now, it scratched just as it always had before. I decided to keep my sandals on. Felix hadn't ordered me to take them off, and I'd have disobeyed if he did. Then I adjusted the crepundia and bulla, both of which I wore around my neck, and made sure the bulla was perfectly visible over my tunic. While I tied the rope that had served as a belt, my wrists and ankles pulsed with a nervous anticipation, as if the chains would logically come next. I shook them, as though it would slough off the feelings, but it didn't help much.

Felix leaned in close to me. "Valerius has a message for you. When this is finished, he wants you to return to his home. He says he is still prepared to honor his bargain with you, if you will honor yours."

It meant he still wanted me to get the key for him. And that he was still planning for Horatio to die in the arena. On the other hand, he had also promised to recover my sister.

"It's time to go now," Felix said. "You can do this, Nic."

I took a deep breath, and then said, "Do me a favor, please. Once I'm gone, get everyone out from the hypogeum. I don't know what this fight will be like. So get everyone out."

"I will." Then Felix ordered men forward to raise me into the arena. When the capstan started turning, he said, "Remember, the crowd wants a show."

I shook my head. "I'm not here for that. My only job is to stop Radulf."

"Exactly." His smile widened. He was as eager for what was coming as I was dreading it. "Stopping Radulf *is* the show."

FORTY-THREE

As I was raised up, a door opened in the arena floor and scorching morning sun poured down on me. White sand on the floor blinded me at first — it was different from the yellow sand that had been here before, and contained minerals that sparkled in the light. That alone was concerning. It suggested there was something different about today's games.

Once I was higher, I realized the crowd in the amphitheater seemed twice what it had been before, but they were all speaking in hushed tones. By the time the top of my head appeared, they had become almost silent. As nervous as their cheers and yells had made me several days ago, the silence was worse. It was unnatural.

I came up directly behind two large ramps in the center of the arena. Between the ramps was a wide platform with images of the gods painted on the sides. Yet as I turned away from the platform, I realized it was hardly the most impressive feature of the arena today. Twelve raised blocks were set around the perimeter. On each was a different person dressed to represent one of the gods. One at the far end looked like Apollo, who carried in his hands a silver bow, aimed directly at me. Of course it was aimed at me. Everything else in Rome had threatened me since I took the bulla. Why not a silver arrow too?

On the next two blocks were men dressed as Mars and Jupiter, each carrying a spear, though Jupiter's was shaped as a lightning bolt. On the opposite side of the arena, Neptune held a trident and Vulcan had a hammer. Every one of them was watching me.

Some of the people on the blocks represented the goddesses. I easily recognized Diana, also carrying a bow and arrow. At first I thought it was a woman in the costume, but then I realized it was still a man, like the others. And he was someone I recognized — the soldier who had been with Radulf when he first came to the mines.

These were Radulf's soldiers.

I heard the sound of another lift and realized it was rising into the center platform. Bit by bit, Horatio appeared, dressed in all his Senate finery. The applause for him was polite, but not enthusiastic. His shoulders fell in disappointment, which made me smile, just a little.

"Friends and Romans," he called into the audience. "Your games today are particularly special, for it pits the gods against the most unlikely of foes." Then he turned and pointed to me. "That boy, Nicolas Calva, is an escaped slave from the mines. You have seen him in this arena before, and you know that he is dangerous. But can he defeat the gods?"

Boos flew at me from all sides, but I tried to shut out the sound. I wasn't here to win their affection, only to defeat Radulf. So where was he?

A popping sound snapped near me, and when I turned to look at it, the floor burst into flame. I jumped and darted away from it, which sent the audience into fits of laughter. Worse still, there were more popping sounds, each one followed by the floor exploding with fire. I thought it was magic at first, but when I ran to another spot, my foot caught in some pipes that had been laid beneath the sand. I was lucky to only have scraped my hands as I fell; at a different angle, I could've been more seriously injured. When I looked more carefully, there seemed to be an entire grid of pipes laid out, probably carrying some sort of fuel for these fires.

Another pop erupted so close to me that it scorched the back of my arm. I gritted my teeth but refused to make any sound of pain. I wouldn't have the mob laughing at me again, and I wouldn't give Horatio the satisfaction of knowing I'd received my first injury.

Only he must've noticed, because in a loud voice meant for everyone to hear, he said, "There is only one safe place in this arena, boy."

More fires popped to life around me, forcing me closer to the ramp. Finally, I had no choice but to get on it. The audience cheered when I did, and began chanting, "Fight, fight, fight!"

"Shall this slave boy take on someone with the power of the gods?" Horatio asked. The audience cheered, but my attention was on the arena around me. By now, the entire floor was filled with flame, except for the twelve blocks where Radulf's soldiers stood, and this platform. The fires worried me. Whatever pathetic plan I'd had ten minutes ago was suddenly useless. To have any chance of winning, I would need to put out the fires. I searched the skies overhead, but there wasn't even a cloud, much less a rainstorm.

"Fight, fight, fight!" the audience chanted even louder than before.

"Then here he is!" Horatio threw a red cloak in the air, and when it fell, Radulf appeared out of nowhere from within its folds. He wore a gladiator's uniform over a fine white tunic, but all in gold and not too different from those his soldiers on the blocks were wearing. If he wanted to give the impression of being one of the gods, he had done a good job of it. The audience froze for a moment at his appearance, completely stunned, and then broke into thunderous applause. Standing at the top of one ramp, I wasn't nearly as fast to recover. Radulf was clearly a master at magical skills I hadn't even dreamed were possible.

Radulf used the moment of my surprise to attack first. He struck me with some sort of magical force that knocked me to my back where I rolled to the bottom of the ramp, inches from a fire. I got to my feet and ran up the ramp again where he struck me a second time before I'd managed to gather enough magic for a first hit.

I fell to my back, but didn't get up again until I felt something churn inside me. It wasn't much for magic, but I tried to aim for his legs. When I did, it scooped him off his feet and dropped him face-first onto the platform. The audience laughed at that, though it didn't last long before Radulf was on his feet again.

We exchanged hits after that, some harder than others. Radulf struck with far more force than I had thought possible, but from the expression on his face, I was sending out my magic with power too. It wasn't an easy fight, but thanks to the strength of the bulla's gems, he was struggling as much as I was. Slowly, I was forcing Radulf backward along the platform, feeling power grow within me.

Then as suddenly as he had appeared, Radulf vanished. I stopped, unsure of what to do, and felt a hand punch at my back, exactly on the Divine Star. I collapsed to the ground, and Radulf's knee went to the center of my back. The audience cheered, and somehow above their noise, my cries could still be heard.

"I thought this would be harder," Radulf said. "Do you have any last words?"

"Only that I'm not through fighting, you miserable roach!"

Radulf laughed and dug his knee in harder. "Yes, Nic. You are."

FORTY-FOUR

I might not have had anything more to say to Radulf, but someone did. From the imperial box ahead of us, Senator Valerius's voice rang out loudly. "My Roman friends, do not think this is the end of the fight. Senator Horatio would never make it so quick or so easy that you don't get your proper entertainment. In fact, he has given the advantage to Nicolas Calva."

He had the audience's attention, and Radulf's too, for that matter. I thought about what Felix had said, that this was theater. Valerius clearly understood that too.

He continued, "To help Nicolas win the fight, Senator Horatio has given him access to a second magical amulet. It is a key that Nicolas now holds, and it is the reason the slave will defeat a general today!"

Radulf threw me onto my back. "You have the key?"

I had expected a trap from Valerius, and this must be it. If Radulf believed Horatio had already given me the key, he would be angry. Angry enough to kill him.

"I don't have it," I said.

Radulf pressed on my chest with something that seemed to punch a hole through my heart. I yelled with the crushing pain of it and he said, "Where is the key?"

Still gasping for air, I choked out, "I would sooner go to my grave than let you get it."

"That can be arranged," Radulf said.

Valerius called down again. "Or does Senator Horatio play his own games with us? Maybe he wishes to keep the key for himself?"

Radulf instantly forgot about me and swung his attention to Horatio, who throughout our entire fight had somehow managed to seem invisible in the far corner of the platform.

Horatio raised his arms in innocence. "Valerius lies, Dominus."

Radulf stopped. "You are the presiding magistrate of the Senate, and yet you address *me* with the superior title?"

"Because you are superior, Dominus. I still have the key. But if you want it, you must accept me as your second in command."

"I do not bargain with fools." Radulf shook his head. "Give me the key, or they will carry your body from this arena."

I got to my feet and yelled, "Fight me, Radulf! Not him."

Radulf turned to me, slowly. "Why do you want this fight? Do you believe you cannot lose? Is that because you have the key hidden, just as you tried to hide the bulla?"

"Valerius is using the key against all of us. Don't fall for his trap!"

"One of you has it." Radulf turned to Horatio. "Is it you?"

And he raised a hand to throw a punch at Horatio, but I used my magic to place a shield between them, much as I had shielded the people near the baths on the Appian Way. It immediately cost the bulk of my magic, and the strain of keeping it in place was quickly wearing me thin.

In his attempts to push through my shield, Radulf was becoming tired as well, and when he paused to rest, I took my chance to change the course of this fight. With one hand keeping the shield on Horatio, I raised another hand to the skies and commanded the clouds to gather. They formed out of nowhere and darkened so quickly that it felt like the daylight had been extinguished.

"What are you doing?" Radulf seemed as surprised as I had been when he first appeared on the platform. He stepped forward, forgetting our fight. "Nic, how are you doing this?"

"I need that arena floor." With that, I directed the clouds to pour down their rain, and they obeyed. It was more than I wanted, as usual, but the onslaught of water quickly put out the fires in the arena, leaving great clouds of steam to mix with the rain and suffocate the air around us. Once the last fire went out, I tried to part the clouds and end it, but the storm was still worsening. Thunder rolled above us, echoing in the skies. That frightened me, more than I wanted to admit. I had never wanted the thunder to come.

I ducked as the storm cracked overhead, and my shield protecting Horatio fell with it. Radulf crouched as well, then cried, "Nic, stop this!"

If only I knew the way to stop it. Where there is thunder, lightning follows. Every storm I'd experienced in my life brought with it the thoughts of my father standing on a tall ridge in defiance of Jupiter's power. But now, Sal's words filled my head — my father had had magic too. He had faced the lightning, hoping to create a Jupiter Stone, and with it, end the war in Gaul. But he had failed, and died.

Radulf grabbed my shoulders, forcing me to look at him. "Nic, we cannot be out here with the lightning! Send this storm away, now!"

I closed my eyes and willed the clouds to part. Another roll of thunder crossed the sky, and so at first I was sure I had failed, but slowly it faded and I saw sun again. The audience cheered at that, which surprised me. I had forgotten they were here.

Radulf sat back, clearly as relieved as I was. I knew why lightning storms frightened me, but I hadn't expected him to be afraid as well.

Before he recovered, I stood and called out to his men, who were still standing on their raised blocks, although they were now dripping wet and significantly less godlike than they had been before. "Drop your weapons," I yelled. "Or they will be eaten out of your hands."

And I raised both arms, then spread my fingers apart. Obeying my will, the thirty-six lifts from the hypogeum below opened into the arena. Felix had said the animals were still in place from what had originally been planned as a hunt this morning. If the mob had expected a hunt, I would give them one. But the animals would not hunt one another.

Out from the lifts came lions and bears and wild boars. There were also tigers and large black cats, and even an elephant. And because I had the bulla, they would hear me and obey.

"Do not harm any unarmed man in this arena!" I told them.

The animals charged, knocking the blocks out from beneath Radulf's men and baring teeth in ways that even made me nervous. Weapon after weapon was thrown aside, followed by the men breaking through the north gate of the arena to escape. The animals went with them, every last one. The audience exploded with cheers.

I figured Rome would probably not have another venatio for some time. Mostly because they had just lost every single one of their animals.

And if nothing else went well for the rest of this battle, that alone made me smile.

FORTY-FIVE

I kept four animals back, to stay with me in the arena, specially chosen for Radulf, who Valerius had told me was terrified of lions.

Indeed he was, for when he saw them coming, Radulf jumped off the platform and went running for a lift that still had its doors open. Except a familiar face was coming up on that lift, with a long knife at her waist and a bow in her hands. I'd never been so happy to see anyone in my life.

Aurelia jumped onto the arena floor and nocked an arrow aimed directly at Radulf. "Another step closer and you'll get poked."

He threw some sort of magic at her, but I had already put up a shield to block it.

"I stand with you, Nic, as an equal!" she said. "This is what friends do!"

"Not here!" I yelled.

"You asked me to stand with you!"

"Symbolically!"

"Can we fight about this later?" she asked.

I smiled over at her. If I won this fight, I would gladly engage in more arguments with her. Radulf was backing away from the lions, but when they began chasing him, he tripped over one of the hidden pipes and fell hard to the ground, unconscious. This was my chance, but I didn't have long.

I crouched on Radulf's left side while Aurelia knelt on his right. She used her knife to cut through his tunic, revealing his Divine Star.

"Exactly like yours," she said.

"Not for long." I started to lift the bulla off my head. When I pressed it to the mark on his back, the bulla would absorb Radulf's magic. In minutes, he would be nothing more than a corrupt general fit for the emperor's dungeon.

"Aurelia, get away from those lions!" Horatio reached down and grabbed Aurelia's arm, then yanked her back with him.

"They won't hurt me," she protested. "Nic would never —"

"He will command those lions to leave," Horatio said darkly. "Won't you, Nic?"

I looked up. When he had grabbed his daughter, Horatio had also gotten Aurelia's knife, which he held to her throat. Despite the fact that Radulf was already stirring, I let the bulla fall back to my chest and then stood with my hands held low, a sign that I would not release any magic. As warm as the bulla was, whatever I tried doing to him might hit Aurelia. Under my breath, I whispered to the lions to go, that the gates were open for their escape.

The audience didn't like that. They had wanted blood, but I didn't much care. This was only a game to them. From my perspective, things were far more serious.

Having regained consciousness, Radulf slowly got to his feet and glared at Horatio, still with Aurelia in his grip. With a snarl, he said, "If you could do this to your own daughter, why would I ever trust your loyalty?"

"I can be of use to you, Dominus!"

Radulf yelled, "You lied to me! You did give Nic the key! There's no other way he could've called in that storm!"

"I don't have it!" I yelled. "Horatio still has the key, and if you harm him, it's lost forever."

Horatio shrugged. "You tried to warn me, Nic. The key is not what you think. We both have it now."

Radulf frowned at him. "That's all I needed to hear."

And he threw out something at Horatio. Calling up what little magic I had left, I put up a shield for Aurelia, still in his grip, but couldn't make it reach Horatio in time. With a brief cry of pain, he crumpled to the ground, instantly dead. Aurelia ran from his clutches into my arms.

"He didn't even have a chance to fight." Aurelia was trembling and struggling to breathe. "Just like that . . ."

She started to turn back to her father's body, but I put my hands on her shoulders and pushed her toward the open gate of the arena. "Get out of here, where you'll be safe."

"What about you?"

"This is my fight. Now run!" And she did.

The audience received Horatio's death with a mixture of jeers and applause, which was horrifying enough. But at least they had seen Radulf kill one of their own leaders. Now they would have to know that he was no great hero, no one worthy of their praise and affection. If nothing else, that was some victory for me. Nobody would follow Radulf now.

Indeed, I saw Valerius stand again in the imperial box and wave his hands for their silence. When he had everyone's attention, he called out, "With the death of Senator Horatio, I am now your presiding magistrate, leader of the Senate and of all Praetors of Rome. And as a representative of Emperor Tacitus, I am ordering all Praetors to surround and arrest Senator Horatio's two murderers: General Flavius Radulf Avitus and the escaped slave, Nicolas Calva."

I turned to him, stunned. He knew I had not thrown the magic that killed Horatio. He knew I wouldn't commit such a crime, not even to save my own life. Everyone would've seen the burst of light from Radulf's hands, different from the shield I had created.

If they had seen it. On the night Radulf and I fought at the baths, nobody had seen the magic but us. They saw the effects of our fight, but not the magic itself. So as far as Rome was concerned, I was part of Horatio's murder. If there were any doubts, then Valerius had just confirmed it for them.

Aurelia had stopped running to hear Valerius's announcement, and looked back at me in total disbelief.

"Shoot me," I yelled at her. "Aurelia, shoot me!"

Even from here, I could see Aurelia's hands were still shaking as she pulled her bow off her shoulder and nocked it with an arrow. I didn't know if the shaking was caused by nervousness from the crowd or horror at her father's sudden death. But as she pulled the string back, her aim seemed true. Once the arrow had flown, she turned to keep running.

Just as it had in Crispus's vineyards, the arrow came directly toward me. Trying to catch it before had thrown off my balance, but not this time. I watched it spin in the air, fluttering slightly in the wind, and aimed at my heart. When the moment was right, I spun around and then caught the arrow in my fist. The audience burst into applause, but I wasn't doing this for them.

I spun again and with that motion threw the arrow into the air, as swift and strong as if I'd had my own bow to launch it. When Valerius realized it was heading to him, he cried out and ducked, but it didn't matter. I stopped the arrow at the tip of his nose, then let it fall.

Laughter and applause followed from the audience, but as soon as they had quieted, I yelled, "I am innocent of your accusations, Senator Valerius. And I'm a free person, not an escaped slave!"

Only then did I realize that Radulf had come up near me and held out a hand for peace. "Come with me, Nic, as my second in command. In our new world, there will be no Senator Valerius. You will become greater than everyone, even the emperor."

"Except for you." I arched an eyebrow. "Right?"

He smiled. "Bow to me, and I'll see that the world bows to you. Or if you refuse, I will kill you, just as I did Horatio."

"You won't have me so easily!" That, I hoped, was true. My magic was nearly drained, and fading fast. If another fight started between us, I wouldn't have enough magic left to squash an ant. Radulf sent another fist of air toward me, but I punched back with something that rattled the ground. I turned to run deeper into the arena, but before I got very far, he shot at my back and flattened me on the ground. I summoned everything I had left into the core of my body and started to get up, but before I could, his foot came down on my shoulder, directly over the Divine Star. It stung beneath his touch, but offered me nothing in added strength.

"You don't need a bulla to pull out someone's magic," Radulf said. "All you need is the willingness to inflict that level of pain."

I didn't waste energy in answering him. Instead, I searched within myself for what magic remained. There wasn't much.

"Everyone you know has betrayed you," Radulf said. "Aurelia, Crispus, Valerius, Felix, even your mother. The list goes on, except for one name and that is mine. How many times could I have killed you, and I didn't. And I won't."

"That's a lie!" I tried pushing myself up but he kept me pinned down. "You've killed everyone whose shoulder is marked."

"For good reason," Radulf said. "I must protect the power for those who should have it."

"That's not your choice!"

"It's *our* choice. Together, our magic will rule this empire. You will not be a slave anymore, not even a mere citizen. We don't need a fool emperor, or a Senate, or the Praetors' secrets. We can defeat them all."

"No!" I struggled again beneath him, but the shield for Aurelia had cost more than I could've imagined. I only hoped something would be left of me at the end of it.

He sighed. "You forced me into this, Nic. I wish you hadn't."

Radulf leaned down and placed his hand on my shoulder, beneath the tear in my tunic and directly over the Divine Star. What had been a mild sting turned to sharp pain as he began to pull the magic from my body. I cried out, both from the pain and the helplessness I felt. If he had been ripping out my heart, it couldn't have hurt worse. This was what Crispus had described to me only days earlier. It was the way Radulf had killed everyone else with the mark, and now he had targeted me. Without strength to fight him, I could only lie there screaming and trying to keep whatever was left gathered in my hands, both of which were wrapped around the bulla. I couldn't let him take it, but I wasn't able to use it either. I squirmed, trying again to stop him, but the pain was greater than anything I'd felt before and was only getting worse. He dug through every vein of my body, seeking out the tendrils of magic that had attached themselves to me and cutting them free. A part of me wanted him to take the rest of the magic, because then this would stop. So I let go of the fight. If it went on much longer, I wouldn't survive the pain anyway.

"General Radulf, that's enough!" a man yelled. He must've come through the gates directly into the arena. "On behalf of Emperor Tacitus and Senator Valerius, the Praetors of Rome demand your arrest."

Hundreds of men had gathered with arrows aimed directly at Radulf. Though my eyes barely remained open now, I looked long enough to notice that each man wore a thin silver band, in the shape of an arrow, folded around his arm. It was Diana's arrow. I wasn't sure how I understood that, but I knew I was right. Radulf stood, and I saw a hint of alarm in his eyes.

Radulf glanced down at me and said, "Neither of us can fight them alone, Nic. The Praetors are more than what they seem."

By the time I looked up to respond, he had disappeared.

Radulf was gone.

FORTY-SIX

Everyone, stay away!" Crispus ran through the opened gate into the arena, then was at my side where I still lay in a heap on the burnt sand. He put my arm around his shoulder, and raised me to my feet. I tried to walk on my own, but it was hard enough to keep my legs from collapsing, much less use them to take me anywhere. My bigger concern was my shoulder, which throbbed with the pain of losing its magic just as it had stung when Caela first gave me the magic. I felt turned inside out.

"Let him pass," Crispus yelled to the Praetors who had also entered. "My father, the presiding magistrate, wishes to speak to him at once. Besides, you know what Nic can do."

That was ridiculous. The magic left in me wouldn't create a slight breeze, much less threaten anyone. Crispus didn't know that. Obviously I was weak, but he didn't know the magic was gone.

I tried not to look at the Praetors as we neared them. Radulf had said the Praetors were more than what they seemed.

Why had they worn that particular armband? And why did Radulf leave so quickly once he saw them here? Perhaps it was I who should fear them. Murmuring amongst themselves, they parted to allow Crispus to help me limp out of the amphitheater.

I took one last look at Horatio's body, still on the ground without a scratch on him. The fact that I had failed to save him tore at my heart. Despite my best efforts, my plan had changed nothing and my shield had not been enough. Aurelia wasn't here anymore. I didn't know where she had gone, or what she must think of me now.

Once out in the corridor, I pushed away from Crispus, determined to walk, or fall, on my own. "Your father is responsible for Horatio's murder!" I snarled. "He used me as bait so he could get the key!"

Crispus looked back through the gates at Horatio's body. "It had to be done. Horatio couldn't be trusted as presiding magistrate, and we couldn't allow Radulf to get the key."

All I wanted was to leave the amphitheater now, while I still had the chance. I focused that thought inside my head and made a silent plea for help. I limped away from Crispus and leaned against a large column for support. It felt like Radulf had done more than steal my magic. He had stolen that part of me that kept my whole self intact. Worse still, Crispus and his father had let Radulf do it.

Crispus stepped forward and in a hushed voice said, "We

needed you, Nic, to bring Radulf into the arena. You helped us, and now we'll help you."

Dizzy with exhaustion, I raised a hand to warn him back. I didn't want help. I didn't need any more of *his* help.

"My father already helped you survive the arena! We knew that if Radulf believed you had the key, he would leave you alive."

"That wasn't help! He wanted Radulf to kill me, and the Praetors to arrest Radulf. Then he could have the bulla."

Crispus cleared his throat. "Yes, that was a possibility. But he hoped you would live. Really, Nic, he did."

"Only because he wants my magic. And now that he's the presiding magistrate, he'll inherit the key to the Malice."

"Horatio said you have it."

"Well, I don't, and I wouldn't give it to you if I did! Even when you're made emperor, I won't give it to you. When will that be, Crispus? Next week perhaps?"

Crispus looked genuinely hurt, but he quickly recovered and said, "All that matters is you must listen. I've brought a message from my father."

"More lies?"

Crispus's expression was flat. "Just cold reality. Radulf will hunt you now more fiercely than ever. We both know he isn't finished with you yet."

In the face of his emotional void, my tone turned sour. "And your father only wants me to live, correct?"

"Yes, *if* you agree to help him get the amulets."

"That's why your father charged me with Senator Horatio's death," I said. "To force me to help him."

Crispus nodded. "There's nowhere else you can go to escape the penalty for that crime. But if you come with me, my father will pardon you, and protect you. He's all you have, even if you don't like what he stands for."

"And what's that?" I yelled. "Corruption? Murder? Lies?"

"He stands for Rome." Crispus drew a deep breath. "My father commands the Praetors now. They will fight Radulf."

I lowered my voice. "Radulf told me there was more to the Praetors than we know. Felix said they were dangerous. If that's true, your father is a fool to think he can control them."

Crispus's eyes darted sideways before he stepped toward me. "Maybe he can't. But it's better than fighting them, which is what you'll have to do if you walk away from here."

He reached out to steady me, but I stepped away. He withdrew his hand and said, "I'm sorry things had to go the way they did. I swear that I didn't know about any of this until Horatio took you away yesterday. I liked being your friend, and I hate what my father is doing as much as you do. But he's your only chance now. One side or the other will get you if you try to survive on your own."

Exactly as Radulf had told me.

I started to walk away, but stumbled. Crispus grabbed my arm and pulled me outside. If it hadn't been for him, I'd have rolled down the marble steps. "Come with me. We have food at home and you can rest there as long as you want. Once you're ready, we'll continue training you in magic and then you will stand at my father's side as the Praetor War begins."

"Nic, are you all right?" Aurelia came running toward us until she saw Crispus, and her eyes narrowed. "You can't be serious about going with him."

"I'm not." I hobbled away from Crispus. "Tell your father that I will not help him with anything again, *ever.* And I will never accept anything from you."

"Then where will you go? You can barely walk right now."

His answer came at just that moment. The sound of flapping wings caught my attention and Caela landed on the ground directly in front of us. With my loss of magic, I was amazed that she'd heard my silent call, and even more amazed that she'd answered. It was the greatest relief to see her again.

I held out a hand to Aurelia. "Come with me."

She shifted her weight and backed away from me. "You put up the shield to defend me — I felt it when you did — but I wasn't the one being attacked. You defended the wrong person in there."

That hurt as much as if she'd slapped me. Maybe I deserved it, but I still wanted her to understand it through my eyes. "You saw what happened. There was nothing I could've done."

"You took the key from my father. Knowing it would make him a target for Radulf, you took the key."

"How many times do I have to say that I don't have it? I have no idea why your father said that!"

"We'll never be able to ask him. Not now."

"Maybe if you—" I could've argued that she never should've come into the arena, that her coldhearted father had been ready to sacrifice her to prove his loyalty to Radulf. But that would've passed the guilt to her, and I wouldn't do that. Better she blamed me than herself. "Maybe not," I whispered. I removed the crepundia and held it out to her. "Thank you for this. It belongs to you, to remember your father."

Her eyes softened as she took the crepundia back. "Those children who were in the sewers with me, I have to find them again."

"I can help you do that."

But she shook her head. "I'd rather go alone. I need time, Nic."

I didn't answer, just shuffled the rest of the way to Caela on my own.

"Please don't go," Crispus said. "My father is your only protection now."

"No," I said. "I am my only protection."

With some effort, I climbed onto Caela's back and let my weight collapse into her as she flew away. She took us at a steep angle into the air and then arced over the amphitheater. I stared down into the arena, hoping the damage from my fight with Radulf hadn't been too great, but what I saw instead surprised me.

The arena was full of thousands of people, and every head below was turned to me. Arms raised up in a salute of honor, and then a cheer rose from their near silence to thundering applause. Caela cawed back, accepting their praise for herself. But I sat taller and even managed a smile. Perhaps some hope remained after all. Valerius had condemned me for Horatio's death, but the mob saw it differently. An escaped slave of Rome had just earned the hearts of the people.

FORTY-SEVEN

The courtyard of the emperor's palace was directly uphill from the amphitheater, so I'd barely had any time to recover before Caela touched down. Surely no place on earth was so beautiful, or fitting, for my griffin. Like many other buildings in the forum, the floor was made of white marble with inlaid mosaics giving honor to the gods. The entire room was surrounded by tall columns that held up a partial roof. The red fresco walls of the courtyard were gilded with gold, which I knew was real because Caela's attention went directly to it. It was so beautiful that at first she failed to notice the emperor's guard filling the room.

But I noticed them, and straightened my back. "I wish to see Emperor Tacitus," I announced as boldly as I dared. "His life is in danger."

"So is yours," one of the soldiers replied.

I raised a hand, palm out. It lacked any feeling of magic, and I was empty of any physical strength beyond what I needed to remain upright, but he didn't know that. "The emperor must know about the Praetor War," I said. "If he rescinds the order of death upon me, I can help him."

"This isn't about the emperor's orders," a voice said from behind me. "He's thinking about my plans for you."

I turned so fast that I nearly rolled off Caela. Radulf stood in the doorway, looking far more rested from our fight than I felt. But I didn't understand. How could Radulf be here, standing in the courtyard of the emperor's palace, as if it were his own?

"You?" I blinked twice to be sure. "Where is Tacitus?"

"His Highness has just returned to Gaul for a military campaign there, leaving me in charge. After five centuries of rule, with millions of my people slaughtered or enslaved, apparently Rome still has not yet conquered it enough. So the wars continue."

"You're a general of Rome," I said. "You were a part of those wars!"

"Was I?" He sounded amused. "Or am I the reason why Rome must still continue to battle those . . . barbarians? Because perhaps Rome has a barbarian at the head of its armies? My soldiers will never betray me."

"Maybe they're just waiting for the right time. Later today, if we're lucky."

Radulf motioned for his men to raise their bows at Caela. "Get rid of that bird," he said. "Or else we'll cook it for supper."

"No!" I raised a hand, hoping for enough magic to repel them, but still there was nothing. That was no small surprise. The bulla was empty.

Caela angrily cawed back at him. Even if she didn't understand his words, she would know the cruel tone of his voice. I nudged her side, urging her to take flight again, but as she reared back, I lost my grip and fell to the marble floor. The bows arced in her direction and I kicked at her leg, urging her into the air. "Go," I said to her. "Leave me — now!"

Caela looked back at me, but I swatted at her again, and then ducked as she spread her wings and flew away. I was alone, once more. Probably never to see her again.

Radulf's soldiers turned their arrows toward me. "How is your magic?" Radulf asked.

With great effort, I got to my feet and stood tall, hoping it would hide the fact that I felt absolutely nothing. The bulla weighed less now, and hung cold against my chest. "How's your reputation?" I countered. "At least fifty thousand Romans saw what you really are. They know you killed Horatio. The emperor can't be far from here yet. How long until he learns the truth?"

"The emperor is probably dead already," Radulf said. "There must be consequences for the bargain he made with you."

That sent a chill through me. Warily, I said, "I proposed that bargain, not him."

"But he agreed to it. Hardly a show of good will for his finest general. A new emperor will be chosen within days. For his sake, I hope that I like him better."

"You've killed the emperor?" I couldn't believe it was possible.

"A blow for the empire on the day Valerius chooses to declare war against me," Radulf said. "And as for the rest of Rome, like rulers of this empire have done for centuries, I'll distract the mob with bread and circuses. They'll do whatever they're told."

"I will stop you," I said.

"You'll save the empire?" He chuckled at that. "You couldn't even save yourself in the arena. And you can't defend yourself now."

I wanted to argue that, desperately, but I couldn't. And we both knew it. Somewhere behind me, something rattled. It was a sound I had heard far too often in my life. My heart lurched into my throat.

Radulf nodded to his soldiers. "Put this runaway slave back in his chains. Prepare the branding iron so he will never forget what he is."

"No," I yelled. "No!" I scrambled to get away, but they brought me down before I could get much of a hit at any of them. The soldiers threw me to the floor, yanked my arms behind me, and cuffed me in manacles, then attached them to chains around my ankles. I cried out, not from pain, but from the horror of what it meant to be reduced once again to property. I had promised myself I would never return to this life, and without any meaningful fight, Radulf had stolen that promise away. Like he had taken Livia. Like he had pulled the magic from my shoulder.

Once I was confined, Radulf knelt beside me. He lifted the bulla from around my neck and lowered it around his. I felt the loss immediately, not only the difference in weight, but as if he had taken away the last piece of my life. It would've been easier if he had taken my heart. I was nothing now anyway.

"Can you feel its magic?" one of his soldiers asked.

Radulf's smile was wicked, but not convincing. "The powers come on slowly. It will take time."

"All hail General Radulf," the soldier said to the cheers of the other men.

"What shall I do with you now?" Radulf asked me. "I can't return you to the mines. You can't work the venatio. So there are really only two options."

"Kill me, then." I spat the words at him. "I won't join you."

"Your willingness to die is admirable," he said. "But will you sacrifice her?"

He nodded permission at a soldier who went out the door and returned with someone in his grip. Livia.

My heart pounded as my sister was brought forward. It felt like years since I had seen her. How much older she looked. How much healthier she already appeared.

The curls in her hair hadn't changed, nor the gentleness in her eyes. This was undoubtedly the real Livia and not some image projected by Radulf, because she reacted the moment she saw me. Her eyes filled with tears and she rushed to my side on the floor.

"Nic! Are you injured? Why are you still in chains?"

I wasn't *still* in chains. I was *back* in chains, and this time they seemed to burn my flesh like never before. I pulled against them, hoping to find some new strength, but the chains held strong. I hated them, and hated myself in them.

Radulf stood and gently laid a hand on her shoulder. "As I've been telling you, Livia, your brother is in more trouble than he realizes. Help him understand."

Lines of sympathy were etched in Livia's face. In her gentlest tone, she said, "It's time to stop fighting. General Radulf will be our *pater familias*."

"Don't call him that!" I yelled. He was not part of our household, much less the head of it. He would not be honored with such a term.

"He saved me from the mines. He'll save you too if you let him."

A burning smell entered the courtyard, and I craned my neck to look for its source. It was one of Radulf's men, carrying the branding iron, white-hot at the tip. Blood rushed to my head as I stared at it, wide-eyed and scarcely able to breathe.

Radulf kept his eyes on me. "They say you can feel the burning forever, even into the next life. Maybe it's cruel, especially for someone so young, but that's the penalty for an escaped slave. Is this who you are, Nic? Nothing more than property?"

"What do I care if you use it?" I growled louder to cover up the shaking of my voice. "You'll only kill me anyway."

Radulf crouched down beside me. "Stop this stubbornness. Who am I?"

I gritted my teeth, resisting with everything I had against the truth that had pricked at me ever since our first meeting.

The branding iron came closer. I heard it sizzle and tried not to think of how it would feel pressed against my forehead.

He grabbed my face, forcing me to look at him. "Who am I? What should you call me, Nic? You know the answer. Now say it!"

Yes, I knew it. It had been the last word on my mind each day and given me nightmares as I slept. The word tasted like acid in my mouth and burned as I spoke. "Grandfather."

FORTY-EIGHT

Radulf motioned the branding iron away, then stood again and smiled down at me. "When did you know?"

"That night we fought at the baths. You spoke my father's name. At first I thought Livia must've told it to you, but I'm certain she's never known his name."

"I know it now," Livia said. "I've learned so much about both him and Mother. Pater taught me."

"I told you not to call him that! He's an enemy to us."

She straightened her back. "Don't talk to me like I'm a child! He's been good to me. And to you too."

I snorted. Maybe he hadn't told her about trying to kill me on more than one occasion. Of course, I'd hardly been an ideal grandson to him either.

"You don't have to love me as a grandfather," Radulf said. "But the blood that runs through my veins also runs in yours, and you cannot deny who you are forever."

"Yeah?" I snarled. "Watch me."

"Our family has the ability to do more than rule Rome. Don't you see, Nic, we can rule the gods! With your help, we can defeat the Praetors, and from their knowledge, succeed where your father failed. We will create a Jupiter Stone, which will make me immortal."

"It will make you insane." I cleared my dry throat. "Or, *more* insane, if that's possible."

Radulf shook his head. "Insanity would be living under the iron boot of this empire when it's within my reach to control it. We can achieve this immortality together!"

"Why should I believe that? After you tried to kill me?"

"I was teaching you, and testing you." He smiled. "And only occasionally actually trying to kill you. But we will work together now." His hand slipped to the mark on my back, which felt like dead space now. "I pulled the magic out, but I could have done more. If I'd wanted to take the rest of you, I would've succeeded."

"And what good do you suppose that mark does me now?" I asked.

"You are still my grandson, Nic." I gritted my teeth and turned away from him, but he continued speaking as if I had just pledged him eternal loyalty. "How did you create that storm in the arena? You must have the key."

I knew for a fact that Horatio hadn't given me anything, nor did I understand what he meant when he said he had given the key to me, *and* kept it for himself. But to Radulf, I only said, "The bulla must've given me the power to call that storm. Though on you, it looks rather childish."

"Yes. Well, don't worry, Nic, I still have plenty of use for you."

"I'd rather eat cow dung." Or better yet, feed it to Radulf.

"Then Valerius wins the Praetor War. Eventually, he will beat us to the Malice of Mars, and find a way to obtain a Jupiter Stone. With them, he will bring the entire world to its knees. There will be nothing beyond Rome, for Rome will be everything."

I wanted to accuse him of lying, to spit the truth back in his face. More so, I wished everything he said could be a lie. But in my heart, I knew it wasn't. I was caught in the middle of a war between two sides I could not support. If I joined Radulf, a city I had come to love would be destroyed. But if I joined Valerius, there would be nothing left in the world but an empire that had kept me and so many others in chains.

Radulf leaned in to me. "I will train you to become as powerful as I am now, and as powerful as your father once was. He was a great man, Nic. It does not honor his memory for you to live in chains. Or die in them."

"Then let me go." I held my chained hands out to Radulf. "In the name of my father, release me. Now."

Radulf requested the key, which was set into his palm. He stuck the key into the lock and released my hands first and then my legs. I scrambled to my feet as quickly as possible, to get away from the chains.

I held out my hand to Livia. "Let's go."

She only stared back at me as tears welled in her eyes. "Let's stay, please, Nic. Our home is with Radulf now."

"Not every chain is made of metal," I told her. "The worst are made of comfort and false promises. You're no more free here than you were in the mines." But she would not budge, so with my heart heavy and torn, I started to walk away.

Except that with a nod of his head, Radulf had his guards raise their swords to block my path. I stopped short of them but refused to look his way. Speaking to my back, he said, "I admire your courage to leave — truly, you are your father's son. But you must know that I can't allow it. If you try to leave, ever, there will be consequences for those you love." Radulf's hand went onto Livia's shoulder.

Livia's eyes widened when she understood Radulf's threat. And only then, too late, did she understand that our family ties weren't nearly as strong as his desire to control an empire. And to control me.

"I will win the Praetor War," Radulf said. "At any price."

He drew his own sword, but it was still in the air before I raised a hand and yelled, "Stop!" Radulf locked eyes with me, and I hated the glint of triumph in his. But there was nothing more I could do. I would not test Radulf against my sister.

"We will join your house," I muttered.

"We will join your house . . ." He raised an eyebrow, waiting for me to finish the phrase.

My hands curled into fists. "We will join your house, Grandfather."

"And you will become part of the Praetor War, as you always were meant to do."

With that, he thrust Livia toward me and replaced his sword. I wrapped my arms around her as she cried on my shoulder.

"We had better leave before Valerius arrives with his victory celebration," Radulf told his men. "I must gather a few things, and by then, you will have my grandchildren in the wagon ready to travel back to my home."

As soon as he left, Livia whispered, "That threat — he couldn't have meant it."

"He did mean it, Livia. You have to accept what kind of a person he really is. That's the only way we'll ever escape him."

"How? We have nothing. Without him, we are nothing."

I shook my head. "That's not true."

The soldier who had spoken before motioned us to walk forward. "You two follow me. Any tricks and I'll poke the person walking beside you."

Livia took my arm where I had received the burn in the arena. "What happened to you?"

I looked at the wound. It had started to heal, but not entirely. And the pain was so minimal that I had almost forgotten about it. It was still healing, despite Radulf having pulled so much magic from my shoulder. Despite Radulf having taken the bulla. It was healing anyway.

"I know about the bulla," Livia said. "Radulf told me the jewels in it come from the gods."

I couldn't suppress a grin. "There are jewels in it, yes. But not from the gods." The ones with the glow were sitting inside Aurelia's crepundia. While still on the lift to enter the arena, I had switched them. There was nothing in the bulla but Aurelia's cheap imitation stones and a fading scent of magic.

"Radulf is making a mistake by bringing us into his home," I told her. "Before I leave, I will know exactly how to defeat both him and Valerius. And I will get that bulla back."

With that thought, my smile widened. The bulla was only part of my magic. The rest was in the Divine Star. And even now, as my strength began to recover, I felt a prickle in my shoulder. Caesar's power had awoken within me once again.

My battle had only just begun.

ACKNOWLEDGMENTS

Readers often ask about the inspiration for a book or character. *Mark of the Thief* began when I happened upon a random fact: Emperor Julius Caesar used to claim he was a literal descendent of the goddess Venus. Historians believe he created this part of his image to make himself seem more powerful, but I began to wonder, what if he had been telling the truth? What if he really did have special powers, if he was a sort of demigod?

That led to other questions, with answers that took my imagination into exciting possibilities. Slowly, ancient Rome came alive in my mind — but now in a time filled with magic, competing forces between good and evil, and a journey where the least likely of all — a young mining slave — rises to save an empire. My stories often begin this way, by asking questions that I can't wait to answer.

But though my stories begin in this simple way, bringing them into readers' hands is a much bigger process, one I could never do alone. So for that, I am forever grateful to Jeff Nielsen, my husband, best friend, and true companion, and to our three children, for their support, encouragement, and willingness to split the last square of dark chocolate. Few things are a truer act of love. Thanks also to my amazing agent, Ammi-Joan Paquette, whose wisdom and knowledge greatly outdistance her years. Heaps of gratitude to everyone at Scholastic — it is a privilege to work with each of you in your various areas of expertise. Finally, warmest thanks to my editor, Lisa Sandell, who does far more than help me shape a story for publication. You are mentor, advisor, teacher, therapist, guidance counselor, and above all, a true friend. You are gold.

One final word — to all those who were my teachers, even in the subjects where I clearly wasn't paying attention — if you've ever wondered whether you made a difference to any of your students, here's at least one answer: For me, you made all the difference in the world.

ABOUT THE AUTHOR

JENNIFER A. NIELSEN is the acclaimed author of the *New York Times* and *USA Today* bestselling Ascendance Trilogy: *The False Prince, The Runaway King,* and *The Shadow Throne*. Jennifer also wrote *Behind Enemy Lines,* the sixth book in the Infinity Ring series, as well as the forthcoming novel *A Night Divided*.

She loves chocolate, old books, and lazy days in the mountains. Born and raised in northern Utah, she lives there today with her husband, three children, and a dog that won't play fetch. You can visit her at www.jennielsen.com.